Praise for *Wyrmhole*

"A fun, fast-paced SF Mystery."   —*Booklist*

"Fascinating and well-imagined . . . A terrific read, combining all the elements of great science fiction: originality, speculation, and consequence."
—Julie E. Czerneda, author of *In the Company of Others*

"Complex, layered, black as night, unputdownable."
            —Stephen Baxter, Hugo Award nominated
            author of *Evolution*.

"Jay Caselberg weaves SF with mystery for a new spin on the PI genre. In a fluid, dreamlike world where everything is changing, Jack Stein, psychic investigator, uses sharp-edged dreams to solve a case of miners vanished off a distant planet. An adventurous romp of a first novel, *Wyrmhole* keeps you guessing. The Philosopher's stone and alchemy shift into the digital age."
            —Wen Spencer, Compton Crook Award-winning
            author of *Alien Taste* and *Tainted Trail*

Jay Caselberg

METAL SKY

A ROC BOOK

ROC
Published by New American Library, a division of
Penguin Group (USA) Inc., 375 Hudson Street,
New York, New York 10014, U.S.A.
Penguin Books Ltd, 80 Strand,
London WC2R 0RL, England
Penguin Books Australia Ltd, 250 Camberwell Road,
Camberwell, Victoria 3124, Australia
Penguin Books Canada Ltd, 10 Alcorn Avenue,
Toronto, Ontario, Canada M4V 3B2
Penguin Books (NZ), cnr Airborne and Rosedale Roads,
Albany, Auckland 1310, New Zealand

Penguin Books Ltd, Registered Offices:
80 Strand, London WC2R 0RL, England

First published by Roc, an imprint of New American Library,
a division of Penguin Group (USA) Inc.

First Printing, September, 2004
10 9 8 7 6 5 4 3 2 1

Copyright © James A. Hartley, 2004
All rights reserved

Cover art by Christian McGrath

 REGISTERED TRADEMARK—MARCA REGISTRADA

Printed in the United States of America

For Jennifer

Acknowledgments

I would like to express my gratitude to my editor Jennifer Heddle and particularly to fellow writers Laura Anne Gilman and Liz Williams. Always, of course, to the Clan, without whom none of this would be possible.

One

Jack Stein swung his feet off the desk and leaned forward to run his hands over the flat surface. It was a good height, a good build. It had taken a full night to remove the old desk and grow the new one in its place, but he was happy with the results. The Yorkstone programs weren't quite as sophisticated as those he'd known back in the Locality, but then Yorkstone wasn't as big a residence.

He sighed and turned his chair to look out the window. Windows were good. That was one thing he didn't miss about the Locality—blank featureless walls. Of course, back in the Locality, Scenics made up for the lack of windows, but they didn't have Scenics in Yorkstone. Semiclear ceiling panels looked out onto sky, real sky, instead of some designer simulation meant to distract the populace from what was going on inside and help them pretend that they lived in a real environment. Yorkstone took a far more subtle approach to things. He could almost believe they lived in a normal, old-style city. It had been almost two years since he and Billie had left the Locality, but there were still things about the place that he missed, despite the many shortcomings. There was just something about daily normality that didn't sit well with Jack.

One of the traps of the programmable residences like the Locality, like Yorkstone, was that you could get caught up for hours growing furniture in new positions, changing the layout of a room. It was just another time sink helping him to avoid facing what was really going on here with his and Billie's existence.

"Diary," he said, and the opposite wall's surface bled lines and shapes until a simulacrum of his handipad's date page sharpened in front of him. He had it set to WEEK, and as he turned to face it, the blank empty page stared back at him accusingly. "Month," he said. A couple of pissant jobs in the last few weeks and that's all he had to show. He stood and crossed back to the window, looking down across a city that at least functioned, and maybe that was the problem. Things worked in Yorkstone. It was a clean city. Clean and ordered. People had less need of the services of the likes of Jack Stein, psychic investigator. Well, he needed to do something about it soon, or he and Billie would be forced into the sort of place that Jack could have put up with if he was on his own, but with her around . . .

He shook his head and made a low sound of displeasure in his throat. It was about time fate started throwing something his way. It had been too long since his inner senses had prodded him into anything that really meant something. His dreams were still full, but the problem was, they were full of crap. The missing relative. The lost object. He'd even had one or two pets crop up in his inner landscape. In the past, even if his dreams had been barren, he'd been able to rely in part upon his other senses, his innate sense of knowing. He didn't even feel anything in his gut, or he hadn't for some time now, and that was unusual. Jack had spent most of his life teetering on the edge of an inner chasm—or at least that's what it felt like—

but even that reassuring discomfort was nowhere to be felt. If something didn't happen soon, he'd have to start thinking about a "proper" job. He had a quick thought.

"Change the window display. Read JACK STEIN, INVESTIGATOR."

The word PSYCHIC bled away and INVESTIGATOR slipped into position beneath the curved arch of his name. Not that people could really see it from the street, but it was something. The letters cast lengthening shadows in reverse across the new, pale desk. Anybody coming into the office would get the right feeling. It was important to convey the proper image, after all.

"Jack, what are you doing? Are you rearranging the office *again*?" There was a sound of exasperation in Billie's voice, but then that wasn't unusual.

He turned to look at her. Billie had shot up since they'd arrived in Yorkstone. She'd also let her hair grow out, but tended to wear it in a tangle of unkempt waves. She stood leaning in the doorway looking at him disapprovingly, her smooth, pale features marked with a frown. She was still slim, almost too slim, but her face had started to gain marks of maturity—slightly longer, less rounded at the cheeks—that sat more comfortably with her attitude. It was almost as if she had started to grow into the sense of age that she already possessed. Damn her. Sometimes, there was no doubt who *she* believed was the real child in their relationship. The kid was trying to run him again.

"Well, it gives me something to do, doesn't it?" he said.

"Uh-huh," she said, nodding slowly, sternly unimpressed. "And what else are you going to do, Jack?"

He sighed. "What do you mean?"

"You know what I mean. You can sit here playing with your furniture or flipping through your diary, but that isn't going to get us anything to eat, is it?" She crossed her arms.

He turned away from her and looked out the window. "All right, you suggest something."

"Nuh-uh," she said. "Not me. It's your turn. You just want to sit here waiting for stuff to happen. I always end up making the suggestions. Why don't you try doing something? Really doing something. How did you get work before? You know, back *there*."

He spun the chair back and forth with one hand. She was referring to the Locality. She still didn't like talking about the place. "I dunno. Talking to people. Bars. Stuff like that. I knew some old contacts back there. Referrals. The Locality was different, Billie. This place, well, it's just too *clean*. You know that. You've seen what I'm talking about. We've been here long enough to know what it's like. Things just don't work the same way here. Everything's too normal. Back in the Locality you knew stuff was going to happen. Here, even looking for it doesn't seem to do any good."

"Yeah, right." She shook her head, her mouth set into a thin line, then disappeared into the other room to continue whatever she was doing. No doubt she was immersed in one of her numerous learning programs. Her capacity to absorb knowledge was just unbelievable sometimes. She liked challenges too. Not that he'd had anything to give her in that regard for a while. She'd be asking—no, demanding—to go out and get something to eat soon. The inevitable accusatory prompt. They were the two things that seemed to drive her: information and food. Ultimately, he guessed that there was more than one sort of hunger.

She was right though; he was just avoiding things.

Okay, they'd picked Yorkstone pretty much at random when they'd left the Locality, and normally Jack would have trusted his gut to lead him somewhere that made sense. The right place at the right time. It had always worked that way in the past. Maybe it *had* been right, as far as Billie was concerned, for what she needed. It had given her a chance to escape the memories of her life back in Old, the tainted existence she'd been forced to lead among the sleaze and the lowlifes who made that part of the city their own. Now and again they talked about it, but her answers were always clipped and reserved. She carried the marks of that life around with her still. For the most part, the subject was strictly out of bounds. Jack had learned that, to both their displeasure, more than once. Two years, and the details were as sketchy as they'd ever been. And as for her family . . . well, there was a limit to the amount of Billie's wrath he wanted to face. He frowned at that thought. Jesus. Who exactly *was* the kid here? He gave a quick snort to himself.

And they were stuck with Yorkstone too. It had gotten to the point now where they couldn't afford to move anywhere else even if Jack had wanted to. He needed a job. One big job and they'd have some choices again. With a sigh, he ran his fingers back through his hair and wandered out into the living room. It was times like these that he missed having a separate office away from the place he lived, but with Billie and the extra expense, that was yet another dream, and not a particularly useful one at that. Dreams. Well, it had been a while since his dreams had given him anything particularly useful anyway.

"Hey, Billie."

She looked away from the wallscreen and gave him a blank look, waiting for him to say something.

"Okay. All right. I get the message." He shrugged. "Do something for me, will you?"

It was Billie's turn to sigh. "What is it?"

He looked at her for a couple of moments before answering. It was hard enough to get her engaged in things at the best of times these days, and if he could get her to feel like she was involved . . .

"Well, you're so eager for me to pick up some work, why don't you get me a list of bars in the area. Maybe I can do what you suggested and find some work. After I've checked some of them out, I might be able to get them to put some discreet notices up or something. What do you think?"

She shrugged. "Uh-huh. I can do that. You'll have to wait. I'm in the middle of something."

He glanced at the screen. It looked like some sort of electrical diagram with a screed of incomprehensible notes. He was glad he'd insisted she enroll in the city's educational program, but some of the things she chose to focus on continued to amaze him. How a fourteen-year-old—well almost fourteen—kid could get buried in that sort of stuff, or even want to get buried in it, he couldn't imagine. Maybe he should encourage her to go out and find some friends. The problem was, with what she'd seen and done, any kids her age were a problem for her and anyone older was going to look at her askance. She seemed happier on her own anyway.

"Okay, well, I'm going to make some coffee. I'll wait. When you're ready, Billie."

She nodded absentmindedly, clearly not catching his sarcasm. "I won't be long. I just want to get through this module."

Jack headed into the kitchen area and brewed himself a cup. It was about his fourth for the day, or maybe fifth. He'd lost count. He'd given up asking Billie if she wanted any long ago.

While he waited for the coffee unit to finish its cycle, he drummed on the counter with his fingers, thinking. Despite all the good intentions when they'd come here, Jack's life hadn't really moved on that much. Sure, he had Billie now, and she did a lot to keep him in line—he hadn't touched a stim patch for months—but that wasn't the point. There had to be more than this. In some ways, he even felt guilty for the life he was offering her, or not offering her. It was better than living on the urges of predators like Pinpin Dan, but how much of a life was it? He needed to do something right for her, or at least make the attempt, though he was damned if he knew what that was.

The coffee finished brewing and he leaned back against the counter, sipping slowly and staring into nothing, waiting for Billie to decide she was ready to help him out.

It hadn't taken long for Billie to compile the list and upload it to his handipad. Out on the street, Jack pulled out the device and flipped it open. What she'd come up with looked comprehensive, but then he wouldn't have expected anything else from her. The local neighborhood boasted a few bars, but Jack doubted that any of them would prove that useful. Standing on the street corner, staring down at the list on his handipad, trying to make a decision, he scratched the back of his head and glanced up and down the street. The nearest was a place called I.D. It didn't sound too promising, not with a name like that.

A shuttle whirred quietly past and headed uptown. Jack watched it disappear into the distance. Maybe he needed to head for somewhere less ordered. There was a seamier side to Yorkstone, up near the port. Most cities had that kind of place—stations, ports, docks— but the Yorkstone facility was a good half an hour away by shuttle. Smaller than the Locality, Yorkstone was still large enough to require decent shuttle transport. Better to start somewhere easy. He might just get lucky. He looked down at the list again, his lips pressed tightly together. So, scratch I.D. It was bound to be full of designer labels and the trendy set. There was another place called the Keg. Okay, a couple of blocks farther away, but it sounded a bit more promising. Sometimes you could get a feel for a place just from the name.

Jack watched the surrounding streets as he walked, more out of instinct than anything else. An old lady strolled up the other side in the opposite direction, leading a dog, tugging at the leash, but her pet had decided to make a stop at one of the trees lining the sidewalk. That was another difference between Yorkstone and the Locality. The local governance had taken the trouble to have real trees, gardens, spread throughout the city rather than confined to central gathering areas like the Locality's Central Park. All very pleasant. All very civilized. There was nothing wrong with it at all.

The dog finished what it was doing and the woman walked on, not bothering to do anything about what her pet had left behind. The city's programming would see to that. The inbuilt biomemory could tell what it could use and what was supposed to be on the streets. And as he watched, a piece of the pavement bulged, hollowed, swallowed the small pile, leaving things as if nothing had ever been there to taint the pristine surrounds. And pristine it was. All around, neat ordered buildings echoed the suburban ideal. Jack shook his head. He really was going to have to do something about this. He and Billie just didn't fit in comfortably here.

They'd ended up in this particular suburb by default rather than by any conscious plan. This area, Grandleigh, was a mixture of small business and residential. The bar he was heading for now was on the border of a warehousing area of the city, but Grandleigh sat in that transitional area between, warehouses on one side and plush apartment blocks on the other. Cheap enough to be affordable, but still pleasant in its layout. Whoever had designed and programmed this city in the first place had been careful about the zoning, making sure that no one area had the potential to upset the careful civic order. Civic order—what sort of background was that for someone like Jack Stein?

It took him about twenty minutes to find his destination. The Keg sat in a narrow side street about halfway along, stuck between two warehouses. A large blank building stood on the other side, probably a local authority parking area by the looks of it. Most of the residents relied on the shuttle, not owning vehicles of their own, but there was always a need for transport for those who kept the place running. The street itself was empty. A small sign, glowing red in the wall above a low doorway, discreetly announced the establishment. The letters weren't even moving. Another quick shake of his head and a sigh, and Jack headed toward the entrance. It didn't look at all like the sort of place where he'd find what he needed. There was something too clean about it. Going in was better than having to face Billie's stern disapproval right now though, and he could do with a drink. Drinking was another thing he didn't do very much of anymore.

Steps led down behind the door. It looked like the owners had taken advantage of unused space beneath

an old office building to set up the bar. As he opened
the door, the smell of beer and the noise of voices and
music greeted him. A long, low bar, simulated wood.
Lines of bottles along a series of mirrored shelves. A
cluster of men at one end of the bar. Even the floor
looked as if it was made of dark wooden boards. Jack
stood at the doorway for a moment, taking it all in.
Round tables dotted the open space in front of the bar,
with low seats around them. This looked like a traditional drinking hole. Whoever ran the place had taken
trouble to make the place have the look and feel of
something old and comfortable. It took real effort to
have actual barstools in a place. You had to have them
shipped in. They weren't the sort of thing built into the
city's programming.

He headed toward the bar. One of the men at the
other end gestured with his chin in Jack's direction,
drawing the barman's attention. The barman, who had
been leaning at the end of the bar in conversation, gave
Jack a speculative look, pushed himself upright after
shoving a cloth into his belt, and wandered slowly
down the length of the bar in Jack's direction. Yeah,
traditional all right. Right down to the barman.

"What can I get you?"

Jack glanced at the bottles arrayed behind the barman's head. "Yeah, scotch, thanks. Better make it a
double."

He flipped out his handipad, placing it carefully on
the bar beside him. The barman was back in a couple
of moments. No casual conversation. He placed the
glass down and pulled a reader from his pocket,
pointed it at Jack's handipad, then slipped it away
again before wandering back up to the other end of the
bar to rejoin his group. That was it.

Jack lifted his glass and swirled the contents before

taking a sip, looking through the golden liquid. Friendly place. He slipped his handipad away and glanced up at the group at the other end of the bar. They were obviously regulars. One of them was watching him, not too surreptitiously either, his eyes slightly narrowed. There were other glances too. The place clearly wasn't used to casual customers. There was something slightly familiar about the man's face as well. Jack's own eyes narrowed as he sipped, carefully looking away, trying to work out what it was. He tried to get a better look in the mirror behind the bar, but the barman blocked his view. He glanced over at a group of three sitting at one of the tables in the corner. A man and two women. Something about them too.

Jack spotted another table in the other corner and headed that way, carrying his glass dangling between two fingers and a thumb, glancing at them as he passed. There was a sort of sameness about them, about the group at the end of the bar. He shook his head as he sat. They didn't look like the sort of people he was here to find, but then why should they be? Another aspect of Yorkstone's clean and proper population. He pulled out one of the low chairs and sat, leaning back, giving himself a good view of the bar's other occupants. No, he'd finish his drink and move on. The port would probably offer more than Billie's list after all.

As he took another large sip, the guy who had been watching him reached up a hand to rub the back of his neck, tilted his head to one side, said something to one of his companions and, carrying his beer, strolled over in Jack's direction. He was a broad, heavyset guy, thinning gray hair, a thick nose, and thick, dark eyebrows, set beneath a contemplative frown. Slowly Jack lowered his glass and leaned forward.

"Don't I know you?" said the man.

"I don't know. Do you?" said Jack.

The man rubbed his jaw with his free hand. Jack took in the details as he did. He wore a plain shirt, barely disguising a middle-aged paunch, and conservative trousers. Sensible black shoes showing a good shine sat beneath them. Jack groaned inwardly. Stupid. He glanced around at the bar's other occupants, then back up at the guy. It suddenly made sense.

"Yeah," said the man. "You're Stone . . . Jack or John or something, isn't it? You're that investigator. Private. I'm right, aren't I?"

Jack gestured at the chair beside him. "You might as well sit down. And it's Stein. Jack Stein."

"I knew I was right. Always been good with faces. You're into all of that weird shit, that psychic stuff, aren't you? I'm right, aren't I?" He waved his fingers in emphasis and then sat down, planting his beer on the table. "I was telling Steve, my partner over there, that I knew you."

Jack looked over at the men clustered at the end of the bar and gave a brief nod. Of all the places to end up. Trust Jack Stein to walk into a cop bar. Here in Yorkstone the police were more like petty bureaucrats than any proper law enforcement. The city's real crime level was minimal. At least they weren't simply corporate muscle like they were back at the Locality.

"Yeah, you got me," said Jack.

"I ran into you on that abduction case, what, last year some time?"

"Uh-huh," said Jack. "Sorry, can't remember your name."

And he couldn't. He remembered their brief interaction. At first the cop and his partner had dismissed him out of hand. The partner had made no bones about how he felt about what Jack did, or anything that hinted at the psychic at all.

His companion thrust out a hand. "Morrish. Jim Morrish."

Jack shook the proffered hand. "Yeah, I remember. Investigator Morrish."

Morrish gestured over at the bar with his thumb. "That one over there's my partner. The rat-faced one." He gave a chuckle. "Steve Laduce."

Jack gave another nod toward the bar end. The scowl on the face of Morrish's partner sat firmly in place. Oh, he remembered Jack too. That much was clear.

"So, what brings you here? You just in the neighborhood or what?"

Jack slowly shook his head. "No, just out sniffing around. See what I might come up with."

Morrish grinned. There was nothing malicious in the expression. "Well, you're not going to find a lot here, are you?"

Jack grunted. Really. A *Yorkstone* cop bar. They were the last people he wanted to make contact with. He was wary of the police, always had been, and he didn't particularly like drawing their attention to him or what he was doing. "No, I guess not."

Morrish leaned forward, looking serious. "You know, Stein, I never did quite get what you did or how you did it, but it seemed to help in that Delynne thing. I don't think we would have found her without you. I remember that." He jerked his thumb back over his shoulder. "If Steve had had his way, we would have arrested you as an accessory at the time. Said you knew too much. Couldn't be natural. He was convinced you were tied into it somehow. I guess I'm a bit more open-minded."

Jack looked up and met another scowl from that end of the bar.

Morrish leaned back, his paunch becoming all the more evident, before taking a healthy swallow of his beer. "And me, I'm grateful for whatever it was. I don't have to understand it if it gets me results."

Jack simply nodded, taking another sip of his own drink, trying to avoid the hostility emanating from the other side of the room.

Morrish leaned forward again, carefully placing his glass down, leaning on his elbows and folding his hands together in front of him. "So, explain it to me again, Stein. I never did quite get what it was that you did."

Jack suppressed a brief sigh. Either the guy was setting him up, just playing dumb, or he really didn't know. He gave a slight shrug. "I feel things. I get impressions from things. You might even call some of them visions. Objects contain their own energies, and some of us can feel things from them. Those feelings are like pointers to bits of information that I can use to solve cases. Sometimes they're just warnings. I also have dreams."

"Yeah, but we all have dreams . . ."

Jack turned his face slowly back from scanning the bar to look at him. "The trick is to know what they mean, Investigator."

Morrish shook his head and grimaced. "I guess I'm not really going to get it. I'm not sure I really understand, and to be honest, I'm not really sure I want to understand. All that stuff makes me sort of uncomfortable. And call me Jim, okay? All I know is that without you, we wouldn't have been able to break the case and she'd likely be dead now. Funny running into you again though. Especially here." He chuckled.

"Yeah, funny," said Jack wryly.

"Can I get you a drink?" asked Morrish.

"No, thanks," said Jack. "I really ought to be going."

"All right, if you think . . ."

"Yeah." Jack downed the rest of his scotch and placed the empty glass down on the table with finality. "I should be going."

"Well, good to see you again," said Morrish. "Here, take my card." He fished inside his top pocket and slid a small, plain card across the table. Jack slipped it away without looking at it.

"Thanks." He pushed back his chair and stood, then headed for the door.

"Good seeing you," he said as he pulled open the door and headed up to the street outside. He could have thought of a number of people it would be good to see, and not a single one of them was a cop.

Out on the street, Jack looked in both directions, his hands shoved deep in his pockets. In the old days he could have walked into a bar, any bar, and it would have been the right one. So much for Lucky Stein. He grimaced and headed up toward the intersection. He might as well face it—he wasn't going to find what he needed this way.

Two

When Jack got back from the bar, Billie was waiting for him, standing just inside the door as he opened it. She must have had the system alert her. There was something about the way she looked, on edge, slightly nervous. He was just about to ask her what was wrong when she desperately waved a hand to still him, her eyes widening in warning.

"Shhh. Someone here. You've got a visitor," she whispered. "A woman. She's in your office waiting for you."

"Well, what's wrong with—?" he started in a normal voice, but she waved him down again.

She wiped some hair away from her face. It was still as tangled as it had been when she got up. "I don't like her."

Jack frowned. "What's that supposed to mean? What does she want? Who is she?"

Billie shrugged. "A client maybe. I don't know. I just don't like her."

"Dammit, Billie. A client? Isn't that what we want?"

"I guess . . ."

"Yeah, well, if she's got a case for me and she's willing to pay, what's the problem?"

Billie shrugged.

"Okay, I'm going in to see her. You wait in the living room, will you? Find something to do."

As he walked past her, heading for the office, Billie grabbed his arm.

"What?" he said.

"Just be careful."

He shook his head and continued into the office. He didn't know what the hell Billie's problem was, but it wasn't going to get in the way of a job. Not now.

Jack stopped just outside the room, waiting, seeing if some sense of the woman beyond the door would come to him. Just as he'd tried to explain to Morrish in the bar, a lot of what he did worked on his extended senses, but the place inside him, high up in his gut where such feelings grew, simply remained blank. He grimaced. It seemed his senses had deserted him for now. He opened the door and stepped inside.

The woman was seated on one of the chairs Jack reserved for clients, though they saw little enough use these days. He couldn't see her face from his position by the doorway, so he pulled off his coat, hung it beside the door, and crossed to his own chair, speaking as he walked.

"Hello, I'm Jack Stein. What can I do for you?"

As he took his seat, he studied her. She was slim, mid-thirties, reasonably attractive, but in an odd sort of way. You couldn't say she was exactly good-looking, but there was something about her. Striking. That was the word. Her auburn hair was done in an elaborate braiding at the top of her head, and her blue eyes looked across at him appraisingly. The cut of her clothes was stylish—nothing cheap about them—but there was a flavor of something exotic, as if they came from somewhere far away. Simple drop earrings complemented her hair color, silver with some sort of red stone in the shape of teardrops. Around her neck she wore a silver necklace with a teardrop pendant matching the earrings. She watched him, waiting.

Jack couldn't see what Billie's problem was. If there was something about this woman, he wasn't getting any real sense of it. Besides, wasn't *he* supposed to be the psychic? He crossed his legs in front of him, linking his fingers behind his neck as he waited for her to respond.

"You were recommended to me, Mr. Stein."

"Uh-huh." Her voice had a slight accent, nothing he could pin down. He didn't know anyone who would be likely to recommend him in Yorkstone, and since they'd left the Locality, he'd hardly made a splash. He decided to let it pass for now. If he needed to, he could find out more later.

She looked at him, clearly waiting for him to say something else. When it became clear that he was also waiting, she spoke again. "I understand you are reliable and . . . discreet."

Jack unlinked his fingers and sat forward. "Yeah, well, that comes with the territory, Ms. . . ."

"Oh, I am sorry. My name is Farrell. Bridgett Farrell."

"So, how can I help you, Ms. Farrell?"

She pressed the tip of her tongue lightly between her lips before continuing. Jack watched with fascination. That simple touch, the barest contact on those perfectly formed lips, drew his attention, held him.

"Are you sure . . ." she said, glancing around the room.

Jack cleared his throat. "Yes, you can talk here. We're perfectly secure and what goes on in this room stays in this room."

She reached across the desk with one hand, touching Jack's forearm with the tips of her gloved fingers. "But what about the girl?"

Jack sat back, pulling his arm out of her reach. Gloves? Who wore gloves? "Don't worry about my niece, Ms. Farrell. She can't hear us in here anyway."

She hesitated before withdrawing her hand, then gave him the slightest smile. "All right. If you say so." Again the slight moistening of her lips with the tip of her tongue, and she folded her hands gently in her lap. Jack was starting to see what Billie meant. This was performance, all performance, designed to keep Jack's attention divided—and it was doing its job. He focused on the single deep-red teardrop suspended at her throat.

Again he cleared his throat. Her eyes widened, blinked a couple of times, and then she relaxed again.

"I have a problem that you might be able to help me with. I *hope* you can help me, Mr. Stein."

Jack was quickly starting to lose his patience, not only with her, but with himself as well. She was dragging this out for too long and his concentration was starting to wander. It had been a long time since . . .

He gave a slight shake of his head. "Go on."

"There's an item of mine that has gone missing. I would like it found and returned."

"Okay . . ."

"This object is something of great significance to me. I would be prepared to offer you handsome payment for its return."

Now she was starting to talk his language. She tilted her head slightly, reaching up to play with one of the earrings, watching him with wide, clear and liquid eyes. The performance wasn't even subtle. Well, maybe she was used to getting what she wanted as far as men were concerned, but on this occasion, she might just be trying to play the wrong man.

"Listen, Ms. Farrell, I don't know what you think you're trying to achieve here. I don't think I'm interested." He stood and crossed to look out the window. Too many complications. Way too many.

"I don't know what you're saying, Mr. Stein. I came here to offer you a commission. If you have a problem with that . . ."

Jack kept looking out the window as he answered. He'd seen the type before, and sometimes you didn't need a psychic sense to be able to read someone.

"Yeah, maybe so, Ms. Farrell. I think there's more to it than that, isn't there? You don't know me. If you think you can play me, then you're making a mistake. Tell me the whole story and I might be willing to take your case. Otherwise, I think our business is finished."

"I don't know what you mean. What are you saying?" she said, all innocence.

Jack whirled on her then, leaning across the table. "Listen. You say this item, whatever it is, has gone missing. That's only part of the story, isn't it? Isn't it?"

She backed away in her chair, looking shocked. But that too was an act, and Jack knew it.

"Well . . ." he said.

"All right. You're right. It hasn't just gone missing. Someone has taken it." She sighed, some of the coquettishness gone from her.

"Better," he said, finally relaxing back into his chair. "Now, tell me the whole story."

She took a deep breath, then nodded. "I'm sorry. Until a week ago, I had the object in my possession. There was only one person who knew about it and I think he's taken it. I need to get it back, very badly."

Jack said nothing, watching impassively, waiting for her to continue. Simple observation had told him what she was doing, but nothing about her had sparked anything in his extended senses yet. Billie was a pretty good judge of character on first impressions. Maybe it was just the woman's cultivated performance that had prompted her caution.

"Okay," he said finally. "What is this thing you're looking for?"

"It's an artifact." Her tongue crept back between her lips and then withdrew, followed by her teeth pressing down on her bottom lip, chewing slightly.

"A what?" said Jack.

"An artifact. It's an object. Metal. Sort of like a tablet, about this big." She held her hands about a foot apart in illustration. "It has symbols across its top surface and tracing along the edges."

"Metal, you say."

"Yes, metal, but it's extremely light. Extremely light and extremely hard. It's a dark gray-black. Slightly wider at one end than the other."

"And how thick is this thing?"

She held her thumb and forefinger apart about midextension.

"And the back?"

"Slightly pitted, but smooth."

"No symbols?"

"No." She shook her head.

"Anything else about it, any other distinguishing marks?"

She shook her head again. "I would have thought it was particular enough by itself."

"Have you got a picture of this thing?"

Again she shook her head. Some of the previous false demeanor was starting to creep back, the uncertainty, the vulnerability, and she was looking at him with a slightly startled, nervous expression.

"Hmm," Jack said, looking down at the desk. He

looked up again quickly, watching as her expression changed. "So, who is this guy who is supposed to have taken it?"

"His name's Talbot. Carl Talbot."

"And what is this Talbot to you?"

She frowned. "Nothing. An acquaintance."

Jack turned his chair back to face the window. "Are you sure?"

"Of course I'm sure."

"If he's nothing to you," Jack said slowly, "how do you know him? Why do you think he took this thing?"

She paused before answering. In the silence, Jack spun his chair slowly back around to face her and leaned forward, elbows on the desk, hands crossed in front of him. Her hand drifted to the drop at her throat.

"He was the only one who knew about it. I'm sure of it."

"Why are you so sure, Ms. Farrell?"

"Because I told no one apart from Carl. No one at all. It was too important."

Jack narrowed his eyes. "So why tell him?"

"Because I trusted him," she said. "We've known each other for some time, only casually. I had no reason to think he'd betray me."

"Hmmm. And there's no chance someone might have stumbled upon it by accident, seized the opportunity."

"No." She shook her head.

Jack watched her, saying nothing. It didn't wash. Why would she tell a mere acquaintance about this thing if it was so valuable? Bridgett Farrell still wasn't telling him everything. For now, though, the prospect of a fee was driving him more than his suspicions about her. He didn't want to think about the other thing that was driving him right now, and it was nothing in his head.

"Okay," he said finally. "I'll take the case. I still have my reservations, Ms. Farrell, but I'm prepared to put those aside for the moment. I think I'm going to need some more to go on though. And despite its apparent importance, you say you haven't got a picture of this thing."

She shook her head.

"Of Talbot?"

"No."

Great. Just great.

"Fifteen hundred a day plus expenses."

She didn't flinch. He nodded. "So where is this Talbot now?" he said.

"I don't know," she said. "Why do you think I'm here, Mr. Stein?"

"I should ask you the same question, Ms. Farrell. Why *are* you here? You're not from Yorkstone."

"No, I'm not. I have reasons for being here. It's a business matter. I think Carl is somewhere here too."

Jack rubbed the back of his neck and sighed. "What makes you think that?"

"We're in a similar line of business. I just have good reason for believing he's here. Isn't that enough?"

"Is that it? That's all?" said Jack. She nodded.

He wasn't happy, but he guessed it would do for now. He said, "Okay, I'm going to have to get you to do a couple of things. We can do the second one in a few minutes, but first I'm going to have to ask you to take off your gloves."

She frowned.

"It's something I need to do," he explained, barely suppressing a sigh. "I need to hold your hand to get an impression, to see if there's anything I can pick up from the contact. It's part of how I work."

There was a little flicker of her brow, and then a

brief half smile. Taking her time, finger by finger, she pulled off the soft, black gloves and dropped them into her lap, then reached her hand out across the desk again. Not once during the entire process did she break eye contact. Trying to ignore the look, Jack reached across and took her right hand in his own.

It was immediate. Jack's head was awash with stars. Black night, sky. He sucked in his breath. Shooting lines, etched in white fire, skittered across the field, sharp, pointed, bladelike tips. The bottom of his stomach fell away. A deep shuddering breath, and he struggled for reality. He couldn't feel anything. He couldn't see. He closed his eyes, drawing on his resources, willing himself to feel his body. Slowly, painfully, he released his grip. His teeth clamped shut. Grimacing, he snapped his head back, remembering how to breathe. Remembering where he was. He forced his eyes open.

He was back in his office. The room was there just as it had been before. Breathing shallowly, he relaxed the pressure in his jaw and then took another deep breath, slowly letting it out and lowering his head to face her again.

Bridgett Farrell was watching him with a wide-eyed expression, genuine this time. "What is it?" she said. "Are you all right?"

Jack took a second to control his breathing properly. It had been a long time since he'd felt anything with that intensity. A long time. His heart was still racing.

"Okay, yeah, I'm fine," he said, forcing himself to speak slowly. He'd been expecting something to do with Talbot, some impression. Not this vast wash of sky and stars. "There's definitely something there, something that has got me interested. What more can you tell me about this artifact?"

"It's something of great importance to my family. It's something old. We're not sure where it came from, but it's been in my family for years."

Okay, so family heirloom. But that didn't explain the whole thing with the stars and sky. No way. He desperately needed to focus. He was awash with the sensation of vast cold and an inability to draw breath. Not good. He needed to get a grip.

"Ms. Farrell, I need you to try and draw this thing for me. Please go over to the wall and just trace your finger across the surface.

"Image," he said to the wall.

She stood, picking her gloves up from her lap and placing them on the desk, and then crossed to the wall, looking a little confused.

"That's it. Just use your index finger." He was still finding it hard to think. The vision's intensity had washed all real thought away, and he could use the moment's respite this little exercise would give him to regain some sort of composure.

Hesitantly, she reached out and traced a line. "Oh," she said, as a dark line appeared across the wall's surface in her finger's wake. She reached out again, this time with more confidence, and traced another line. Within moments she had sketched a shape. She stood back, nodded to herself, and then made some markings on the area representing the upper surface. It was a crude drawing, but it was giving Jack the general idea of what he was looking for.

"Save," he said. The whole wall flickered briefly and Jack frowned. What the hell was that? The home system just didn't get interference. He looked around the office quickly, but there was nothing else to suggest anything was out of place.

Bridgett Farrell moved back to her chair, crossed her

legs after sitting, then reached across to snag her gloves, pulling them on and adjusting the fingers one at a time. She seemed not to have noticed the brief aberration on the screen.

Jack took a couple of moments before speaking.

"Right. Ms. Farrell. Um . . . describe Talbot for me. Tell me what he looks like."

She peered across the desk at him, sizing him up. "Dark hair, a little shorter, a little bigger than you. Square jaw. Five o'clock shadow."

"Bigger?"

"Yes, you know . . ." She pressed her hands to her shoulders.

"Hmmm."

"How does he dress?"

"Smart. He has style."

Okay. And Jack didn't. He shrugged. He had a picture forming in his head, but he had no idea whether it might be accurate. If this Farrell woman was anything to go by, there'd be a touch of something foreign about Talbot's look, his clothes, something. Something out of the ordinary. He might be making assumptions here, but it was a fair bet. Jack didn't think it very likely that Talbot came from Yorkstone, especially as she'd said he was "here too," implying that it was for the same sort of reason she was.

"Does he come from around here, Ms. Farrell?"

She gave a little shake of her head. "No. But does that matter?"

"Not really, but it gives me some pointers about who I'm looking for. I think I've got enough to go on for now," he said finally. "It's a pity you haven't got more I can use. Clear image," he said. He could recall it later, get Billie to work on it. "Where can I get hold of you?"

There was a slight quirk of her lips at that. "I'm staying at the Excelsior."

Jack nodded. He knew it well. Yorkstone didn't have too many luxury hotels and The Excelsior sat bang in the middle of the main shopping district. You could hardly miss it.

"Fine. I think I have enough. Just one last thing. I'd like to start with a retainer. Three thousand should do it."

She reached into her bag and pulled out a handi-pad. There wasn't the slightest hesitation. She keyed a few commands and then swung around to face the wall.

The transfer went through in moments, the wall mapping the success of the transaction.

Jack nodded slowly. "Yeah, that'll do it," he said. "I'll see you out." Whatever the hell it was, she wanted this thing back pretty badly—and whatever it was, it had to be worth a damned lot more than she was prepared to pay for the services of one Jack Stein.

Jack stood, waiting as she also got to her feet, then walked her out of the office and to the door. Billie was nowhere in sight.

At the door she paused, turning to place one gloved hand upon his upper arm. She was little, this Bridgett Farrell, small and petite, but her presence was bigger than Jack might have at first expected. Somehow he'd thought she was larger. She barely came up to his shoulder.

"When will I hear from you, Mr. Stein?" she said. There was something deep and throaty in her voice.

"I'll be in touch."

She gave a quick nervous smile and turned, walking off down the hallway toward the elevator. Jack stared after her, watching the prim measured steps, the careful carriage. Billie had seen it; there was something not quite right about this woman, but for fifteen hundred a day, plus expenses, Jack could ignore that fact, at least for now. And there were other things that might just keep him interested for a little longer too.

Three

Jack came back into the living room to face glaring eyes and firmly crossed arms. Billie stood in the room's center, staring at him accusingly.

"What?" he said.

She turned away from him, her arms still crossed. She said something that he didn't quite catch.

"What, Billie? *What?*"

"I told you I didn't like her."

"Yeah, fine. What about it? She's a client. We can do with the money."

She spun about, her chin stuck out. "So why were you holding hands with her?"

"Jesus. Were you spying on me?"

"Nuh-uh." She shook her head.

"I don't believe you."

That was what that flicker in the wall had been all about. Billie had programmed the home system to spy on his office. She probably had it set up to work from her bedroom, somewhere strictly out of bounds to him by mutual agreement. Damn, but she was good. He pursed his lips. Okay, she was smart, but how the hell was he supposed to maintain some sort of order in their life, when she was starting to do whatever she wanted without even consulting him? It wasn't good

that she was listening in either. Sometimes there were
things that he'd just rather she didn't hear.

Jack sighed and sat, running his fingers back
through his hair. "Listen, I wasn't holding hands with
her. She's given me limited stuff to go on. I was seeing
if there was anything else I could pick up on.
That's . . . all."

It was as if she was being possessive. The last time
he'd seen her like that was with the Van der Stegen
woman, over two years ago. This time, there was another edge to it. Not one that he could afford to let get
out of hand. Their relationship was taut enough as it
was, without the other implications. Implications that
he really didn't want to think about. There was no
way he was going to let on to her about the other
thoughts he'd had, right now.

She held her lips in a tight line, but her face relaxed
a little.

"Yeah, and you're right," he continued. "There's
something about her that I don't quite trust. But we've
been there before, Billie. You know as well as I do that
we need this job. She's going to pay, we can live with it."

She humphed, but his words seemed to have molli-
fied her. She sat on a chair opposite, pulling her legs
up in front of her. "So tell me?"

"Location. Retrieval. She's lost something." He
shrugged.

"What else?" She was looking down at her fingers,
picking at the nail on one finger.

"She says this thing has been taken by some guy
called Talbot."

"What thing?" She looked up at him.

"Last image," said Jack. The quick sketch bled into
existence on the living room wall. He jerked his head
at it. "That thing."

Billie studied the drawing and then frowned. "Huh? What is it?"

Jack sighed. "Don't know. She called it an artifact. Something old. Not much more than that. She said it was a family heirloom. I don't think that's enough to go on though. I need you to find out what this is, Billie."

She was still staring at the sketch. "Uh-huh."

Jack waited till her attention swung back to him.

"There's something about this thing, Billie. I don't know what, but I think there's more to it than it seems. I got some pretty strong impressions in there. The same with this woman, Bridgett Farrell. I need you to do some work on her and on the Talbot guy too."

Her eyes narrowed and she gave a quick nod. "Talbot. What Talbot?"

"Carl."

"Uh-huh."

"And that's it for now. Me, I need to work out what they're doing in Yorkstone. She's staying at the Excelsior."

Billie rolled her eyes. "I know she is."

Of course she did.

"Okay. I need coffee. You want anything?"

"Nuh-uh. Soon."

Jack frowned. Billie shook her head, then mimed pushing stuff into her mouth with her fingers, looking at him like he was an idiot. "Got it?"

"Yeah, yeah. All right. Soon, okay?"

He pushed himself to his feet and headed into the kitchen to leave her to it. He knew better than to disturb her when she was focused on her particular talent. He'd talk about the whole sky/stars thing later when she'd tracked down some more information. Billie accepted what he did, what his inner senses told him, but she was just as likely to take whatever impressions he'd received and run with them, distracting her from the matter at hand. Sometimes that simply confused the process rather than helped it.

As he waited for the coffee, he decided he missed having a window in the kitchen. It would be good to be able to stare out at the street while he was waiting for things to happen, not that there was that much to see. Instead he was left with his thoughts to play with. If they'd been in a different place in the building, he would have been able to program one, just like he could program the furniture and the other parts of the apartment, but he doubted the neighbors would appreciate a new window looking into their bedroom, even if the building would have let him.

He and Billie had been together for two years now, and in the beginning they'd been through a fair bit. The life he gave her was better than anything she'd had back in the Locality, but there were times, like now, when he suspected it might not be enough. The way she talked to people, the way she reacted. It wasn't so different, he supposed, from when he'd first met her, but he sometimes wondered whether too much of his own attitude and brusque approach to life had somehow rubbed off on her. That attitude was part of the reason they functioned so well together, but it couldn't be good for a young girl like Billie. And she was just that—a young girl.

The coffeemaker announced it had finished its cycle, and he poured himself a mug and headed back into the living room. Billie was squatting on the couch, head tilted up, staring at a list on the wallscreen. She barely glanced at Jack as he reentered.

He sipped at the coffee, watching her focus and concentration, envying it a little. Too much distracted him to do such detailed searching—little echoes, resonances that set off tangents in his brain. She seemed to be able to refine her attention, streaming it into an almost obsessive directedness. Ten minutes later, she was still scrolling through screens and his coffee mug was empty.

"Food, Billie."

She waved at him for quiet.

"Come on. It's getting late. And let me guess . . . Molly's, right?"

That stopped her. She glanced at Jack, back at the wallscreen, then back at him again. "Save," she said.

As they left their building, Jack scanned the surrounding area, looking for anything out of place, not expecting to find anything in particular, but old habits died hard. Yorkstone's social planning had done much to make the city cleaner, more friendly to normal life. The grime and underlying sense that everything might fall apart was absent. Despite himself, Jack almost missed it, that edgy sense of being just on the lip of a yawning gap. The shuttle stop was not too far from the apartment, but whereas Jack's old place in the Locality had been on a main thoroughfare, here they lived in a pleasant little side street.

Yorkstone had invested more in the maintenance end of the programming spectrum, and though there was the inevitable decay as the pseudo-organic builders reached the end of their lifecycle, it seemed to happen much farther down toward the city's tail. In the Locality, you would have seen the marks of that crumbling edge closer to the city's center. In the Locality, people still lived and worked right within that urban tarnish, the falling apart a constant reminder in the back of the consciousness. Yorkstone's owners and designers were more careful. The residential areas were defined well away from those sections where things slowly stopped working. You could almost believe you were in one of the old, fixed cities, rather than a mobile, half-alive urban containment.

Jack and Billie strolled up their street, heading for the shuttle. It was dark now. Far above, the ceiling panels revealed a clear, cloudless sky beyond their transparent vault. Jack looked up as they walked, swallowing back the slight chill that came with the starry black picture above them. Outside it would be cold, far colder than the regulated temperature inside. Cold white light, touches of something else tracing the edges. The vision washed back into his senses, prompted by the night sky. The sensory flash had been intense. Too intense. He hadn't had anything like it for well over a year now, and that sudden forgotten power was unsettling. He knew, without thinking about it, that they were about to get involved in something big. He tore his gaze from the sky above and glanced across at Billie. No point in worrying her about it right now. He could wait until they'd eaten and gotten back to the apartment to broach his suspicions.

Billie was humming as they boarded the shuttle, and her apparent quick mood change set him thinking again. As they took their seats, a couple toward the other end of the shuttle smiled at them, then politely looked away to watch the passing scenery. So different. Everything about this place was different. The shuttle cars were clean. The people were clean, friendly, polite. The education program was certainly better than anything offered back at the Locality. Back there, you made your own existence. Everything was available, as long as you could pay for it. Here, money was still involved, but it was a different equation. Society functioned in an ordered fashion. In the Locality, you made your own luck and that was how things worked. That was the funny thing. For years and years Jack had done just that, made his own luck, as haphazard as that had been. But now, here in Yorkstone, that facility no longer served in the way it had. Maybe he just didn't need to be lucky here.

A sharp nudge brought him back to himself.

"Jack?"

"Yeah, sorry." It was their stop.

"What is it?" she said.

"Nothing. I was just thinking." She peered up at his face, but seemed content with his answer. She tugged at his arm.

The shuttle slowed, the doors hissed open, and together they stepped out into balmy, temperate air in a tree-lined plaza. This, their nearest commercial area, was open, lines of stores on either side with glasslike fronts. Advertising crawled up walls and across lintels, but it was in subtle, muted tones, not glaring. There were no advertising drones in sight. Back in the Locality, a place like this would be full of the short mobile devices, programmed to tag passersby and hit them with bursts of light and noise. It was one of the many things he really didn't miss.

Molly's sat diagonally across from the shuttle stop and he and Billie walked across, the lightness still present in her steps. Funny, Jack thought as he stepped through the door into the slightly cooler temperature of the store itself, he'd even become used to the taste of Molly's. There was a time when he wouldn't go near it to save his life. It was some vague principle thing. He'd always objected, for some reason, to the prepackaged synthetic muck, but now . . . now, he seemed to eat the stuff more often than not. He wasn't the only one doing the influencing in this partnership. Billie was influencing him in her own, sometimes less than subtle, way.

They ordered—Billie her standard Mollyburger and fries, and Jack the fried onion rings and a salad as well as a burger, a couple of drinks—and headed for a table by the front window. Jack picked slowly at his fries.

"Tell me, Billie. What was it about Bridgett Farrell that you didn't like?"

She shrugged, taking a big mouthful and chewing enthusiastically, swinging her legs back and forth under the table. She reached for her drink.

Jack watched her. "Listen, I'm curious. What was it?"

"I dunno. She was fake. I could tell as soon as she walked in. That fake voice. The fake way she held herself. It wasn't real. I don't like people like that. You can't trust them." She shrugged again, more interested in the food in front of her than pursuing Jack's line of thinking.

Jack thought that over. Okay, he knew that, but Billie seemed to have made the decision in an instant. She would have taken the Farrell woman into the office and left her as quickly as possible. What was it? He'd never really worked out whether that sense she had was innate, something similar to Jack's own talents, or something born of experience gathered in the life she'd led down in Old back at the Locality. Could you learn survival sense or did you have to have it in the first place? Because that was what it was all about—survival.

"Ever since I've known you," he said, "you've been quick to make up your mind about people, haven't you? Was it always like that? Before, I mean."

She shrugged again, reaching for her fries.

"No, come on, Billie. I'm trying to work something out here."

She stopped with a fry halfway to her mouth and stared at him. "What for?"

"Just an idea I'm working with."

She finished the action, popping the fry into her mouth and reaching for another. He sat waiting for her to answer, but the answer never came. He knew better than to push her if she didn't want to talk about something. Maybe he'd try again later. He speared a forkful of salad and lifted it to his mouth, inspecting it before popping it in. The salad was merely a reaction to their constant diet of processed pap. Fooling himself that he was making some attempt at being healthy. But then, Jack had always been pretty good at fooling himself.

Clang. The sound reverberated around and through him, loud, sonorous. *Clang.* There it was again. He could feel it in his guts, in the back of his teeth. Slowly he opened his eyes. He was standing in the middle of a flat plain, dark gray, featureless. *Clang.* Ask not for whom the bell tolls.

This was a dream. Had to be.

Clang.

Jack tried to pick out something, anything that would pin down where he was supposed to be. The surface upon which he stood was smooth and dark. Hard. He could sense the hardness through his feet. Above him there was . . . nothing. No, that wasn't quite right. It too was gray and featureless, but if he concentrated, he could feel rather than see a roiling motion in the reaches far above.

He willed himself larger.

Clang.

He was stuck. Too much inactivity. He was out of practice, knew he was. He bunched his will and tried again. This time it had an effect, but instead of growing in size, his feet left the surface he was standing on. Okay, so this was going to be a flying dream, was it? Gradually he floated upward, slowly picking up speed, heading . . . no, it wasn't skyward . . . what was it?

Clang.

The sound seemed to propel him with greater speed, pushing him up into what was evident now as a swirling gray fog. His head, his body, eased into it. And then it was all around him. There was no feeling to the wafting nothingness, no taste, no smell. He had expected clammy dampness, but it was swirling nothingness. He could see shapes and patterns in the gray, but that wasn't why he was here, he knew. He willed himself farther. In the midst of the blankness, he couldn't tell if he was moving at all.

Then, suddenly, his head was clear, then his shoulders, then the rest of his body. He floated in a between place. Below him was a cloudscape, dark, the color of thunderstorms and threatened energy. Above him . . . Jack narrowed his eyes, trying to work out exactly what it was that lay above him. It took a moment to make sense of it. It was like the slightly arched ceiling panels of Yorkstone, but instead of being clear, they were matte, dark gray. The roof space swept over him and off into the distance till it merged with the mist in one blurred continuous line. Behind him it was the same, and off to either side.

Clang.

Again he willed himself higher. He picked up speed, rushing toward the hard, flat surface above him—but no, it wasn't flat. Now that he was closer, he could see there were marks on the vault's underneath. Vast protrusions in curves and lines, spelling out incomprehensible symbols. They were hard, solid, and he was picking up speed. If he didn't do something, he was going to crash into those ridges. He clamped his jaw tight, painfully willing himself to slow.

Clang.

The noise was coming from the surface above him, an echoing vibration pulsing down through the surrounding space. It was like that. It was like some giant metallic heartbeat. He was slowing; he could sense it.

Right then, he knew, he reminded himself. This was a dream. Things could happen to him in a dream. He could slam against that solid surface and wake, shaken, but undamaged. But that was logic, and dreams weren't always logical. With another effort of will, he forced his passage slower, feeling a rising sense of panic.

Success.

He was hovering now, floating just below the vast surface. There was no feeling of height. It was natural just to float here. No fear of falling.

Clang.

The vibration shook him. It rattled his teeth, his bones.

He tried to make out the symbols, but they were too big. They stretched away on either side, far too large to see the sense of the shapes. He was too close.

And then darkness was replaced by light.

Jack opened his eyes and stared at the ceiling—his bedroom ceiling.

"Arghh," he groaned to himself. He wasn't finished yet. He needed to get back into the dream and work out what it was telling him.

He closed his eyes again, trying to force himself back into the dreamstate, but it was gone. He could feel the last vestiges trickling away.

He groaned again and rolled over onto his side.

Just before he'd surfaced, there'd been light, bright

and blue-white. Illumination in the distance. Traceries, almost spiderwebs of light. That had meant something. It was almost as if that huge, stretching surface had been like a sky, but a sky that was solid, stretching out to eternity. The growing light—it was almost like a sunrise, shafts of blue-white shooting across the surface, casting shadows in the distance.

No, he didn't have enough. There was nothing there yet. Not anything he could hold on to.

Four

Jack was puttering around in the kitchen when Billie finally arose. She appeared in the kitchen doorway rubbing her hand through a tangle of blond hair, eyes half shut, stifling a yawn.

"Hey," he said.

"Hmmmmph."

"How long do you think it will take to get something on this Talbot guy?" He could start the work himself, but Billie was so much better, so much quicker than he was, and he didn't want to waste any time. Since they'd been in Yorkstone, she'd gotten even better. It seemed to take her mere moments to make connections, draw the references that would lead her down a path, mining information like she was almost scenting it. She seemed to sense patterns innately. But not in the morning.

She screwed up her face and looked at him blearily through narrowed eyes. She wasn't very good in the mornings, but then neither was he. Not that Jack ever had any proper sense of what time of day it was. Living in and out of dreamstate did that to you. There was no defined sleep pattern, no regular hours of unconsciousness to order or organize his life. With Billie, it was just morning.

"Okay, take your time," he said. "But I need to get moving on this pretty quickly. If we're not careful, Talbot will skip, if he hasn't done so already."

She waved a hand at him and headed for the freezer, looking for the boxed synthetic milk.

"Okay," he said. Better to leave her to struggle into consciousness in her own time. Half an hour either way wasn't going to kill it. He poured another mug of coffee and headed for the living room, leaving Billie to clatter and fumble around in the kitchen behind him. He placed his coffee down and leaned forward. "Last image," he said.

The sketched object took shape in the wall and he stared at it, chewing at his bottom lip. The Farrell woman had said it was dark gray, metal. That certainly coincided with his dream image from last night. And those squiggles she'd drawn on the upper surface could have been the vast shapes above him while he'd floated just beneath the endless ceiling. It was only a rude sketch, and there was not enough detail to tell whether there was anything to indicate light, or a sun, or something like that. This thing was a chunk of metal. It wasn't particularly big, and it certainly didn't look like it was a part of something larger. The designs along the side edges meant that it hadn't been broken off from something else along those sides, but he didn't know what was on the other edges at either end. For all he knew they could be rough and unmarked, meaning the thing could have been snapped off from something, anything, larger.

Billie stumbled past, heading for her room and the shower. Jack closed his eyes, holding on to the sketch, trying to give it solidity and shape. Nothing there. Nothing sparking inside his head or in his guts. He grimaced and opened his eyes again. Really, he'd seen nothing quite like the object before, but as far as he could tell, there wasn't anything about it that would make it particularly valuable. There was no accounting for the taste of people who collected things though. Rarity, age, all gave objects value. As far as Jack was concerned, the real value lay in the energies that objects accumulated over the years, but he wasn't going to get anywhere near those from a simple hand-rendered sketch.

Billie reappeared, dressed in pale, loose, comfortable clothes. Her hair was as messed up as it had been before she went for her shower. She moved over to the couch and shoved Jack out of the way.

"Hey!"

She gave him a dismissive look. "Well, do you want me to do this stuff or don't you?"

"Yeah, yeah. Okay, I'm going for a walk and leave you to it." He had no other option really. He could go back into the office, but he'd only end up playing with the furniture or the window displays again, or simply staring at his empty diary. He had far too little to occupy himself with. What a life.

He actually ended up getting on the shuttle and heading into one of the shopping districts, to wander among the storefronts and the people. Large department stores clustered together, one on top of the other. In between lay cafés, bars, and restaurants. He wandered for a while, browsing along the catalog boards inside the stores, randomly flicking from page to page, watching as the images formed and re-formed in front of him. He tapped at them randomly, not looking for anything in particular, just seeing what there was to see. Appliances, new media toys, top-of-the-range handipads that put his own to shame. They were there, page after page. You could do all of this from the comfort of your own personal wallscreen, but there was something about the ritual of "going shopping" that people still clung to, regardless. He wandered out of the store and into the next one.

This one was a fashion chain, and Jack, realizing where he was, glanced down at his old long coat. It had lasted for years, but it wouldn't survive for years more. Maybe it was about time he did something about it. He headed for the relevant department on one of the upper floors, all the while watching. People browsed, calmly, unhurriedly. There was a pace of life here. Where was the edge?

He wandered over to the coat section and scanned the boards, feeling slightly foolish. Nothing really grabbed him. He liked his old coat. He ran his finger down the displays and tapped on something vaguely similar. An image of Jack Stein sprang into being in front of him, wearing the coat in the catalog. The store system had automatically mapped him as soon as he'd started browsing the displays. He walked around the image of himself, considering, casting a semicritical gaze. It was slightly disconcerting to be standing behind yourself, seeing yourself from the back as others saw you. He reached up a hand to smooth down the back of his hair. Maybe he needed a change. He crossed back to the board and changed the color, watching as dark brown bled into gray-black. Yeah, maybe. The problem with these images was that you couldn't adjust things like lifting the collar. They were set for optimum display, but optimum in the mind of the marketing functions. He glanced at the price, then shook his head.

"Forget it, Stein."

A voice came from the board. "Can we be of further assistance?"

"No, that's fine," he said, tapping at the board to kill the display.

"May we suggest the latest seasonal line?" Images flashed in quick succession across what had been, moments before, a straightforward catalog display. All of them were Jack, dressed in a range of different coats and outfits. The yellow, as it flashed past, was just simply obnoxious. He thought he'd killed the display.

"No, that's fine," he said a bit more forcefully, and headed for the exit shaking his head.

He found himself out on the street a few moments later, suddenly realizing that without even thinking about it he had come to a section quite close to the upper end of Yorkstone. Not too far away sat the Excelsior. He glanced about, establishing his bearings. The hotel was about two blocks virtual north. The problem with living in any of the urban structures, such as Yorkstone or the Locality, was that direction was transitory. As the cities crawled across the landscape, seeking the replenishing materials, constantly renewing themselves and their structures, they changed direction, driven by the autoprogrammed sensors built into their leading edges. This meant they often moved in vast arcs, shifting their compass bearing as they traveled. But city maps were still city maps, and the top of the map was north, whichever way they were facing. So Jack turned "north" and started walking. It was close enough that he didn't need to hop a shuttle.

There was no mistaking the Excelsior. The gold and glass entrance portico shone in the middle of its block, stylized with pillars and rotating doors reminiscent of a bygone style. He stood, hands on hips, looking at it, just appreciating it for what it was for a few moments before heading to the front doors. He was here; he might as well visit Bridgett Farrell and see if he could work out what she was hiding.

The large glass doors whooshed open to allow him entrance, and he walked into a wide polished space—shining marble, bronze pots, plants, and real people. There was a front desk, wide and richly polished, looking like it was made of granite. He knew it couldn't be the case, but the effect would have taken some programming. He'd never been inside the Excelsior before, and despite himself, Jack was impressed. He wandered over to the desk, wondering what he was supposed to do for attention. A smiling person, crisply uniformed, was instantly in front of him.

"Can I help you, sir?"

Jack ignored the slight flicker in the man's eyes, the unspoken *And what precisely do you want here? You don't really belong, do you?*

"I'd like to speak to one of your guests."

"Certainly, sir. The guest's name?"

"Ms. Farrell. Ms. Bridgett Farrell."

The clerk fiddled with something on the desk's surface, and a scrolling list appeared. He tapped once or twice and then nodded. "I'm afraid Ms. Farrell is not in."

"You're sure?"

"Yes, quite certain, sir. If you'd like to leave a message, perhaps . . ."

"No, that's okay. I'll catch up with her later."

So, a wasted journey. Well, not entirely wasted. He had the confirmation that she could afford his services. Anyone who stayed in a place like this had to be able to afford someone like Jack Stein.

As he walked away from the front desk, he could

feel the clerk watching him. But that was not all he could feel. Someone else was watching him too. He knew that feeling of old. Slowing his pace a little, he glanced around the lobby, trying to make it not too obvious. There. Over to one side, on one of the large, comfortable pseudo-leather lounges, sat a small man. He caught Jack's look and quickly averted his gaze. The observation had been more than casual. Jack was sure of it. Behind him, the clerk was saying something to a coworker. Sound carried well across this lobby, and he could almost make out every syllable. Jack moved over to one of the information displays and started scrolling through, keeping one eye on the guy on the couch.

Was it the Farrell name that had drawn the attention, or was it something else? Something was sparking inside him, telling him, a knotted expectation nestled in his abdomen. The man was round-faced, dark mousey hair, dark eyes. He was dressed nondescriptly, a plain jacket and trousers and a casual shirt. Right now, he was studiously not making eye contact with Jack's carefully undirected gaze. Pretending that he had found what he was looking for, Jack headed for the entrance. As the doors swung open with his approach, he turned, looking back over his shoulder. The guy was watching him all right, and he quickly looked away again. Nodding to himself, Jack stepped out of the lobby and into the street. All right, that had been strange.

He strolled casually a few doors down, then slipped into a doorway, watching back the way he had come. Nobody else appeared through the tall hotel doors. Maybe he'd just been imagining it, inventing things he could chase to keep himself occupied, but he didn't think so.

"Hmmm," he said to himself, barely noticing that he'd made the sound.

Something to think about anyway. It probably wasn't Jack who was being watched—it could just as well be Bridgett Farrell, and that put an interesting spin on things. His guts were telling him something anyway, and that was progress.

Shoving his hands in his pockets, he walked slowly back toward the department stores and the shuttle that would take him home.

By the time he got back to the apartment, Billie had made real progress. She looked up as Jack walked into the living room. She had that look of accomplishment on her face, and the set of her shoulders told him she thought she had achieved something.

"So . . . ?" he said.

"Well . . . Talbot, Carl."

"Uh-huh?" He sat down on the seat opposite her, waiting while she drew the moment out.

"Antiques."

"Good. Yes. That doesn't surprise me. What else?"

"Arrived in Yorkstone four days ago. Registered at the Excelsior."

She gave Jack a pointed look and he frowned at that revelation.

"What the hell?" That didn't make any sense at all. If Talbot was registered at the Excelsior, then . . . No. That just didn't make any kind of sense. Farrell would hardly hire him to look for the guy if he was staying at the same hotel, would she? The place was small enough, exclusive enough that she'd have to have some idea if he was there. It was possible she didn't, but not likely.

"And?" he asked, ignoring Billie's told-you-so look.

"Hasn't checked out."

"Okay, this makes absolutely no damned sense at all. If both of them are registered at the Excelsior. . . . Dammit. I was just up there." He sat forward and scratched rapidly at his temple, grimaced and shook his head. "You got a picture?"

"Uh-huh," she said. "Carl Talbot file. Picture," she directed at the wall.

A man looking just as Bridgett Farrell had described appeared on the wallscreen. It wasn't a good picture, an identity shot or something like that, but all the features were there. Front on, dark hair, square jaw, slightly shadowed. Widely set dark eyes beneath fine dark brows. Olive skin. Slightly tight mouth. He stared out of the wall arrogantly.

Jack whipped out his handipad and directed the system to download the image. He looked at it, trying to divine anything from it, but it was just a picture.

"Antiques, Billie. Anything more than that? What about antiques?"

"Dealer. Import/export. That's all." She shrugged. "Getting that much was hard."

"Is there an address?"

"Not here. It's not onworld. Somewhere called Utrecht. Balance City."

He'd never heard of it. But then the universe was no longer a tiny place. There were worlds upon worlds that he'd never heard of. The new jump drive developed by Outreach Industries had opened up the known universe to everyone. No longer did people have to rely on the old, conventional means of travel. What had once been an impossible dream for those without the wealth to afford it was becoming accessible, well within the means of common people, and now those common people were moving to places previously inhabited only by corporations and the impossibly wealthy. There were other implications as well. Knowledge was growing at an exponential rate, and there was no way anybody could possibly keep up with it, let alone someone with limited resources like Jack. Just as well Billie was so good at ferreting out information from the vast array of systems that spanned the increasingly known worlds.

So this Carl Talbot, offworld antique dealer, had taken this artifact. Maybe he'd done it as a commission job. Something for a collector. It was not unheard of. The heirloom story was becoming less and less likely. He didn't even know what Bridgett Farrell did. She'd said this Talbot was nothing to her, but that didn't seem very likely either.

"Jack?" Billie was looking at him, expectantly.

"Yeah, sorry. I was thinking. What is it?"

"I haven't had enough time to find anything about this thing you're supposed to find."

"Yeah, but. . . ."

"There's more." This time she was looking more than pleased with herself.

"Okay, give."

"There is no Bridgett Farrell. Couldn't find her anywhere. Apart from the Excelsior, there's nothing."

That wasn't good. He narrowed his eyes at her and sat back. "Nothing at all?"

"Nuh-uh."

"Shit." Billie might see it as a victory, but it more than complicated things. "Do me a favor? Look for any known links to Carl Talbot. People. Especially women. It might be a long shot, but it's worth a try."

She grimaced, but nodded.

So, his mystery woman was more than a simple mystery, and she was certainly being less than honest with him. Now that he had confirmation, he had a bit more work to do. Part of that would be to work out the exact nature of the game she was playing with him. The prospect intrigued him. He was starting to get more interested. Probably more interested than he should be.

Five

Jack paced back and forth in front of his desk, trying to work out what the best course of action would be. So what if the Farrell woman was a fake, and in more ways than one; he'd kind of expected that. Still, she had seemed convinced that Carl Talbot had taken the artifact. If he could find Talbot, he could find what she was looking for. He could feel it.

He wandered past the shelves on one side of the office and noticed the card he'd casually dropped there the day before. Pausing, he picked it up and looked down at it thoughtfully. He hadn't even bothered to upload the information to his handipad yet. JIM MORRISH. INVESTIGATOR. He dug out his handipad, swiped the card, and then flicked it back to lie on the shelf. He'd file it away later. You never knew when a contact might come in useful, cop or not.

"Call Excelsior Hotel," he said, turning to the wall.

The desk personality took shape in the wall in front of him, and he leaned back on the edge of the desk. "Welcome to the Excelsior Hotel. How may we assist you?"

"Could you put me through to one of your guests, please?"

"Of course, sir. Guest's name?"

"Talbot. Mr. Carl Talbot." If Talbot was there, Jack

could pretend to be a collector, looking for what Talbot might have to offer. He'd at least thought that much through. He waited while the hotel program did its stuff.

"I'm sorry. We have no guest by that name."

"What? You're sure?"

"Yes, sir. We have no guest by that name."

"Look, put me through to a person, will you?"

The program paused again. "How may I assist you?"

Dammit. The programs were good, but sometimes there was a limit to what they could do.

"Put me through to . . . ah . . . Reservations."

"Connecting you now."

Moments later, another program took shape on the wall in front of him. He didn't want a program. This time the program was a pleasantly smiling female replica.

"Reservations. May I be of assistance?"

"Can I speak to a person, please?"

"Please state clearly your requirements and I will try and fulfill your request. We currently have a weekend special in effect. Would you like to hear the special rates?"

"No, thank you."

"How many people would you like to book for?"

"Listen. Can I talk to the manager, please?"

"Connecting you now."

There was a long pause, and Jack could feel his frustration building. A bored-looking young man in hotel livery—red jacket, dark shirt—took shape on the screen, looking away at something to one side. Jack coughed. The young man looked up, momentarily confused, then regained composure, smoothing his jacket and sitting up, looking slightly abashed at having been caught doing something else.

"Yes, sir. How can I help you?"

"Sorry," said Jack. "I was having a few problems with your desk programs. I'm trying to track down one of your guests. We have some business together."

"Certainly, sir. Can you tell me the guest's name?"

"Carl Talbot. We were supposed to have a business appointment this evening."

The reservations manager fiddled with something beside him, then looked up at the screen again, obviously watching a split display.

"I'm sorry, sir. Mr. Talbot has checked out."

"Can you tell me what time?"

"Yes, about three o'clock."

"Was there any forwarding information left?"

"No, I'm sorry. But there is a message waiting for him. We were instructed to hold any messages that came in."

Okay, so someone else clearly knew Talbot had been staying there. "Can you tell me who it's from?"

"I'm sorry. I'm not able to give you that information. Would you like to leave a message too? Though if he has checked out, I can't guarantee that he'll collect it."

"No, that's okay," said Jack. "Thanks for your help." He cut the connection; then, rethinking, he called the hotel again.

"I'd like to speak to one of your guests, please."

"Yes sir. Guest's name?"

"Bridgett Farrell."

There was another brief pause as the desk program processed. "I'm sorry, sir. That guest is not taking calls at the present time. Would you like to leave a message?"

Jack suppressed a growl of frustration. "No, that's okay." He cut the connection again.

He had no choice but to go up there and confront his client with what he knew, try to get some more information from her about what was really going on. Finding an extra excuse for having a face-to-face was just an extra bonus. He grimaced. He had to stop thinking like that. The woman was trouble.

He shut down the wallscreen and headed into the living room. Once again Billie was staring at the screen, cross-referencing index material. The display was split into multiple panels. One held the finger sketch that Bridgett Farrell had left, another showed an article, yet another seemed to be some sort of catalog listing, and yet another showed scrolling text. Billie's gaze flicked from one to the other.

"Right panel. Hold," she said. "Pause." She looked up at Jack, a question on her face.

"I have to go up to the hotel again. Bridgett Farrell or whoever she is isn't taking calls."

Billie just nodded.

"You okay?" he asked her.

"Uh-huh."

"Okay, I'll see you in a while." She'd already lost interest in him and was back watching the scrolling displays.

Jack nodded to himself and headed for the door. It looked like she was going to be occupied for a while yet.

As he left the apartment, something snagged his attention. He stopped in midstep, looking up and down the street, slowly turning, trying to find out what had set off his internal alarms. The street was fairly empty. An old guy walked farther down the same side of the street, heading in the opposite direction from the shuttle stop. A slight breeze riffled through the leaves in the surrounding trees and a couple of leaves floated down to be quickly snatched up by the pavement. He looked around again. Nothing unusual at all.

He tried to shake the feeling away from him and

headed toward the shuttle stop, walking slowly, his hands shoved in his pockets. As he neared the end of their street, the feeling was back. He stopped again. The slightest flicker of movement from the other side of the street drew him. Across from where he stood, on the other side, someone had been standing in a doorway, partially shadowed. As soon as Jack had looked in that direction, the figure had slipped quickly back inside. It had been too quick for Jack to make out any real details, but whoever it was had been short and male, dark haired. He had picked up that much. The face had been a mere pale smudge. He stood watching the doorway for a couple of minutes, waiting to see if whoever it was would reappear. Maybe it had been nothing, his imagination working overtime again, but he'd learned long ago to trust those feelings. When it became clear that whoever it was had gone, he shook his head and wandered on. If he was really being watched, he'd find out about it soon enough, but it added an interesting element to the mix. Why would anyone be watching him particularly? Was it the guy from the hotel lobby?

There was no shuttle in sight, and he waited, riffling through the possibilities. What about Billie? If there was someone watching the apartment, or watching him, then it affected Billie by default. No, she'd be fine. Billie knew how to look after herself. Besides, the shuttle had appeared farther down the street. He watched and waited for it to pull in, and then climbed on board. A family group at the other end looked like they were heading for a shopping expedition near the end of the line, just as he'd done earlier. Despite the system access to everything you needed, people still went shopping. People liked going shopping. Maybe it was the actual social nature of it, but even that wasn't true anymore. Maybe it was like the entertainment center. You went with crowds of strangers and sat there, not interacting with them, but sharing it all the same. He shrugged. Not Jack. He preferred watching a vid at home, the old stuff with real actors and real settings— not that you could really tell the difference these days. He could do without the crowds and the people. Mostly, he could do without the people. Billie was no different. She was just as happy as he was with their strangely cosseted existence. He wondered briefly if that was partly his influence or whether she was like that naturally. Whatever, it seemed to suit them, together. Too much analysis and he could drive himself crazy. He grimaced at himself. For someone who spent his time analyzing impressions and the feelings he got from people, he didn't do a very good job of it when it came to himself. Nor, come to think of it, as far as Billie was concerned.

He was still musing when they reached the end of the line, and he looked up, semisurprised that they were already there. He stepped out of the shuttle into the stop, the curved white arcs above him blocking the outside view. Plenty of people still walked between the stores and sitting areas, looking perfectly content with their Yorkstone existence. Jack gave a little sigh. He too had become part of this. At least, for now, it looked like he had something he could get his teeth into.

He strolled in the direction of the Excelsior, taking his time—checking not only with his eyes, but also with his inner senses, testing if there was anything out of place. His internal alarms were out of practice, rusty, and he wanted to give them the time to trigger if there really was anything there, though the place was really too public for there to be much of a risk.

The Excelsior's lobby was just as it had been before. He walked up to the front desk, giving the place a quick scan. A couple of businessmen sat in tall lounge chairs in front of a table, deep in conversation, but apart from the staff, they were the only other occupants. There was a different person behind the desk.

"Welcome to the Excelsior. May I help you?" She had a bright smile, and Jack felt himself smile back.

"Good afternoon. I'd like to speak to Ms. Bridgett Farrell. She's staying here. I don't know the room number."

The woman gave him another smile. "Of course, sir. One moment."

Again the ritual with the desktop and a brief frown.

"I'm sorry," she said. "Ms. Farrell has checked out."

"What?"

"Ms. Farrell has checked out. I'm sorry." She spread her hands in a gesture of apology.

Jack shook his head. "But that's impossible. There must be some mistake."

"I'm sorry, sir. No mistake. She checked out about twenty minutes ago. You've just missed her." Her glance flickered to the side, as if seeking backup in case Jack was going to turn difficult.

"Were you here when she left? Do you remember her?"

"I'm sorry. I've just come on."

"Yeah, well, thanks." He turned away from the desk and stalked over to one of the large comfortable couches that now sat empty around the lobby. Twenty minutes. She could be just about anywhere in York-stone within the space of twenty minutes. He sat heavily, propping his elbows on his knees and staring at the floor. She was gone. Not good. So, if his thought processes weren't betraying him, was his fee. The three thousand retainer was a start, but it wasn't anything like he expected out of this case. Nothing like it. He shook his head again. What the hell was going on? Maybe she had cause. He was probably just being paranoid. For whatever reason, she'd needed to take off, and all he had to do was wait for her to contact him. Or maybe something had happened to her . . .

Whatever this artifact was, it was valuable, but, presuming he found the thing, he could hardly get it to her if she had disappeared too. Somehow, though, he suspected that someone would pay for its return. All he needed to do was work out who that someone was.

Right about now, Jack really needed Billie to determine what the object was, how it was significant. He also needed to find Carl Talbot and work out how he was tied into things, what his connection to Bridgett Farrell was. He should just walk away from this, he knew, but he was in too far. He straightened, ran his fingers through his hair, scratched his head and stood. He didn't have much of a choice really. He could feel this was big, had the potential to be big, if only he could start to tie off some of these loose ends that kept appearing without a moment's warning. Damn the Farrell woman, anyway. He'd come all the way up here for nothing. He gritted his teeth and let a slow breath out through his nose. Stupid, Stein. Stupid. He was letting the woman influence his thinking.

When Jack got back to the apartment, Billie was nowhere to be seen. He stood in the center of the living room, trying to ignore the spark of cold growing deep in his abdomen. He shouldn't have left her. His guts had been telling him something as he'd left for the Excelsior and he'd ignored them. His memories flashed back to the Locality and the cold spot in his middle grew colder.

He'd come back to an empty apartment once before with Billie nowhere to be seen. That time she'd been taken . . . taken by Pinpin Dan. But there was no Pinpin Dan here. Heironymous Dan was dead and the network of people he dealt with was far behind, back in the Locality. No, this couldn't be the same thing. Yorkstone was different. He swallowed.

"Billie?" he called.

A few moments later she appeared in her bedroom doorway, her clothes rumpled.

"What?"

"Oh, shit, sorry. I thought for a moment you weren't here." He felt himself relax.

"Got tired. Couldn't think."

"Yeah, sorry."

She wandered into the kitchen, poured herself a glass of water and came back in, clambered onto the couch, pulled her legs up in front of her and took a couple of sips.

"Well?" she said with a big sniff.

Jack collapsed into the chair. "She's gone."

"What do you mean?" Billie frowned across at him.

"Gone. Checked out. Don't know where she is."

Billie shook her head. "Great. What are you going to do?"

Jack leaned back and looked up at the ceiling. "Don't know yet. I need to think about it a bit more. There's something going on here." He lowered his face again and looked at her. Her lips were set in a thin disapproving line and her eyes were narrowed. He ignored the expression.

"Did you get anywhere with the artifact?"

She sighed and pushed a tangle of hair away from her forehead. "Maybe." She shrugged. "I need to look some more."

"Okay."

Jack glanced at the time display. He still had about an hour before things started shutting down for the evening. "Listen, I've had a thought. I'm going to try something."

She gave a half shrug and then took another sip of the water. He left her sitting there and went into the office, heading straight for the shelf where he'd dropped the card. Investigator Jim Morrish. He'd run into Morrish again for some reason, and right now it was time to put that coincidence to the test. Taking his seat, he put in the call.

"Yorkstone police." Another front desk program.

"Investigator Morrish, please."

"Connecting you now."

Jim Morrish's big doughy face floated into the screen. "Morrish," he said, all business, but then his face broke into a grin. "Stein. Hello. I didn't expect to get a call from you so soon."

"Yeah, well, you know. It's funny how things happen."

"What can I do for you?"

Jack paused for a moment, collecting his thoughts before continuing. "It's a case I'm working on," he said. "I was just wondering if you'd heard anything."

The grin faded and Morrish leaned forward. "What is it?"

"I'm looking for this guy called Carl Talbot. I was wondering if you'd heard the name."

There was a flicker of a frown and Morrish leaned in still closer. "You know I'm happy to help you out, Jack, but there are other people around here who might not be so happy. It's not proper procedure, you know."

"Yeah, I know," said Jack. "But . . ."

Morrish looked away to either side, then back at the screen. In the background Jack could see movement, the vague shapes of other desks, other people. A police station was still a police station no matter where it was. A large board was on one wall with papers and pictures stuck on it. They didn't even use the building's programmed capacity. Morrish frowned and then shook his head. "No, the name's not familiar, but I'll keep my ears open for you."

"I'd appreciate it, Jim," Jack said. He didn't want to mention the Farrell woman, not yet. He was certain that if he found Talbot, then he'd find her and possibly the artifact too. "You know where I am," he said.

"Yeah. It's on file somewhere. I can look it up. See you sometime for that drink, hey?"

Jack nodded and cut the connection.

Six

It took Billie two days to come up with something relevant to the artifact, and even then Jack wasn't sure how useful it was.

"So tell me."

She was grinning from ear to ear, standing in the middle of the living room, waving a hand at the wall—very different from her usual huddled position in the corner of the couch.

"It was really hard, but I did it. It's archeology."

"It's what?"

"*Archeology*," she said triumphantly.

"I don't get it."

"There's this planet and they're doing all this archeology stuff there. Only it's different. Xeno-archeology."

"Huh?"

"It's like archeology, but it's alien archeology." She sat down, waiting for him to catch some of her excitement, pulling her legs up in front of her and clasping her arms in front of them, rocking slightly back and forth. Jack couldn't share the enthusiasm. It made no sense to him. What the hell did archeology have to do with finding a missing object, and a family heirloom at that?

Jack paced the room. "I don't get it. I don't know anything about aliens. What aliens?"

She'd stopped rocking and had started to acquire that set to her jaw that told him she wasn't impressed.

She sighed. "Don't you read anything, Jack?"

He shrugged. "Yeah, sure. But I don't see . . ."

She rolled her eyes.

He came back and sat. "Okay. Tell me."

"It was on the newsfeeds a couple of years ago, but I found something and I remembered about it. It was an article. They said they'd found something on a planet called Mandala. There's been a big project there, digging through what's left from some alien civilization. It's really interesting."

If it had been a couple of years ago, his attention had probably been elsewhere. "Yeah, okay. I remember something a few years back about some alien ruins or something, but what's that got to do with this thing?"

"Well, they found something there." She was half grinning again.

"Don't tell me . . ."

Billie nodded. "The article was talking about this tablet, made of some metal that they didn't know anything about. Well, they thought it was metal, but they weren't sure. There wasn't anything they could test it with. They were really excited back then, but then things sort of went away when they made no progress. The interest kind of died. Anyway, this thing had designs on it, and they thought that it was some sort of translation device, or a key or something. Because of where they found it, they said it had been left as a pointer."

Jack leaned forward, suddenly interested again. That would tie in with the dream he'd had, that cast metallic sky stretching to the horizon with strange markings all over it, shafts of light heading into the distance. But what would someone like Bridgett Farrell want with something like that?

"Jack?"

"Yeah . . . sorry. Thinking."

"Do you want to see the article?"

"No, it wouldn't make any sense to me probably anyway. You just tell me about it." Jack scratched his head. "I didn't know there really were any aliens. I think I dismissed it as speculation at the time."

She nodded. "They don't know if they're still alive. All they've found is a few ruins and things on a couple of planets. They're still trying to work out what they were and whether it's some ancient civilization that all died out, or whether it was the end of an empire or something like that. They haven't even worked out what they looked like yet. There's been a team on this place Mandala for nearly two years."

"A team from where?"

"Some university. I can't remember the name, but I can go back and find out."

Yeah, okay, that made sense, but he still couldn't see that there could be anything to link either Bridgett Farrell or the mysterious disappearing Carl Talbot to an archeological dig on some deserted planet. At least he assumed it was deserted.

"Which university?"

"I said I can look it up," she said, a hint of exasperation creeping into her voice.

"No, don't bother now. Later will do." There were other things about an operation like that that they'd need to find out too. Something that big didn't exist in a vacuum. He grinned at the thought. Maybe it did. He didn't know anything about Mandala, what sort of planet it was, anything. It could be an airless rock for all he knew.

Billie was looking at him strangely. "What's so funny?"

"No, nothing, sorry. Tell me more." He sat forward, his hands linked in front of him, totally attentive. "So how do you know this thing is the same one from Mandala?"

"They had a picture."

Jack nodded. "Okay, I'm going to need you to find out anything you can about the archeological team, about the university and about this planet Mandala. We also need to find out if there's any record of our Bridgett Farrell leaving Yorkstone. Somehow, I don't think she has. What's she doing here? That's the question. Why here and not somewhere else? It's hardly the place for interplanetary commerce. I've got a hunch that whatever brought her here in the first place is going to be keeping her here."

A low insistent chiming from the wall interrupted his flow. Damn. He knew that sound. It was different from the normal tone indicating a call. He waved Billie away, and she jumped quickly off the couch and disappeared into the bedroom. She knew the sound too. Police.

"Answer," said Jack. Morrish's face, larger than life, appeared across the wall.

"Hello, Stein."

"Hello, Investigator," said Jack, waiting.

"I thought I'd give you a call."

"Uh-huh. What can I do for you?"

"Well, you know that guy you were asking about, Carl Talbot?"

Jack nodded.

Morrish waited a couple of seconds, his eyes narrowed slightly. The guy was like an open book. He was clearly waiting to see if Jack gave any reaction.

"Well, we found him."

Jack leaned forward. "Great," he said. "Where is he?"

"This is strictly off the record, Stein."

"Yeah, okay."

"I should have said we found what's left of him."

Jack felt a chill run through him. "Where? How?"

"That's not important right now. Someone had taken to him with a high-powered energy weapon. Not a pretty sight, Stein."

So that's what this was about, and that's why Morrish was calling him on the police channel. He could just as easily have used a private line. Or maybe Jack was just reading too much into it.

"Jesus, I'm sorry."

Morrish looked down, and then slowly looked up again. "What do you know about it, Jack?"

Jack stood. "Nothing. This is the first I've heard of it."

"Why did you want to find Carl Talbot?"

"You know better than that, Morrish. I can't tell you." He walked around behind the couch and leaned forward, his hands on its back, thinking hard. Someone had taken Talbot out of the picture and there had to be a reason for that. This artifact had suddenly become even more interesting.

"Listen, Stein, I'm doing you a favor calling you, now do me a favor. Why did you want him?"

Jack walked back around in front of the couch and spread his hands. "I can't help you, Jim. As much as I'd like to. I just don't know, right now. I have no idea why someone would want to kill this guy and I have no idea *who* might want to kill this guy. I just wanted to find him. I don't even know if the case has anything to do with whoever got rid of him or why they might want to do so. Who knows what this Talbot was into? I don't. Do you?"

Morrish gave a short unamused laugh. "Pretty

good, Jack. Not good enough though. I can't tell you anything either. You know that."

"Yeah, well, give me the same respect, Morrish. If I could give you anything I would."

Morrish pursed his lips and nodded. "All right. But keep in touch. We'll be talking again." The wall blanked and Jack stood where he was, staring at it.

Talbot dead. No Bridgett Farrell. It was getting better and better. And now he'd probably pissed off Morrish, his only decent contact in the department.

"Billie?"

She appeared from her room, glanced nervously at the wall, and then took up her usual position on the couch.

"Did you listen?"

"Nuh-uh," she said.

"Talbot's dead."

She blinked a couple of times as she processed the statement. "So I guess we don't have to find him," she said, and shrugged.

"Yeah, you guess right," said Jack, shaking his head and turning away. "But I guess we have to find Bridgett Farrell now, don't we? She's the only link to finding this artifact, and finding the artifact is the only way we're going to turn this case into something that's worth anything." He turned back to face her. "So, the task now just got all the more simple. We have to find Farrell."

She shrugged again. "I guess."

"Well, you're damned right we do. Listen, I think now's the time for *me* to do some work. You do what you want for awhile. I'm going to need a bit of space in the office undisturbed. Okay? You've got enough to do, don't you?"

She looked at him, her chin thrust out. "I want to go out."

"Yeah, you do that, Billie." For some reason, her sudden threatened petulance was starting to annoy him, especially after what he'd felt on coming back to the apartment and thinking she was gone.

"Aren't you going to come?"

"No, Billie. I told you. I have to do some work, some real work for once, okay? You go out."

He turned, headed into the office, and closed the door. She'd be perfectly all right on her own. She'd probably catch the shuttle up to Molly's or somewhere, and she had enough credit on her own handipad for whatever she needed to do. Besides, if she got into trouble, she could call, couldn't she. He stood behind the door, debating for a moment, and then shook his head. No, she'd be fine.

"Lock," he said. "Dark."

The windows opaqued, turning from transparent to darkened gray, letting the minimum of light through. In the dimness he stripped off his coat, shirt, shoes and trousers, then stepped across to the couch that sat at one side of the office. He reached up to a shelf above the couch and pulled down the inducer pads that would force him down into sleep state. It had been a while since he'd done this. In Yorkstone, he'd been forced to adapt his office space into a workroom as well, putting up with the dual purpose. Back in the Locality, he'd had separate space for these procedures, but here, with Billie, he just couldn't afford the luxury.

With a wry grimace, he affixed the inducer pads to his temples and lay back on the couch, forcing his breathing slower, trying to clear his mind.

"Commence," he said quietly. He closed his eyes, shutting out the gray dim shapes of the office, trying to clear them from his consciousness. He felt the waves starting to press in on his awareness as the inducer started working, teasing him away from consciousness, away into darkness and sleep. That was his cue. Jack conjured an image of Talbot in his mind, trying to forget what Morrish had told him. He brought the artifact into his perception, trying to hold the two images together in his mind as he drifted farther and farther downward into blackness.

There was light. Blue-white light picked out details of a landscape unfamiliar to him. Jack stood in a pretty field, squinting against the glare. Grass, wild and tangled and sprinkled with tall wildflowers, stretched out toward a low hill in one direction, and what he presumed were trees in the other. They didn't look like trees, but they grew out of the ground and were clustered together. In place of trunks, four large branches stuck into the ground, and they were slick, reflecting back the bright light. A single spire reached skyward on each one, making it look like a cluster of framed cathedrals. The air carried a tang. Jack wrinkled his nose. It was a bit like old sweat. He turned slowly, looking for some clue that might tell him where he was. Which way was he supposed to go? He thought about heading for the trees, but there seemed to be nothing prompting him to go in that particular direction. For a moment he tried willing himself upward, but in this instance he seemed confined to the ground. No flying here. Pity. With a shrug, he started walking in the direction of the low hill.

As he neared, a figure crested the rise, silhouetted with glare so he could not make out the features. He stopped walking and waited. The figure stood at the top of the rise, seeming as though it was looking down at him. Jack couldn't quite tell. The figure started down the gentle slope and started to become more distinct. It was a man, and as he drew closer, Jack could see exactly who it was. Carl Talbot was heading down the hill in his direction, wearing a pale suit and half-open shirt, his hair slicked into place like something out of the old vids. Talbot took his time, and Jack waited. He glanced behind him once or twice, but the cathedral trees were still there, so he turned his gaze back to watch Talbot's steady approach. When Talbot was about ten feet away—though distance was always deceptive in the dream landscape—he stopped.

"Hello," said Talbot.

"Hey," said Jack.

There was a silence, followed by a slight buzzing in the air, like the sound of insects.

"What are you doing here?" said Talbot.

"I guess I'm looking for you," Jack answered slowly.

Talbot nodded. The sweat smell was joined by the hint of ozone.

"Where are we?" asked Jack.

Talbot shrugged. "I wish I knew. You wish you knew."

Sometimes dream statements weren't quite what you expected, but Jack just accepted it for what it was.

"Who killed you?" he asked.

Talbot frowned, puzzling over the question. "Am I dead?"

"Yeah, sorry."

Talbot's eyes widened. The buzz had grown louder, pounding in Jack's ears.

A bright flash lit the landscape, a sizzling rush, and then the buzzing was suddenly gone. The sharp smell of burning filled the air. Talbot still stood in front of him, but half his face had been burned away; one arm was gone, leaving just a blackened stump. His remaining eye was still wide.

"See wha' you done," he said with what remained of his mouth.

"I've done?" said Jack. "That wasn't my fault. I'm not responsible."

He glanced back over his shoulder, but when he looked back, Talbot was gone. Even the awful burning smell was gone.

Suddenly Jack was standing on top of the hill, looking down into a wide valley. Down at the bottom in the valley's center sat what looked like another forest of cathedral trees. Something moved between the spires, flashing in the light, sending star-shaped flashes across the valley floor. Still the glare was interfering with the clarity of his vision. Perhaps they were birds. Some sort of shiny bird. But then he realized that couldn't be right, not at this distance. They were just too big.

Talbot's voice came from the air around him. "'Ere, Yack. 'Ere. 'At's 'ere you going." The words were almost incomprehensible. The sight of the damaged Talbot had unsettled him, and as he headed down into the valley his heart was pounding. Sometimes he wished he could just conjure things in the dreamstate; a pair of sunglasses would be really good right now, but as much control as he had, he could only push and cajole the dream, prod it into a direction that might yield results. He shielded his eyes with one hand as he walked.

The buzzing was back, muttering in the back of his consciousness and working on his back teeth. He kept walking, glancing around, looking for details, checking for anything that could possibly be a clue. The sky, though washed out with brightness, was slightly wrong. Beneath the glare there was a greenish tinge. A clump of cathedral trees appeared to one side, and this time they really were trees. Something dark and spiny lumbered between the legs and disappeared from sight. Jack swallowed. He turned his attention back to his destination and continued walking.

He'd been walking for what seemed like hours now, and still the shining target seemed no closer. It was far, far away, and the valley stretched on in front of him. He stopped, staring into the distant structures. He was convinced they were structures now. Some vast, artificial construction.

"Jack."

He looked to one side. There sitting on the ground, her legs crossed, picking at the stalks of vegetation in front of her, was Billie.

"Billie?"

The buzzing got louder.

"You'd better get down, Jack."

There was a bright flash and a loud crack. Jack threw himself to the ground as something sizzled through the air above him. The smell of burning followed. Jack's face was buried in the grass. He clambered to his feet, brushing himself off and looked around. A broad swathe of ground had been seared clean. Billie was gone again.

Clearly, it was not a good place to be. He willed himself closer to his destination, but that didn't work either. This was getting nowhere. Again, the buzzing was starting to intensify. No, he'd had enough warnings. Pushing hard, he willed himself awake. The brightness faded, drifting away into a tissue of smoke, and he struggled up through layered clouds toward consciousness. He broke through the mists, and he was awake. Fuzzy, but awake.

Working his mouth and reaching for his water bottle, Jack sat up. Well, that had given him nothing. He worked his thumbnail under the inducer pad at one temple and glanced at the wall display.

He'd been under for about an hour and a half. Maybe there were no clues for him to find in his subconscious extra senses. The dream seemed to have been fed by things that had happened: Talbot's death, Billie's discussion about alien archeology. He needed more, but right now, he didn't quite know where he was going to find it. With a grimace, he scraped off the other inducer pad, placed them both on the shelf above the couch, took another sip, and swirled the water around in his mouth before swallowing. He would have at least expected some appearance of Bridgett Farrell in the dream if she was truly connected to Talbot and the artifact, but there had been no sign of her. That was the problem when he had nothing really to work with. Normally he would have had some sort of object he could use as a psychic cue, feeding from its energies, but right now he had nothing as substantial as that. He really needed something more physical to work with. He had to work with energies, not mere speculation.

He pushed himself off the couch and reached for his clothes. As he pulled them on, he wondered again whether he should just drop the whole thing. He had the retainer, the so-called client had disappeared, and Talbot was out of the picture. Somehow, he had the feeling this was going to turn out to be a lot bigger than a simple three grand retainer though. There had to be something that was dragging offworlders to a safe little backwater like Yorkstone.

"Windows clear," he said.

The opaque toning faded and his office filled with light, but it was fading light. It was starting to grow dark outside. He stepped out of the office and into the living room.

"Billie?" There was no sign of her. He thought about calling her handipad, but then reconsidered. If she thought he was checking up on her, he'd be in trouble. It had only been a couple of hours though, hadn't it? He couldn't help feeling uneasy, but it was probably just a hangover from the dream. Ultimately, it was a hangover from other things too, but he preferred not to think about those.

Seven

The system announced someone at the door. Jack frowned. He'd been looking through Billie's notes, waiting for her to appear. If it was Billie, she would have used her own access commands.

"Who is it?" he said. "Show me."

Two men stood at the door—two men he didn't really want to see right now. Jim Morrish and his partner, Steve Laduce. Morrish was looking slightly uncomfortable and rocking back and forth on his heels, looking at his feet. Laduce was staring at the door, a set expression on his face, arms crossed.

Jack sighed and headed for the entrance. He wasn't going to let them in. He could deal with whatever they wanted at the front door.

He opened the door and stood looking at them, one face to the other. Morrish looked up from his feet, meeting Jack's gaze with a sheepish expression. Laduce hit him with a hostile stare.

"What can I do for you, gentlemen?" said Jack.

"I think you know, Stein," said Laduce.

Morrish waved his partner to silence. "Listen, Jack. We'd like you to come with us, answer a few questions."

"Uh-huh," said Jack, shoving his hands in his pockets and leaning against the doorway. "And why would you want me to do that? What's wrong with right here?"

"Listen, don't make this any harder than it needs to be. There are just a few unanswered points we'd like to clear up."

Jack crossed his arms. "We can clear them up here and now, can't we?"

"We'd prefer if you came to our place," said Morrish.

"Get your coat, Stein," said Laduce.

Jack nodded, taking a heavy breath, and headed back into the living room to do just that. Morrish's earlier call had been the first probe. Now they wanted to take things further. As he reached for the coat, he spoke.

"Message. Billie, police have taken me. I'm down at their offices answering some questions. Should be back soon. End."

Laduce had walked in after him and stood in the doorway, looking around the room, a slight sneer on his thin, pointed face. "Come on, Stein."

Jack turned, narrowing his eyes at the man. "I didn't ask you in. I'd thank you to wait outside. I'll be with you in a moment."

Laduce shrugged. "Whatever," he said, making no move to shift from his position.

Jack sighed and shook his head, pulling his coat on. He stepped across to the coffee table and scooped up his handipad. All the time Laduce watched him, the hostile glare unwavering.

"You're not going to need that."

"Yeah, well. Let me decide what I need and don't need," said Jack, shoving the handipad in his pocket. No way he was going to let them stop him taking it; his handipad was his link to Billie if he needed it. He pushed past Laduce and headed for the door. Laduce took a moment, giving the living room one last scan, and then turned to follow. Jack didn't know what he'd ever done to this guy, but there'd been clear animosity from the start. Jack assumed Laduce was the sort of hard-nosed practical cop who wanted nothing to do with anything weird or out of the ordinary. To him, Jack was definitely that, and therefore suspicious.

At the doorway, Morrish refused to meet his gaze.

Together Morrish and Laduce, one on either side, accompanied him down to the street and to a waiting police transport. Across the road there were faces at windows, clearly watching what was going on. Jack closed his eyes briefly. Okay, so now he'd become the point of excitement in their otherwise ordered and ordinary lives. He pressed his lips together and allowed himself to be shepherded to the transport.

"Listen, guys. Do we have to do this?" said Jack.

Laduce snorted and Morrish said nothing. Okay, so that was the way it was going to be. They eased him into the back and then took positions in the front, giving the transport directions. Police headquarters. Fine. He glanced out the back as the vehicle took off, watching as the faces tracked his progress up the street. Standing outside a building a few doors up, a short man stood watching, unremarkable round face, blank expression, dark hair, his hands in the pockets of a short brown coat. Jack had seen that face before. And in that moment, Jack's concern for Billie suddenly grew. Who the hell was this guy, and why was he watching them? He tracked the man until they turned the corner and he was obscured from view.

He settled back in the seat to wait, reminding himself all the time that Billie was perfectly capable of looking after herself. Right now, he had to worry about what the police had sitting in their often slow-moving minds. They didn't have that much to keep them occupied in Yorkstone.

They pulled up behind the police building and Jack was led past the front desk, through the main reception area, and into the offices proper. Doors opened automatically, the police identification program easing the way. Morrish and Laduce led him to an interview room—a bare empty space, a desk, three chairs—and left him there. There was no need for anything else in the room. The walls themselves could relay images to adjoining rooms. Everything would be recorded. They were probably in a nearby room right now, watching him and working out the strategy between themselves. Jack pulled out a chair and sat behind the desk, ready to wait. If they thought they were going to make him sweat, they were in for a surprise. He pulled out his handipad and occupied himself spinning it around and around on the smooth table surface with one finger. After about ten minutes, both investigators appeared—the pride of Yorkstone's detective force. He slipped the handipad away, then smiled at them and tilted his head. It brought an immediate reaction.

Laduce crossed quickly in front of Jack, planted his fists on the table surface, and leaned forward.

"I don't think you've got anything to smile about," he growled.

"Yeah, whatever," said Jack, and looked away. He didn't want to get caught up in Laduce's little game.

Morrish had been standing by the door with his arms folded. He joined his partner at the table and pulled out a chair, then sat.

"Jack, it'd be better if you helped us out here."

Jack looked from one to the other. "Look, I don't know what you want me to say. I guess this is about the Talbot case, right? I've already given you everything I know."

Morrish nodded. Laduce leaned forward across the table again. "And what do you know about that, Stein? It's a bit funny, don't you think? You start asking around for this Carl Talbot, and then he winds up dead. What have you got to say about that?"

Jack shrugged. "Stuff just happens, doesn't it? I didn't know this Talbot. I was looking for him for a client. I didn't find him. You found him first. End of story."

"Yes, we know you were looking for him," said Laduce. "You were at the hotel. You called a couple of times. And all this happened just before Talbot met his unfortunate demise. So, what exactly have you got to do with it, Stein? You can't tell me you're not involved."

Jack leaned back and crossed his arms, pulling back from the intensity of Laduce's probing stare. "Absolutely nothing," he said. "I've told you everything I can."

Laduce turned away from the table, stepping back to lean against the wall near the door, shoving his hands into his pockets, but not breaking the hard, accusatory gaze. The guy really didn't like him. Jack shrugged the glare away and turned his attention to the table in front of him.

Morrish rubbed the back of his neck, then looked at Jack's face. "You know, you say this sort of shit happens. Well, shit doesn't happen in Yorkstone. Not this kind of shit, anyway. Do you know the number of murders we've had here in the last few years? You can count them on the fingers of one hand. You have to look at it from our point of view. It's kind of suspicious, don't you think? Everything's quiet, you start asking around, and then someone winds up dead. How do you think it looks from our perspective?"

"That's just dumb, Morrish," said Jack, a bit of exasperation starting to feed into his voice. "Look, I get called in on a case. You get called in on a case. It just happens to be the same case in a roundabout way. I can't do anything about that. I'd be a lot happier if that wasn't the way it was, but it is. What can I tell you?"

Laduce strode across to the table, spun a chair around and sat, one hand leaning on the back. "You can tell us everything you damn well know about this Talbot. I don't care what you say, Stein. You stink. I can smell it on you. You've got something to do with this. I wouldn't be surprised if you're the one who took the guy out."

Jack glared back at him. "What's your problem, Laduce?"

"I don't like you, Stein. That's what my problem is. You're my problem."

"Oh, give it a rest."

"What?" said Laduce, nearly spitting the word at him. "I don't have to like you or that crap you pretend to be able to do. You don't fool me, Stein."

So that was it. What Jack did, what he *was*, threatened some people. They were afraid of it, and sometimes that fear simply translated into hostility.

"Can't help you, Laduce."

Laduce quickly stood and strode back to the door to glower across the room. Meanwhile, Morrish just sat there looking on. He was giving Jack a half-apologetic look. "I don't know what to say to you, Stein. I'm half willing to give you the benefit of the doubt, but you have to admit it's all pretty strange. Steve here isn't so ready to cut you any slack. I think it would help if you told us what you were working on. That's going to help us rule you out. Doesn't that make sense?"

"No can do," said Jack, and shook his head. "Client confidentiality." He wasn't really in a position where he could even feed them some line yet. He couldn't afford to have them messing up the trail. If the police got involved, they would only get in his way.

His answer brought a snort of derision from the door. Jack ignored it.

At that moment, Jack's handipad chose to vibrate; a trilling tone came from his coat pocket. He went to reach for it, but Laduce was across like a shot, grabbing the handipad from his grasp, right out of the pocket, none too gently, and holding it aloft.

"And I think we'll take care of this too."

Jack growled through gritted teeth, but he knew there was little he could do about it. Laduce thumbed the handipad off and the sound died.

"Well," said Morrish. "I think we'll leave you here to think about things for a while."

"Hey, come on. You can't hold me," said Jack.

"We can do anything we damned well please," said Laduce with a grin.

"If you change your mind," said Morrish, "we'll come and talk to you again."

They left him sitting there, nothing to look at but the empty chairs and the walls. No doubt they were in the next room watching him again. There wasn't even anywhere he could lie down.

He sat and thought about what they wanted. He couldn't tell them about Bridgett Farrell. She was the only link to this whole thing, and the only link to his fee. If he brought her into it, it was just as likely that any of their efforts—his and Billie's—would have been for nothing. No, he couldn't risk it.

Whether he liked it or not, he wasn't any closer to a solution either. He was certainly no closer to tracking down this artifact, and when it came to it, he suspected that the artifact itself was the ultimate key to all this. He ground his jaw and drummed his fingers on the table.

An hour later and he was still grinding his teeth and drumming his fingers on the table. He was debating stretching out on the table itself, or on the floor in the corner, when the door opened. Morrish walked in. This time he was alone.

"Well, any thoughts, Jack?" said Morrish, standing in the doorway, the door half open.

Jack shook his head. "I can't, Morrish. There's nothing I can give you."

"Well . . . it doesn't look good then, does it?" Again Morrish's expression was almost apologetic. "It looks like you're going to be spending a little more time with us."

"Oh, come on. You've got to be joking."

"My hands are tied. Come on." He gestured for Jack to get up, led him out of the room and down a corridor. They passed Laduce on the way, who gave him a malicious little smile, and then he was led down into the bowels of the police complex. Plain, unadorned corridors, neutral walls. At least the holding cells in a place like this were going to be clean. This wasn't the first time he'd spent a night locked up, but this time, the injustice of it was rankling.

As Morrish led him into the standard, small space—bed, chair and waste facilities—he sighed. "Come on, Jack. It doesn't have to be like this. Give us something to work with."

Jack said nothing.

With a shake of his head, Morrish sealed the door behind him.

Jack headed for the low bed, stripped off his coat, laid it across the chair and clambered upon the bed and lay back, his fingers linked behind his head, ready for a long wait. It wasn't too bad. As he'd suspected, it was clean and functional, not too different from his old workspace back in the Locality. Hopefully, Billie had gotten his message by now, and she'd know what to do. Sit tight and wait. It was unlikely she'd come looking for him. Since her time living with the fringe dwellers in the Locality, and more with Pinpin Dan, she had a real aversion to authorities. He could hardly see her turning up at the police station of her own volition. It was probably she who had called before. As soon as Laduce had switched off Jack's handipad, she would have drawn her own conclusions. But maybe, in the meantime, it would give her more time to come up with something.

Meanwhile, Jack was hoping that Morrish and Laduce would tire of this game. He thought they wouldn't be able to hold him for too long, or at least he hoped they couldn't. Maybe they could. He shook his head. It was unlikely. Not in a place like Yorkstone. Anyway, he'd be here until the morning at least. Morrish and his partner would be leaving for the day soon. He glanced around, realizing that he had no way of knowing what time it was. With a long low sigh, he settled back and closed his eyes.

Jack spent a dreamless night, despite the similarity of the environment to the places in which he was used to dreaming, the Spartan, featureless nature of his workrooms. There still wasn't enough to prompt his subconscious mind to lead him down the path he needed to travel. He woke early and spent the time pacing back and forth across the small space, waiting for someone to come and see him. The last contact he'd had was when a uniformed officer had brought him something to eat. He'd merely picked at it, finally gotten sick of looking at it, and disposed of everything, tray and all, into the wall unit.

When someone finally did show up, it was Laduce, rather than Morrish. He entered the small holding cell and looked down at Jack with a smug expression.

"Seems you had a visitor last night, Stein."

"Huh? Who?" said Jack.

"Young blond girl. A bit wild-eyed, according to the guys on the desk."

Billie. Billie had actually come to police headquarters?

"So, what are you doing with a girl that age?"

Jack gave him a disgusted look. "You can check if you want. She's my niece. I left her a message before we left the apartment."

"Oh, don't worry, we *will* check."

Jack shook his head and reached for his coat. The sooner he could get out of here, the sooner he could do something to divert attention from Billie. He didn't want her involved.

"I don't know where you think you're going," said Laduce, the smirk still there.

"What do you mean? You can't hold me here anymore."

Laduce took a step forward. "That's where you're wrong, my friend. We can keep you here as long as we want."

Jack dropped his coat back on the chair. "Fine. If that's the way you want to play it. I want to see Morrish."

"He's not in yet."

"I'll wait," said Jack, and sat. Laduce gave a sniff and left him there, locking the door behind him.

It was about another half hour before Morrish made

an appearance. "Morning, Jack. You've had some time to think, I see."

"Yeah, I slept well, thank you for asking."

Morrish shook his head, pulled out the chair and sat. Jack knew he had no choice. He was worried about Billie. Already she'd been alone for the night, and there was that little guy hanging around the apartment. If she'd been concerned enough to show up at the police building, he needed to get out of here. Spending another night here wasn't going to get him anywhere at all. He had to give them something, though it went against everything he normally kept to. He sat back on the bed and looked up at the ceiling before finally looking back at Morrish.

"Okay," he said with a heavy sigh. "I'm working on a case for some woman called Bridgett Farrell. She wanted me to find this Talbot guy and get back something she thought he'd stolen from her."

"I see," said Morrish slowly. "And where is this Farrell woman now?"

"I have no idea," said Jack with a shrug. "I wish I did."

Morrish leaned forward on the chair. "Okay, well, where was she?"

"She was staying at the Excelsior."

Morrish narrowed his eyes and frowned, processing that.

"Yeah, I know," said Jack. "It's all screwed up. I know. Talbot was staying there too. I didn't know that at the time."

"It doesn't sound very likely, Stein." Morrish was staring at him with narrowed eyes, testing for a chink, waiting for him to slip.

"Yeah, I know that too. That's partly the reason I didn't want to say anything before I'd worked out what was going on. I was going to sound like an idiot."

"Uh-huh. And what about this thing Talbot was supposed to have taken?"

Jack shrugged. "Some sort of antique. All I was supposed to do was find Talbot and deliver it to Farrell once I'd gotten hold of it. She didn't give me much to go on. Whatever it was, it sounded like it was valuable."

Morrish sat back again, testing what Jack was telling him. Finally he shook his head. "And you had nothing to do with Talbot's death."

"Come on, Morrish. What do you think I am?"

There was silence for a couple of seconds. Finally, Morrish heaved a sigh. "Well, we know this Talbot was an antique dealer, so that much makes sense, but I don't like it. Of course we're going to have to check your story. Steve's going to like it even less. If Talbot was supposed to have this artifact, where is it now? Maybe we should search your apartment, Jack."

Jack responded with a slight shrug.

There was a pause as Morrish considered his reaction. After a moment, Morrish stood. "Okay, I'm going to let you out. Maybe against my better judgment. Don't go too far away. We might want to talk to you again soon."

"Thanks," said Jack.

Morrish waited while Jack pulled on his coat. "Go home. Get yourself cleaned up. If you're smart, you'll stay out of it. And on the way out, stay out of Steve's way, okay?"

"Yeah," said Jack. Right now, the prospect of getting back to the apartment, climbing into a hot shower and checking that Billie was okay was foremost in his mind, not necessarily in that order. Laduce could think what he wanted.

Eight

"Jack? Is that you?"

Billie appeared in the kitchen doorway, one hand behind her back.

"Yeah. Sorry."

She slowly withdrew the hand, revealing a large knife.

"You can put that down, I think. Not a good idea anyway, Billie."

She slowly slipped the knife away out of view. "I was worried." With her free hand, she pushed her hair out of her face. "And there's been this guy hanging around outside. I could see him from the window. He couldn't see me."

"He bothering you?"

She gave a slight shrug. "Dunno."

"What did he look like?"

"Short. Brown coat. Brown hair. Kind of ordinary."

"I think I know the man you mean. I've seen him too."

Jack shrugged off his coat and let it fall over the back of the couch. Billie stepped forward and touched his arm.

"I tried to call you."

"Yeah, I know. That bastard Laduce took away my

handipad. At least I got it back before they let me go. You did more than that though, didn't you?"

She looked down at her feet.

"Well, listen, I really appreciate it, Billie. There was no need to come down there, you know?"

She looked up, nodded, and stepped back again.

"Listen, Billie, I need to take a shower, get into something clean. Then we can talk, okay?"

"I found out some stuff," she said. She was checking his face, his body, clearly testing to see if he was all right.

"Look, I'm okay," he said, heading for the shower. "Let's have a look at what you've got when I get out."

She gave a quick nod, her teeth pressed against her lower lip, and then disappeared into her own room, leaving him to it.

Jack took his time under the shower, letting the sharp, hot stream pound away at the stiffness he'd developed sitting and lying in the same position in the police cell. There hadn't been much space to move around in there. He felt a need to get clean, feel fresh, and he even took the time to shave. A while later he emerged, feeling somewhat human and smelling slightly less like something half dead. Billie was waiting for him, her position and expression telling him that she'd relaxed a little bit. She was still checking him out as he sat.

"So, what did they want?"

Jack sighed. "You know what they're like. They can't work out things for themselves so they have to point the finger at someone. They think I had something to do with Talbot's death."

She pursed her lips.

"Anyway, tell me what you've found out."

"Uh-huh." She turned her attention to the screen. "File. Mandala."

Step by step, Billie guided the screen through various

pictures and images. The information she'd gathered was comprehensive. Mandala itself was an oxygen-rich world, fifth in a system of planets having six in total. Its sun was slightly toward the blue end of the spectrum, but far enough away from Mandala itself to make it habitable, if a little warm. There was a thriving colony there, and they'd used the weather patterns and vast stretches of unspoiled landscape to sell the place as a playground destination for the rich and famous, where they could vacation undisturbed by those less well-off than themselves.

"Okay, so that's Mandala. Funny place for an archeological site," said Jack. "It doesn't look like it's the sort of planet that would encourage it. How do they deal with the tourists?"

Billie shrugged. "This is the site. There's not much I could find. They use it as an attraction. Tours and stuff. Exclusive visits with tour guides. I found a few articles and things, but they don't seem to know very much about it."

"Well, how the hell can it be a tourist attraction?" said Jack.

Billie shrugged. "Something to do with being exclusive, I guess. Only give it to people who can afford it."

A picture blossomed on the wall and Jack leaned forward. From what he could make out—the image was not very clear—large square structures stood grouped in fours, side by side, clustered buildings. They were blocky and thick, square in shape, and apart from small doorways at their bases, they seemed to have no other features. He couldn't tell how big they were. The doors could be as tall as buildings on their own. There were no internal shots.

"Well, that doesn't tell us much. Do you know what they're finding there?"

She shrugged. "Too hard. I need some more time."

"Okay, Billie. That's good. Is there anything else?"

"Uh-huh. Whoever is paying for all this work doesn't want people to find out. There's the university, but the real funding is coming from another company. It's a shell and there's a trail, but I don't know where it ends. I couldn't find it yet."

"Anything about the artifact?"

She grinned. "There was a tiny news article about stuff being stolen from the site. I nearly missed it."

"Uh-huh." Now they were getting somewhere. "Did they say anything else?"

"Yeah. Something about archeological significance."

"I bet there was. Hmm, okay, I think things are starting to come together. I'm not sure how yet, but this is great, Billie."

She seemed to be waiting for something.

"Well . . ."

"The university, Jack."

"What about it?"

"UBC. The University of Balance City."

"Utrecht," they said together.

She sat back and crossed her arms triumphantly. Jack nodded slowly and, just as slowly, he started to grin.

Talbot came from Utrecht. The archeological team was from Utrecht. There was the connection.

Jack stood and started pacing. He was thinking, and Billie sat watching as he worked it through in his head. He paced around the living room and into the office. He was being stupid. Of course there was a link between Farrell and Talbot, but if he had stolen the artifact from her, what were they doing in the same hotel? Who was to say that she'd even had the damned thing in the first place? The whole family heirloom story was becoming less and less likely. As was the fact that she'd hired him. Why in the hell would she hire someone like Jack to track down someone who was staying at the same hotel? That still didn't make sense.

Jack scratched at the back of his head and looked out the window and stopped in midaction. Across the other side of the street, standing in the doorway, was the guy who seemed to have been appearing everywhere over the last couple of days. Something nasty was working in the depths of Jack's guts. He curled his lip. The man was clearly watching the windows. Jack couldn't tell if he could see him, but right now, he didn't care. He was going to do something about this. He walked back into the living room and grabbed his coat.

Billie looked suddenly panicked.

"It's all right," said Jack. "It's about time I found out what our little friend wants."

He strode quickly to the front door, out to the elevator, and down to the street. He wanted to catch his new friend by surprise. Once in the lobby he paused, hanging back, giving a quick surreptitious glance around the doorway, confirming that the guy was still there. He was, still staring up at the windows. Jack dashed across the street. He was fully two-thirds of the way across, his coat flying behind him, when the man looked down and noticed. His bland round face paled, his jaw dropped open, and he reached into his coat and started backing away. Jack was on him in an instant. He pushed, his hand flat in the man's chest, forcing him back.

"Who are you? What do you want?"

The little man's gaze flickered nervously from side to side, his hand still buried in his coat pocket.

Jack shoved again. "Come on. Talk," he said from

between closed teeth, reinforcing the words with yet another shove. The man's face went from shocked to hostile.

"I wouldn't do that," he said quietly. "Not if you know what's good for you."

"Is that right?" said Jack, giving another shove.

The man was a good head shorter than Jack, but Jack felt no qualms about monstering him. Jack didn't like being watched, and he liked it even less when Billie was involved.

The little man had had enough. He shoved forward with the hand buried in his right jacket pocket, and Jack felt something hard pressing against his abdomen. The guy looked down significantly at the bulge and then back at Jack's face.

In one quick motion, Jack seized the guy's jacket, pulling the shoulders back and down around his arms. Then he slapped him, hard, once, twice.

"You go away now, little man," said Jack. "Don't come back until you're ready to play with the big boys."

The guy's eyes widened and his face blanched again, this time in fury, the marks of Jack's hands standing out clear and red on his cheeks. Even though his arms were pinned by his own jacket, he shoved forward with whatever he had in his pocket.

"You're going to be sorry."

"Yeah, we'll see about that. You go and tell whoever you're working for that if he wants to talk to Jack Stein, then he should talk to Jack Stein. He shouldn't send his lackeys." He grabbed a good handful of jacket and shook. "You got that?"

The fury grew. Jack slapped him again, and in the next motion, he spun the little man around, dug his hand into the right jacket pocket and wrenched the obvious weapon out of the guy's hand. He grabbed his shoulder and spun him back around. He waved a nasty little gun in the guy's face.

"And before you start playing with toys, you better learn how to use them." He gave him another slap and pushed him out of the lobby entrance and onto the street. "Now get. Don't come back." He shoved the gun deep into his pocket and watched as their erstwhile watcher pulled his jacket back on, adjusting it as he walked quickly up the street, looking back over his shoulder with a glare of absolute hostility. Jack stared back. Whoever he was, this guy was just what he'd said, a lackey. He was the sort who wouldn't spit without his master's permission.

He was just about to head back over to the apartment when he had a thought. He dug in his pocket and drew out the gun, turning it over and over. No way was this the weapon that had seen to Carl Talbot. This would put a small and nasty hole in someone, but it wasn't going to take off half a face and an arm. He put the gun away again and crossed the road, first checking to see that their watcher was truly gone. A couple of minutes later, he was back up in the apartment.

"Well, I don't think he's going to be bothering us again. At least not for a while." He tossed the gun onto the low table. Billie reached for it. "No," said Jack quickly. "Leave that alone." He leaned over and swept it away, shoving it up into a high shelf. She knew it was there, but he thought she'd take his warning. Billie wasn't stupid.

"What did you do?" she said.

"Just showed him that he needs to be a little more respectful of other people's privacy. I sent him away, back to his boss with his tail between his legs."

"His boss?"

"That sort always has a boss. Can't do anything on their own. Somehow, I think we're going to be getting another call. Maybe I'm wrong, but you know . . . I've got this feeling . . ." He grinned and turned away. Billie just shook her head.

There was still one thing that didn't make sense in the middle of everything else that was adding up to a tangled confusion. What the hell were these people doing in Yorkstone? Yorkstone was a nice city. Carl Talbot, Bridgett Farrell, they just didn't belong in a place like this. Even Morrish had said it. It made him question again what he was doing here himself. Jack had simply been coasting for too long, but this time it was a different sort of coasting. In his previous existence, before he'd met Billie, he'd let fate play its hand, always counting on circumstance to lead him in the right direction, allowing his inner senses to do the work for him. Now, in this environment, it was different. The place itself had become the excuse. Nothing turned up because there was nothing *to* turn up.

And now he was getting frustrated. The suspected call had not happened, Billie was getting nowhere further with her research, nor was there any sign of Bridgett Farrell. At least the police had not been back, but he suspected that wouldn't last either. He couldn't imagine that they'd managed to work out anything on their own.

Laduce's snide comments had set him thinking about Billie again too, and that wasn't a good thing. Their relationship was full of unexplained tension recently. Maybe it was just because she was getting older. He'd thought, maybe, that getting to Yorkstone would have given her what she needed.

Regardless, there were more important things to

deal with, matters more pressing. He was achieving nothing sitting in his office, fiddling, resisting the urge to play around with the furniture. He called up the notes Billie had been working on and scanned through them, looking for clues. He went back to the pictures of Mandala, studying them. There had to be something he was missing. He narrowed his eyes at the picture of the archeological site, trying to blur the image, looking for correspondences. He sat back and shook his head with a sigh. Nothing was coming. Once again he called up the sketch of the artifact, staring at it till it too blurred into a meaningless smudge. He stood, cleared down the screen, and walked over to the window, his hands clasped behind his back. He'd wasted almost an entire day since the incident with the guy on the street and had nothing to show for it. He felt like growling, growling at the world and growling at Yorkstone in particular.

The system announced a call and he turned slowly, a half smile forming on his face. This was it. It had taken longer than he'd expected.

"Answer. This is Jack Ste—" His voice drifted off to nothing. Bridgett Farrell was looking at him from the wallscreen. She moistened her lips with the tip of her tongue and spoke.

"Have you got it, Jack?"

"Have I got what?"

She lifted a finger to her lips and spoke in an even quieter tone. "The object, of course." She was clearly nervous, glancing off to the side.

"Where are you, Ms. Farrell?"

"I can't tell you that. Not now. I need you to help me, Jack. I think I'm in trouble."

Jack walked closer to the screen. "Why would that be, Ms. Farrell?"

"Have you found Talbot?"

Jack looked down at his fingernails, then slowly back up at her. "Talbot's dead."

She gasped. She looked shaken. Either she was being genuine or she was really good. At this point, he didn't know which one. She looked as if she was struggling to maintain calm.

"If Carl's dead, then someone else has to have the artifact." She bit her lip. "You have to help me. I'll double your fee. I'll double the amount. Just help me find it, Jack."

Jack's head was ticking. He had to find this woman. She was going to lead him to the artifact one way or another, unknowingly or with full knowledge of what she was doing. Somehow, he thought it was the latter. He still didn't know how much she really knew and how much she was telling him, but he was going to play along for now and see if he could come up with the answer. There was some reason she was keeping things from him. Maybe she really was scared.

"Listen, Ms. Farrell."

"Call me Bridgett, please." Her hand was playing with the pendant at her throat.

"Why" said Jack. "What do other people call you?"

There was a slight flicker of her eyes at that, but she let the comment pass. "Can I trust you, Jack?"

"I don't know, Ms. Farrell. Can *I* trust *you*? What can you tell me about a place called Mandala? Or maybe Balance City?"

She looked away. The hand that had been playing at her pendant drifted up to touch her hair, and she moistened her lips once more. Again she glanced to the side, then leaned in closer.

"None of that's important, Jack. All that matters is the artifact."

Jack leaned back on the desk. "It's been a couple of days, Ms. Farrell, and you're nowhere to be seen. I'm afraid your retainer has run out. I'm going to have to see some sort of mark of good faith."

She tutted and sighed. "Why?"

"Because you've been taking up my time on what seems like a pointless exercise. If you expect me to keep working on this, I'm going to need some more. Show me that you mean it, Ms. Farrell."

"Is that all it's going to take . . . I would have expected a little more trust from you, Jack." Her handipad lifted into view. "How much?"

"Six, no, ten should do it."

She pressed her lips together and nodded. A small split panel emerged at the bottom of his screen showing the transfer taking place.

"Okay," said Jack. "I need to know where you are."

"I'll be in touch," she said. The wall went blank.

What the hell was this woman playing at? Jack ran his fingers back through his hair and grimaced. He'd just ensured that he was truly tied in now. He turned away from the screen to see Billie standing in the doorway watching him.

"What are you doing, Billie?"

She shrugged. "I heard voices . . ."

"How much did you see?"

"Enough." She shook her head, turned, and walked back into the living room, leaving him standing there.

"What am I supposed to do, Billie?" he said, but she had already gone.

"What am I *supposed* to do?" he breathed.

Carl Talbot was back. The "after" Carl Talbot, not the "before."

Jack suppressed the gag reflex that threatened to

overwhelm him. It was just a dream, but the natural reaction was there, forcing him to fight it.

"Yack Stein," said Talbot from his ruined face.

Jack tried to look away, past the blasted features, trying to determine where they were. Above him lay a broad ceiling. No, it wasn't a ceiling. It was farther away than that, far, far above. It was . . . it was sky, but dark, leaden gray. That was all he could see. They were standing on nothing, floating. Quick traceries of light shot back and forth below them. Jack tried to look everywhere but at the face that was speaking to him.

"You . . . haf . . . to go."

"What is it, Carl? Where do I have to go?"

Talbot tried to wave his arm. His remaining eye looked surprised. He gestured with the other, good arm. The sky disappeared. The lights in the darkness disappeared. Blankness remained. They floated in nothing. Jack peered into the nothingness, trying to work out what he was supposed to be seeing. There, over Talbot's maimed shoulder, something was forming, far away now. He concentrated. Quad shapes. Quad shapes like four thick, stocky legs, joined to a central spire that reached up into the sky. The same shapes he'd seen before.

"'Ere!" said Talbot emphatically. "You haf to go."

"Why do I have to go there, Carl? Tell me."

Talbot drifted into vaporous wisps and blew away, saying nothing more. Jack was left with the structural image in front of him. He stared at it, imprinting it deeply.

Then he was somewhere else. He was standing on a plain. Silver shapes whipped above his head, almost too fast to follow. One zipped silently past, whipping his head back as he tried to track it.

He turned to follow it into the distance.

Something was standing behind him. It was tall, with four legs spaced evenly around a thick central body. It seemed smooth, featureless, shining slightly with a sleek, silvery slickness. At first he thought it was some sort of sculpture, the same sort of structure as the other things he'd seen, but on a smaller scale. And then it moved. Jack took a step back. Again, one of the four legs swung forward, repositioning the body. The top of the thick central shaft tilted forward. The whole thing looked ponderous, awkward. About halfway up the shaft, something slowly bulged, then separated. A section folded down and then another. Behind one of the sections there was a hollow. Jack shook his head. This was just weird, and the weirdness was working in his chest, making his heart pound faster. There was something in the hollow. Despite the fear starting to rise within him, he looked closer. There was a shape in there, something flat, rectangular. He recognized that shape. It was the artifact.

The sections that had folded down swung back up, and the hollow was concealed once more. The bulging torus slowly merged back into the shaft, and then the thing was gone.

Jack swallowed.

He woke, staring at the ceiling in the darkness, knowing what he had to do, but struggling with a deep sense of unease. How do you deal with something that's truly alien? He was used to things that he could control, even in the dreamstate. Thoughts, symbols, had their place in the human psyche, and they were things he could come to grips with. If his visions were suddenly taking him into an area where the energies had nothing to do with humanity, he had no guarantee that he could control that. He had no guarantee that there were any psychic anchor points he could hold on to. What would stop the dreams from sweeping him away completely? Maybe this time he really was getting in too deep—lost subconsciously in an alien civilization. He didn't think it was possible, but sometimes, even he didn't know how his abilities worked. Alien sendings? Alien minds? No, it didn't bear thinking about.

It was a long, long while before sleep found him again.

Nine

Jack wasn't quite sure how Billie was going to take his news, so he waited till she was showered and well and truly awake before he mentioned it. As it was, he needn't have bothered.

"We need to go on a bit of a trip," he told her.

She stopped running her fingers through wet hair, waiting for him to continue.

"I had a dream last night. I think I know how to work out this whole mess. I thought about going alone, but with you along, it's the perfect cover. I'm about to be your rich uncle, Billie."

"Okay. Where?"

"We're going to Mandala."

Her eyes widened. "Really?"

"Yeah. We have to go to the archeological site. I don't know why, but that's what we have to do."

"Yes!" she said, jumping up and spinning around on the spot.

He stared at her. He'd been expecting something, anything, but not this. Billie just didn't get excited about stuff. Just when he thought he had her all figured out, she went and did something that screwed it all up again.

"What . . . ?" he said slowly.

She grabbed his arm and swung it. "It's great. I never thought . . . It's great. We're really going there?"

He carefully extricated his arm from her grip and stepped back out of range. "I don't get it, Billie."

"What's not to get? Just imagine it. Think about it." She thrust her arms wide. "*Aliens.*"

"Yeah, well, we're going to have to get some bookings worked out. Find out where we're going to stay. It's going to cost, but despite what you might think, that little conversation yesterday afternoon with Bridgett Farrell seems to have come in useful."

She shrugged and turned away, heading straight for the wallscreen.

"What are you doing?"

"Looking for timetables and prices. And checking out Mandala bookings. Who do you want to be?"

"It's that easy for you?" he said.

"Uh-huh," she replied without turning around. "Who do you want to be?"

"Yeah, well, we can't use my name. Think of something, will you, Billie? Whatever it is, we've got to make it believable. You're my niece and I'm taking you to Mandala as a treat because you really want to see the alien ruins."

"What is there to believe?" she said, looking back at him over her shoulder with a grin.

"What do you mean?"

"I *do* really want to see the alien ruins."

He left her to it. She'd have the best deal set up soon, and whatever ID they needed she could set up in a matter of minutes. Her time with Pinpin Dan sometimes came in useful. She already had a file of prepared IDs that Jack had used in the past.

The problem of Morrish and Laduce still remained. How would it look if he suddenly skipped town? Not only town, but the planet as well. If Laduce found out, he'd be after Jack like a man on a mission. Hopefully the pair of them would be slow-moving enough not to get around to him before he and Billie got back, if they did get back. And if not, he'd deal with it when he had to. All he knew was that he had to do this. The dead Carl Talbot had told him so.

He was Jack Stinson, CEO of Carmody Industries. The company name was vague enough to be any of a number of conglomerates that stretched across the system. Mining mainly. He looked down at the ID. Okay, but there was something wrong about it. It didn't *feel* right.

"Billie, what's wrong here?" He scratched his head.

"Look at you, Jack."

"What?"

"Look at that coat. Look at your clothes. Do you look like a CEO?"

"Mirror," he said.

The wall realigned itself and became reflective. He looked at himself critically. Billie was right. He looked nothing like a CEO. Forget the clothes, the slight stubble was okay, but the unkempt hair, the whole demeanor. He straightened his stance and pulled at his sleeves, trying to smooth things. It wasn't working. They had to go shopping. He grimaced. They had little enough of Bridgett Farrell's funds left, maybe a couple of grand after Billie had made the bookings. The resort had taken up most of the money, the transport a good slice of what was left. Maybe a couple of grand would be enough. Billie needed some stuff too. High end.

"Yeah. Okay. We're going shopping," he told her. She grinned and gave a little jump. Suddenly it seemed that everything they were doing pleased her. She was happier than he'd seen her in a long time. It made him wonder. Was he really giving her enough? He knew that a lot of her attitude was simple bravado, but underneath that, he didn't know if she was really happy. She seemed content with him, but that didn't mean she was happy, did it? He shook the thoughts away and checked the handipad to see how much they did have left. Two thousand three hundred and fifty-eight. Well, it looked like they weren't going to be getting room service when they got to Mandala.

"Come on," said Billie, dragging at his sleeve. "What are you waiting for?"

"Can't we do this here?" he said.

"No, Jack. Are you stupid? Not for the kind of stuff we need."

She was probably right. He slipped the handipad away and followed Billie out of the apartment, wondering now, for a totally different reason, what he was getting himself into.

As they climbed aboard the shuttle he grabbed her shoulder, pulling her down to one end of the compartment. Up at the end, they were far enough away from the other passengers to talk.

"Okay, let's go through what we need to do," he said as they sat.

"It's simple," she said, glancing around the carriage.

"Yeah, okay, it may be simple, but I need to hear it again."

She rolled her eyes, then became all serious. "You're Jack Stinson. We're visiting Mandala as a vacation treat for your niece, Susan." She tapped her chest, then continued. "We get on a transport out to the port. We catch a ship to the relay station. We jump to Antioch. From Antioch we get the private liner to Mandala.

There's a shuttle there that will take us to the resort. It's called the Mandala Country Club."

He nodded. It seemed simple enough. They could work out the way to get to the archeological site when they got there. The resort pages had talked about organized trips out to the ruins. He suspected it was a fairly standard excursion from the place. It was just the sort of thing that rich tourists would love to brag about when they got back home. "So, is there a city name? You've only talked about this resort."

She frowned. "No. Mandala's kind of funny. It's all Mandala this, Mandala that. The site has a name and that's about it. It's called the City of Trees."

"Huh," said Jack. "Why?"

"Well, they say it looks like a big forest of square trees."

"Hmm," said Jack. He remembered the strange forests that had populated the dream. That structure in the distance suddenly made more sense. The City of Trees. It had to be the same place.

"How long are we going to be traveling?" he asked after a few moments.

"Altogether? Probably about a day." She shrugged again. "Mostly we'll be waiting. You know, the ships take almost no time at all."

He did know, and so did she. The new drives developed by Outreach had totally changed travel. Now, getting from one place to another between the stars was almost instantaneous. The routes were expanding daily. Despite the ease, he felt a certain level of discomfort traveling on ships developed and supported by Outreach. Merely thinking about it sparked a nagging nervous unease. There was too much history there with Outreach, and mostly, history he would prefer to forget. In many ways, he just couldn't. Outreach had used the mining crew from Dairil III as experimental subjects in their initial tests of the new drive, often with disastrous consequences. There were places people just weren't meant to go. He swallowed, pushing the thought away.

"Okay, that seems to all work," he said.

They changed shuttles about halfway up. The shopping district they were heading for was at the more exclusive end of the spectrum, and Jack, picking intermittently at his coat and light sweater, felt slightly uncomfortable. There was a change in their fellow passengers. They were better turned out; there was an aura of affluence about them. He could see the style, sense the difference, but it was nothing he'd ever really aspired to. He sniffed, trying to suppress the feelings. They were irrational. Billie was fine; she was watching the outside, everything they passed, the people, the buildings, the streets. He wished she'd done something about her hair before heading up here, but it was a bit late now.

As soon as they alighted, Billie dragged Jack straight away toward a huge glitzy department store. He let himself be dragged, knowing who was in control here. He just had to keep an eye on the funds. They went from department to department, Billie leading the way, Jack looking at things she suggested, shaking his head when the price was too high. Finally, they ended with a couple of tops, two pairs of trousers, some new shoes, a jacket, and a coat. Then it was Billie's turn. She was easier, and the results were less expensive. Jeans and tops and a well-cut jacket. He guessed it was enough. They chose to take the purchases with them, rather than waiting for them to be delivered. Delivery, though reasonably efficient, was variable in timing, and they were due to leave on the following morning. At last, Jack was relieved that Billie seemed to have decided they had enough.

"Okay. Can we go home now?" he said.

"Nuh-uh."

He stood outside the store, arms full of packages, and shook his head. "Why not? What now?"

"Luggage," she said simply. "We need to have the right luggage."

She was right. If they were truly going to look the part, they couldn't only dress it. Luggage was the perfect prop. He put down a couple of packages and reached for his handipad. They'd already taken a healthy chunk out of the remaining funds. He chewed at his bottom lip and then looked up at her impatient stance.

"Okay, you're right, but we need to do it carefully. I'm not sure this is the right place to get what we need."

She looked at the surrounding stores and finally nodded. "Leave it to me." Barely leaving him time to grab the packages, she dragged him toward the shuttle stop.

A short ride later they were in another shopping area, but this one was in a section of the city marked by more moderate appointments. Billie headed straight for a small store. Jack stopped, waiting for her to realize that he wasn't following.

She turned. "What?"

"What is this, Billie?"

"Trust me," she said, waving him forward.

With a shake of his head, he followed. THE COPY SHOP sat atop the doorway in muted letters. Jack wandered in, putting the various packages down on the floor behind the doorway. Billie was already leaning across the counter talking to someone. And this was a real someone instead of some program.

The man behind the counter nodded and then disappeared into the back of the store. Moments later, he appeared carrying two finely crafted travel bags, one larger, one smaller, in front of him. He planted them on the counter. Jack walked over, nodded to the man, then reached out a hand to the bags. They looked like top-of-the-line leather and they felt like it. Real leather was something well out of Jack's usual range, particularly in something as practical as luggage. The man mentioned a price and Jack frowned, believing he'd misheard. Billie said yes, immediately.

Jack had some doubts. "Is this legit?" he said to the storekeeper.

"Well, certainly," said the man. "The big labels recognize that people are going to copy their look and feel. As long as we display the official hologram"—He reached over to one of the bags and opened it, turning a small label out so Jack could see it—"then everything's fine. The difference is durability and, ultimately, quality. That's what you pay for with the originals."

"Well, okay," said Jack, but he was still a little dubious.

"Would you like me to have them delivered?"

"No, we'll take them with us," said Jack, pulling out his handipad to make the purchase. He reached for the bags, took them over near the door, and started piling their packages inside them.

Within moments, they were outside the door.

"You want to explain this to me?" said Jack, repositioning the bags till he felt comfortable.

"Sure," she said. "They're programmed copies. They look like the real thing, feel like the real thing, they have the labels, but they break down after a while. They cost a lot less and they last a lot less." She shrugged. "They're what we need, right?"

And she was right. Not even thinking in those terms, about labels and designers and things like that, he hadn't even known such things existed. So how was it that Billie did? He suddenly felt guilty, realizing that he knew far less about what she occupied her time with than he probably should. If he'd taken on the responsibility, the least he could do was follow it through.

Billie was looking thoughtful.

"What is it?" asked Jack, wondering what was next.

"We need some accessories. People with money always have accessories."

"And how do you know that?" said Jack, putting down the bags and waiting for her to answer.

She gave a little shrug. "I've seen people with money, haven't you, Jack? It's not hard." She was looking at him with that faintly exasperated expression again. Finally she gave a little shake of her head and headed off toward another line of stores. "Come on. This way. I know what we need."

With a frown, Jack stooped and hefted the bags again. "Okay, wait," he said. "Where are we going?" He didn't even want to think about how much more they were going to eat into the remaining funds.

"Just down this way. It's not far," she shot back over her shoulder, not even waiting for him.

As she disappeared inside a doorway, he quickened his pace to catch up. The store was full of stuff. That's the only way he could think of it. There were glasses and small trendy little bags, handipad cases in bright colors, all sorts of things—he couldn't even tell what purpose they might serve. It was stuff, and all of it stuff that meant nothing to him. Billie was standing, leaning over a counter, peering down at the contents. There were no display boards here. Jack guessed that this kind of merchandise people wanted to pick up and feel, to play with, to try it on. Jack joined her at the counter.

Billie looked up at him as he stepped up and pointed down at a pair of glasses.

"These are great," she said. "You can touch them and they change color according to a voice command. They can be really dark, or you can mirror them, or do anything you want."

"But we don't need sunglasses in here," said Jack, confused.

Billie shook her head. "We don't *need* them, but they look good. Everybody's wearing them."

Jack grunted. "Not everybody."

"Yeah, well . . ." said Billie, looking back down into the case. "Those ones, I think," she said. She glanced back up at Jack's face. "Uh-huh. I think they're good."

She thumbed the pad at the side of the display, and an assistant was with them in a couple of seconds. "We'll have those, I think. Can we try them on?"

The assistant opened the case and handed the glasses over. Jack slipped them on, and Billie nodded approvingly.

"Yes, they're good. Do you want to look?" she asked Jack.

He shook his head and she sighed. "Yes, we'll take them," she told the assistant.

The assistant started to launch into a spiel about the various features, but Jack cut her off with a wave of his hand. "That's fine," he said, and opened up his hand-ipad to pay. The assistant looked slightly disappointed, but put the payment through. Billie was leaning back over the display case, looking at other items. She found something for herself, and again, Jack paid.

"Don't worry," she said as he slipped the extra purchases into the bags. "I'll explain them to you when we get back."

Jack just shook his head and let himself be led out of the store.

When they did get back, Jack was all for dumping the purchases and getting something to eat, but Billie insisted on taking out all of the articles they'd acquired, arraying them across the back of the couch and disappearing into her room, only to appear moments later parading a different combination of outfit, the wall turned to its mirror function so she could check that everything met with her approval. Eventually, Jack looking on, she tired of the game, packing the clothes away, ready for the morning. When she was done she reappeared in the living room, looking at Jack expectantly.

"No," he said. "I'm fine, Billie. Everything's okay. How could it not be? You chose it."

She grinned and accepted that.

"There is one thing though," he said. "I think you're going to have to do something about that hair."

The grin slipped away and was replaced by a half pout, and she reached up to play with the tangled waves on top of her head, but then she slowly nodded and sighed.

"In the morning," she said.

When she did appear the next morning, Billie looked almost demure, with her neat little jacket, well-cut jeans, and simple white top. What she'd done to her hair was astounding. When Jack had first met her, she'd had a simple straight bob, but then as her hair grew, the tangles came into being. Now the tangles had been straightened out, the ends were even, and it fell in soft waves to her shoulders. She looked cute. She could be anybody's daughter. Jack stood and stared at her.

"What?" she said.

"Nothing. Doesn't matter. You just look so . . . I don't know. You look great, Billie."

She suppressed a smile. "Uh-huh. You look okay yourself."

"Come on. We need to move."

And they did. It was still early, but they had limited time to get up to the port and make their transport on time. Jack grabbed the prepacked bags and headed for the door.

"Wait," said Billie. "Let me take mine."

That was unusual too. What had come over her?

They traveled to the port in silence. Even though Jack had managed a morning coffee before they headed out, he was still in that half-awake morning state. In that less-than-good frame, he was mulling over the actions they were just about to take. They'd spent thousands on the mere whim of a dream prompt. As accurate as his dream pointers had been in the past, it was still pretty tenuous. It had been a while since he'd been able to rely on his dreamstate with any certainty. He didn't even know if there was any way he'd see Bridgett Farrell again. Her cat and mouse games didn't fill him with confidence. So, he was headed out into the wild unknown with no good reason for doing so. He screwed up his face and readjusted the bag on the seat beside him.

He glanced across at Billie. She seemed content, the bag clutched in her lap, kicking her feet slightly back and forth, looking into the distance. She was probably thinking about their destination. He didn't dare do that yet. It made him think about the process of how they were going to get there. And with that, there was just too much uncertainty.

They reached the port after one shuttle change. It was early yet, and there wasn't too much activity. Yorkstone wasn't one of the trendy destinations and vacation season was much later in the year. Their ground transport sat waiting, doors already open. There was a small covered waiting area and a check-in desk in front. They headed in that direction. Just before they reached the desk, Jack dug out his handipad and made sure the right identity had been loaded. He set his bag down and strode forward to the desk, placing the handipad down on the small recess designed for that purpose. There was a pause; then their reservations came up with a series of question and answer touch points. He answered the security questions, the baggage questions, and confirmed the fact that they had a connecting flight. The screen accepted the answers and displayed an instruction to await further boarding information in the waiting area. Jack grabbed the bags and headed for a vacant seat. There was one other passenger already waiting. As Billie and Jack settled into place, the man, dressed in a conservative suit, turned to Billie.

"Hello, young lady," he said with a smile. "Where are we off to today?"

Billie, uncharacteristically, returned the smile easily. "We're going on vacation."

"Oh, yes? Anywhere special?"

Jack felt his heart lurch.

Billie nodded enthusiastically. "Yes. My uncle's taking me offworld to Mandala. We're going to visit the ruins."

The man's eyes widened a fraction and he glanced over at Jack, took in the coat, the luggage, cleared his throat and nodded. "Yes, very special indeed." He adjusted his jacket and looked away, pulling out his handipad and pretending to bury himself in the morning news. Jack wondered briefly whether the man thought himself out of his depth or whether there was some sort of subtle disapproval there. No, it was probably the Mandala reference that had done it. It was out of most people's reach.

Billie turned to Jack and gave him a little grin. He just shook his head.

When the boarding announcement came and their luggage was stowed, they found seats up near the front of the ground transport's passenger section. The businessman found a seat in the corner, looking out a window. That suited Jack fine.

The drive to the spaceport took just over twenty-five minutes, through open countryside. Had they still been at the Locality, they would have been forced to take a flyer, but Yorkstone was currently in close proximity to the port. In a couple of years its slow crawl would probably take it farther away, necessitating different connections, but now it was within striking distance.

Once there, there were more check-in procedures, security questions, but this time they were ushered into a lounge—wide comfortably padded seats, a bar, snacks, multiple screens showing different programs. Jack headed for the bar and made himself a coffee. Billie made a beeline for the free snacks and started loading up her pockets. Jack tried to ignore her. He also tried to ignore the chill growing steadily in his chest. Flying was fine. Spaceflight was fine. It was just this new drive, the jump. He'd seen what it had done in Outreach's experimental stages and he didn't want the same thing to happen to him, nor to Billie. Gilbert

Ronschke and his severed hand kept floating up inside his head. It was probably just as well that they were in the lounge and he couldn't see their intended transport. He carried his coffee back to a chair and tried to lose himself in one of the screens.

An hour later, the boarding announcement came. Billie tugged at his arm and Jack nodded. He reached for the travel bag and followed her reluctantly to the boarding gates. What the hell was he doing?

The boarding went without a hitch, and they were led to big comfortable seats toward the ship's front by one of the ship's personnel who obsequiously fussed about them, making sure they were all right. They had the section to themselves. Jack just wished the steward would leave them alone. Right now he could feel the slightest sense of panic working up inside him. When the steward leaned in close and warned them that the jump sometimes resulted in nausea, then asked if he wanted a patch to counter it, he waved the man away. He was close enough to being sick as it was, but he wanted to do this on his own. He needed to face the fear and conquer it—just in the same way he'd schooled himself out of reaching for a patch every time he needed to concentrate. It was discipline. Meanwhile, Billie was prodding and poking at controls and playing with the screen in front of her, flicking from channel to channel.

Jack closed his eyes and took deep, steadying breaths. He heard the doors close and the launch announcement. It would take about forty-five minutes after launch to the jump point, and then another forty-five minutes to landing. It was certainly different to weeks and weeks, but it still didn't make him feel any better knowing it. The ship thrummed into life around him, and Jack gritted his teeth. He knew, rationally, that they were nowhere near jump yet, but the feeling still worked inside him. He felt the ship slowly rise, pick up speed, then accelerate further, pushing him back into his seat. One thing, it was a hell of a lot more comfortable than his usual mode of travel. It would be a while before they'd be traveling like this again.

After the acceleration eased, he opened one eye a crack and then the other one. Billie was absorbed in a game. They had the cabin completely to themselves. He loosened his grip on the arms with an effort of will. He knew he was being stupid. Ever since the start of the drive's more widespread use, there'd not been a single report of any problems with it. No accidents, no disasters, everything seemed to work.

About ten minutes after takeoff the steward reappeared, asking if they wanted drinks. Billie took an orange juice and Jack just asked for water. He couldn't face anything else. Ten minutes later, the steward reappeared and cleared away their glasses.

"Fifteen minutes to jump," he told them. "Please make sure you're strapped in securely."

He fussed around, making sure their restraints were fastened properly, then disappeared again. Jack closed his eyes again, far from reassured. Billie just seemed to be taking it all in her stride.

He was expecting some buildup, some warning apart from the brief internal announcement that jump would be in two minutes, and then it was upon them. He felt his stomach flip, a strange sucking sensation that seemed to pluck at every one of his cells, individually, and just as quickly, it was gone. They were through. Jack opened his eyes, glanced at Billie, but she was still absorbed in the game as if nothing had ever happened.

"Was that it?" said Jack.

"What?" said Billie, not even looking away from what she was doing.

"Is that all? The jump?"

She shrugged.

Forty-five minutes later they landed at their stopover.

Again they were ushered into a lounge, but this time it was even more plush. They had two hours, and Jack busied himself with Billie's notes. When they at last boarded the ship that was to take them to Mandala, it was much the same routine, but the ship was smaller, only room for about a dozen passengers, and they seemed to be the only ones on board. There were no lower classes of travel. Jack looked around, grunted at the sheer plushness of the fittings, and strapped himself in. This wasn't him. This wasn't Jack Stein. No way. At least the nerves had gone.

Ten

Mandala loomed in the viewscreens, a veldt world, green-brown, with mountains on the main continent, small icecaps, and just the edge of an ocean visible. Jack knew from Billie's notes that most of the planet was landmass. The seas were more like vast salt lakes than oceans. There were no industries, a few nonsentient native life-forms, and little else apart from the resort and the ruins. Jack could see nothing of either the resort or the archeological site from this distance. He watched the planet grow larger and larger. Billie, beside him, was staring fascinated. He didn't think it was the fact that it was a new world that had piqued her interest—she'd traveled offworld before, after all—but rather Mandala itself.

The descent was quick, and they touched gently down at Mandala's port before they knew it. The ship settled and the door slid open. Jack and Billie unstrapped themselves and stood, heading for the steps that would take them to the ground, their steward ushering them to the door. At the bottom stood a woman dressed in the hotel uniform, deep green with a simple yellow blouse. She smiled broadly as they descended step by step.

"Mr. Stinson, welcome to Mandala. Welcome to the Mandala Country Club."

Jack nodded.

"And this must be your niece, Susan." Jack glanced at Billie, then back at the woman, and smiled. Billie smiled widely at the woman.

"Welcome, both of you. My name is Stella. I'm here to make your journey to the resort as comfortable as possible."

"Our bags?" said Jack.

"Have already been taken care of, Mr. Stinson. Your transport is waiting for you."

"When do we get to see the ruins?" said Billie.

The woman smiled. "Oh, I think we need to get you settled in after your trip. There will be someone at guest services who can answer all your questions and make all the arrangements. If you'd follow me, Mr. Stinson."

She led them to a low white transport, helped them into the back, and then climbed up front. A driver already sat waiting for them. He turned as they climbed in, smiled, and then turned back to the front. Of their bags there was no sign.

Stella glanced back over her shoulder. "You'll have a good view of the countryside and the resort itself when we get a little closer."

"Can we see the ruins from here?" said Billie. Jack narrowed his eyes at her to shut up, but Stella's smile didn't waver for an instant.

"No, the ruins are actually some distance away," she said. "But there's plenty to see on the way in. If you're lucky, we might get to see some of the local wildlife."

The "plenty to see on the way in" consisted of miles and miles of rolling, grass-covered hills and valleys.

Off in the distance there was a semienthusiastic mountain range—nothing forbidding there. Looking around as they drove, Jack couldn't quite work out what the attraction was. Maybe it was the simple exclusivity of the place. Of course, back in the days when travel between the stars took weeks and months, Mandala would have been more exclusive still, but now . . .

The Mandala Country Club appeared as they crested a rise. Dark, low buildings clustered across one side of a valley. Several pools, gardens, a golf course, stables, they were all there. Jack felt a growing sense of trepidation. They didn't belong here. It would be so easy just to give everything away. What did he know about lifestyles of the rich and famous?

They drove down the valley and pulled up in front of the main building. Stella climbed out and opened their door for them, standing back to let them approach the front doors. The main building was a little taller than the others that clustered around. Dark wooden pillars flanked a simple glassed door. There were no signs, nothing to announce what the place was. Jack presumed they didn't need it. Twin lines of large potted plants led up to the doorway. He could smell the vegetation, the clean earth and air. It was different from the recycled atmosphere of Yorkstone, the ships, the terminals. It was fresh. An undercurrent of something sharp, indefinable, sat beneath the cleanness—something he couldn't identify. Probably something to do with the alien atmosphere. Just inside, a slim young man with dark hair, also decked out in the resort's colors, met them and ferried them to the front desk.

Another smile greeted them. "Mr. Stinson. Susan. Welcome to the Mandala Country Club. If you have any needs during your stay above and beyond what is

provided with your residential facilities, please don't
hesitate to contact me. Here at the Mandala Country
Club, service is our watchword. We have prepared the
Kalama residence for your stay. Hopefully it will be to
your liking. If there are any problems with it, or it's not
completely to your liking, again, please don't hesitate
to call me immediately. My name is Stefan. Markus
here will show you to the residence."

Jack glanced around to see a young man, blond,
with fine, tanned features, who had appeared behind
them as if out of nowhere. He too smiled and nodded.

Stefan continued. "A couple of points before you
see your accommodations. Dining is available at the
City of Trees Restaurant, twenty hours a day. Of
course, Mandala has a twenty-hour day, so it's open all
the time. I guess you could say it was open twenty/
nine, because of course we operate a nine-day week. Is
there anything else I can do to help you before Markus
shows you the way?"

Billie opened her mouth, but Jack grabbed her
shoulder and she quickly shut it.

"No, that's fine," said Jack. "We've had a long trip.
I think we'll just go to our rooms."

"Of course, Mr. Stinson. Markus, would you show
Mr. Stinson and his niece to Kalama, please? Markus
will look after you now."

Markus held out a hand, indicating the way.

Jack nodded and smiled, taking Billie by the upper
arm and leading her in the direction that the young
man had indicated. Jack was feeling even more uncomfortable, right out of his depth, but he tried to re-
tain his composure. They were led down another path
flanked by thick vegetation, past a glassed-in dining
area that Jack assumed was the City of Trees Restau-

rant, and farther to a small wooden building, looking more like a cabin than anything else.

The young man called Markus flashed something and the door opened.

"The door is now keyed to you and your niece, Mr. Stinson. It will only open to you." He stood back, letting them enter.

Inside, the cabin was much more than a cabin. Modern chairs sat around a wide glass table in a central room. Broad windows looked out over the low rolling slopes stretching out in front of the resort complex. A plush couch and lounge chairs sat to one side. One complete wall was blank. Jack assumed it was their personal system for the duration of their stay. Several doors led off from the central room. One by one, Markus walked from door to door, opening them and standing back for Jack and Billie to inspect the rooms. One held a kitchen unit, another a bathroom, all marbled with gold taps, still another bedroom, yet another bedroom, an office area. Jack's luggage was already sitting in one of the bedrooms, Billie's in the other.

"Can I get you anything, Mr. Stinson? A drink? Something to eat?"

"No, that's fine, Markus. Thanks."

"If you would like to change the room choice we have made for you, I can shift your luggage now."

"No, that's fine," said Jack.

The young man dipped his head and withdrew. There was no tipping at the Mandala Country Club.

Jack stood in the center of the main room and looked around, slowly shaking his head. Billie was going from room to room, touching things, opening cupboards, playing with control panels.

"Billie, cut it out for a minute, will you, and come here."

She came and stood with him, then glanced out of the windows. "Wow! Look at that."

Jack turned to see what had prompted such a reaction. With slow, stately grace, a pair of peacocks was strutting past the window, their iridescent plumage shining in the bright afternoon light. Jack watched them walk past, his jaw half open. Peacocks? He hadn't seen peacocks for years, and that was back on Earth, off in some zoo complex he'd visited during some foreign mission. It had been pretty close to the hotel they'd been staying at, and all he could really remember was how they'd kept him up at night with those damned cries of theirs. What it must have cost to ship them out here . . . Billie had her face pressed up against the glass, her hands spread on either side as she watched the birds disappear from view. Slowly she turned around.

"Wow," she breathed. "They were beautiful."

"Yeah," said Jack, walking over to the control screen to see what their options were. Billie had gone back to the window and was pressed up against it again, watching the outside.

The door chimed.

"Enter," said Jack.

Markus was back, bearing in one hand a tray of exotic fruits which he proceeded to place on the table's center.

"Are you sure there's nothing I can get you, Mr. Stinson?" he said, sounding a little as though he was actually failing his guests by not being able to help them.

"No, that's okay. Actually, wait. There is. Where can I find the information about excursions to the City of Trees?"

"It's all on your room system," said Markus, "but

we have qualified guides taking trips to the site twice daily. You will have your own guide. You can reserve the space through the room system. Would you like me to show you?"

"No, that's fine," said Jack. "What do you mean, qualified guides?"

"Well, most of the guides who work at the Mandala Country Club are archeologists, mainly doing post-graduate work. They come here from the university so they have an opportunity to be close to the ruins without necessarily being attached to the main archeological party. Of course if the party needs some extra work, then they're available. It's the sort of opportunity a lot of them can't pass up. Many students take the option."

"Of course," said Jack. "Very interesting. University?"

"Yes, UBC. The University of Balance City. They're the ones who specialize in the City of Trees, mainly. There's been a team here for a couple of years now."

"Thanks," said Jack. "That's interesting."

"Of course, Mr. Stinson." Seeing that there was nothing else, Markus ducked his head and withdrew.

Billie had opened the double glass windows leading to a small patio and was standing outside, looking over the facilities. The light was starting to fade, but the temperature was still warm and comfortable. Jack sat at the table and called up the system to have a look at what options were available. After a couple of moments, he noticed something, something that didn't seem quite right, and in the next instant, he realized what it was—the silence. Somewhere off across the grounds a peacock called, clear in the early evening air, but apart from that . . . Yorkstone, the Locality, they all had this underlying hum of activity, barely perceptible and deeply embedded in the back of the consciousness, so far that you didn't even notice it. But

now that it wasn't there . . . Jack sat back and listened.
So quiet. He'd forgotten what it was like.

Before he'd moved to the Locality Jack had spent
time in many and varied places, especially during his
time in the military. Deserts were quiet. Tundra was
quiet. Even the jungle was quiet, in its own way. When
you were hundreds of miles away from civilization,
you noticed it, whether on an operation or simply on
maneuvers. This was like that. People paid for peace
and quiet, as they called it, and just now he could see
why. He followed Billie out onto the patio and just
stood there listening.

The next morning, they breakfasted in their room.

Jack thought it better that they stay in the rooms as
much as possible, but Billie wanted to try everything.
The pool, though she'd never learned to swim—the
stables, though she'd never learned to ride—even the
golf course. He let her go, with the admonition that she
should keep as quiet as she could about their background and their life. She had charged out of their
cabin and disappeared without a word of argument.
Meanwhile, Jack had occupied himself with the wealth
of information on Mandala available through the hotel
systems. There were lengthy guidebook-style articles
on the City of Trees, pointing out particular features of
note, detailing the history of the site's discovery, and
suggesting walking routes through the vast complex.
Jack studied them, page after page. Certain areas were
out of bounds. They were the subject of the archeological work being carried out by the UBC team. He noted
those, then downloaded the walking maps to his
handipad.

He'd made the booking for their first trip just before
Billie had left, with her standing behind his shoulder

bouncing up and down. He needed to check the details. The system quickly confirmed the booking and flashed up details and a name. Their appointed guide was called Hervé.

He looked at the time display, registering that Billie had been gone for a couple of hours. There wasn't much she could get into trouble with, so he spent some time flicking through the various other infoscreens provided by the hotel. He had to keep in mind that their time was actually more limited, what with the shorter day. Hopefully they wouldn't need too much time at the site for Jack to get what he needed, but there was no telling how and when his senses were likely to kick in. His sleep last night had been dreamless, when he'd finally managed to sleep, and there'd been nothing to tug at his subconscious workings since they'd been here.

He killed the wall display and wandered over to the window to see if he could catch sight of Billie, but their cabin was facing away from the main complex, just as all the other cabins were. He glanced around at what he could see of the place, once again feeling strange about the whole thing. He almost felt dirty. How could people live like this? He turned away, shaking his head.

"Jack!" Billie was standing in the doorway, looking slightly out of breath. "The guide will be here soon. Aren't you going to get ready?"

He frowned and looked down at himself. He wore the same coat, trousers, and top that he'd had on yesterday. She was right. If they were going to be trekking around the ruins, he really ought to be wearing something a bit more appropriate. With a nod of acknowledgment he disappeared into his own bedroom to change into something more casual. He emerged just in time for the system to announce their guide's arrival.

Hervé was a young man with a deep olive complexion. The hotel greens failed miserably to cover the wide expanse of belly jutting out and barely covered in a white T-shirt beneath the jacket. A round jolly face seemingly stretched to its maximum beamed at them from the doorway.

"Hello," he said. "I am Hervé. I'm going to be your guide to the City of Trees. Mr. Stinson. Susan. I am right, aren't I?" A clear accent marked his words.

"Yes," said Jack. "So tell me, Hervé. How far away is the site?"

"It will take us about an hour to drive out there. I can assure you, the vehicle is very comfortable. It is, of course, air-conditioned. Have you got everything you need?" He looked them over and nodded, watching as Jack reached for his small travel bag. "It might be a good idea to take a bottle of water or two with you," said Hervé. "It can get hot and dusty in the ruins and we will have some ways to walk."

"Will we be going anywhere near the archeologists?" said Billie.

Hervé chuckled. "Well, no, it is not on our planned route, but I'll see what we can do, eh?" He gave her a big wink. Billie grinned in return, then gave Jack a quick pointed glance. He nodded. Sometimes she knew exactly how to use what she had, the innate charm of a young girl. Just now and again, she played it for all it was worth.

Hervé waddled out to the parking area, leading the way to one of the low white resort vehicles. He clambered up in front, leaning back in the seat, his arm draped across the back, thrusting his wide belly forward. He waited politely for Jack and Billie to get settled in the back, then turned around to talk to them.

"I will give you some more information when we're at the site, but I believe you're going to find this a truly memorable experience. Just to see the City of Trees is a wonderful thing. It is such an important site."

Billie nodded enthusiastically.

Jack chose the moment, just to verify what Markus had told them about the guides. "Hervé, are you an archeology student? The reason I ask is that one of the hotel staff said something about most of the guides here."

"Yes, it is true. I am working on some postdoctoral studies to do with the site. There is no better place to be close to the work, and of course, it helps to pay the bills, you know. We live pretty well here at the Mandala Country Club."

Jack settled back. "So I guess you can tell us quite a bit about the site, more than just the standard guidebook stuff. You know, about the theories to do with what it is and things like that."

"I will try," said Hervé with another broad grin. He turned around and sparked the vehicle into life.

All the way to the City of Trees, Hervé regaled them with anecdotes about various visitors to the resort. Billie seemed to lap it up, but quite frankly, Jack felt his interest waning and he tuned them out, turning to watch the landscape. He was more interested in what he was going to find at the ruins than whatever had happened in some playground for those who had too much money for their own good. They wound up through rocky outcroppings and then down the other side. Their vehicle rounded a bend, and there, at last, below them lay the site. Billie craned forward, trying to get a better view, and Jack found himself doing the same.

The information pages back at the hotel had barely prepared him for the site itself. Thick, square structures, clumped in groups of four, reached up toward the sky, stretched across a wide expanse of plain. The tops were uneven. He had expected them to be level. Even at this distance, the dark mottled surfaces reached out to them with the uniformity, the evenness and vastness of the constructions themselves. It was immediately clear that this was nothing man-made. The simplicity and order spoke of a different kind of intelligence.

"It is something, isn't it?" said Hervé from the front. He was concentrating on negotiating the winding path down to the valley floor, but even he risked a glance or two as they descended. "It always fills me with a kind of awe. Perhaps you might say respect."

Jack was reaching for some sort of spark deep within himself, but there was nothing there apart from natural amazement at the site itself. Billie was leaning almost across him, trying to get a better view. Okay, she was excited, he was impressed, but there had to be more than that. The Talbot figure in his dreams had told him he had to be here. There was nothing yet to tell him the vision had been more than just a conjuration from his true subconscious, rather than that part of him that put him in places he was meant to be. He would have expected something to be working by now, this close to their destination. If it turned out that he'd simply blown all of Bridgett Farrell's funds on some subconscious whim, he was not going to feel good about this at all.

It didn't take long to descend to the valley floor proper, and as they came closer and closer, the sheer size of the structures started to sink in. Whoever or whatever had built these things didn't believe in doing things by halves. Jack leaned back, peering up through the transport's ceiling at the shattered tops—because that's what they were, shattered, crumbling uneven ends to square fingers pointing to the sky.

"Are all the tops like that?" asked Jack.

Hervé looked where Jack was looking and nodded. "Yes, all of them are the same. They are all buildings. There are floors within them and entrance places as we shall see, but not a single one has a roof or a ceiling. We suspect that the damage is simple exposure to the elements over time. No one has yet been able to establish an accurate dating for the city, but we know that it is very old. After perhaps thousands of years, you expect some deterioration from exposure. We are very lucky, perhaps, that the buildings themselves are still standing."

They pulled into a parking area. There were a couple of other resort transports similar to their own, and a few other vehicles which Jack presumed were from members of the archeological team. Hervé clambered down from the front and opened the rear doors to let them get out. He stood for a couple of seconds waiting as both Jack and Billie stared at the first clusters of buildings, craning back to see their tops. When they'd had enough time to appreciate the true majesty of what they were seeing, Hervé began his spiel.

"These are the outer buildings. You can see they are positioned in clusters of four. The entire city is laid out in a grid pattern, itself a square. The area between each of the sets of four buildings is exactly the same, leading us to believe not only in the ordered nature of the builders, but that the number four has some special significance to them. Clusters of four. Four sides to the square. Four pathways leading to each intersection. The pattern continues throughout the entire city."

Yes, all of that made sense. Jack pulled out his hand-ipad, thumbed it on and called up the map. "Have you any idea what the builders looked like?" he asked.

"No," said Hervé. "Unfortunately there are no pictorial representations within the site, or none that have been found. Of course time and the elements could have obliterated any that were there. That's one of the things the on-site team is working on, trying to discover something that might give some clue as to the nature of these beings. If we were to find something like furniture, or maybe something else, it would give us some clues, but so far, there has been nothing."

Still Jack was feeling an absolute internal void. The site was interesting and impressive enough, but there was nothing sparking inside him. He grimaced and glanced up at the buildings' tops again. Where was it? Where was the thing he had come to find?

Eleven

All the literature, what Hervé had told them during their meander through the vast columns, everything had been right; the site was nothing less than impressive. Dark mottled stonework thrust up above them as they negotiated the spaces between the buildings. Each tower had its own broad entranceway, and they peeked inside a couple, but whatever had been in there, if there had ever been anything, was long gone. The doorways had four sides as well. The tops of each entranceway were pointed, something like a squared-off arch, the two top edges shorter and narrower than the sides. Jack glanced from side to side as they progressed, looking up each of the side streets—well, he presumed they were streets—seeking anything that could act as a prompt. All he saw was ordered uniformity. There wasn't even any rubble to fix on.

They'd been wandering for about an hour, Hervé giving them a running commentary, when Billie spoke up.

"Where are they working?" she asked.

Hervé stopped, looked at her speculatively, leaned one hand against a nearby structure, wiped his forehead with the back of one hand, and then scratched his ample belly. "Well, let me see. We are in sector six now.

That would make it . . . over there." He gestured back
behind them.

"Have you been to that section?" she asked. "Have
you worked there?"

"Well, yes, as it happens, I have had the good for-
tune to spend some time on the site. It's more to the
center of the city and seems to have been less affected
by time and the elements. There are one or two interesting features there."

"Wow, that must have been exciting," said Billie,
her eyes wide, rubbing at one arm.

"Yes, indeed it was," he said. "I hope to have such
an opportunity again soon if I am fortunate."

Billie glanced up at Jack, for once seeking some sort
of approval before heading farther down the path she
was pursuing. He gave her a quick nod. It couldn't
hurt. So far he was no closer to a spark than when they
had arrived.

"Can we go and see? Please?"

Hervé chuckled. "All right. Let us see what we can
do. I'm not really supposed to take you down that
way, but I cannot see it doing any harm. You won't be
able to see too much, but you might see a little."

"Really? We can?"

"Sure." Hervé pushed himself off the wall and
beckoned them down one of the straight avenues running between the building clusters. By now the paths
were deep in shadow, but a warm breeze stirred,
bringing the smell of old earth and stone, the taste of
dust.

"Do you think the buildings were always this
color?" asked Jack, staring up at a wall, mottled in
brown and deeper gray-brown patches.

"No. It is a good question," Hervé answered without turning around, continuing his waddle down an

adjoining street. "Some of us believe that the buildings were once covered in some material. We think it's likely that they were smooth. There have been discoveries of flat, metallic sheets, with designs on one surface, but there have not been enough of them to confirm the theories. If it had been so, we suspect the buildings would all have been covered like this, giving them a vague shine, like dull mirrors."

Jack glanced up again, trying to picture it. A slight shine. How would that have looked from a distance?

Before long, their path was stopped by a broad barrier. Flat panels blocked access to one of the streets, temporary wide, flat boards, locked together in an interlocked wall. A couple of names and dates were hastily scrawled across a couple of these. Even out here there was graffiti—the need for someone to stamp a record of their presence. On one side the fence continued, turning sharply and heading off toward the city's other end. On the other, the panels made way for metal fencing. Signs affixed to the fence's outer side warned of restricted access.

Hervé waved Billie forward, and they headed off toward the right.

"I don't know how much you will be able to see from out here," said their guide, "but if you look through this fence, you might be able to catch sight of something."

Jack followed a little behind. When he caught up to them, Billie had her hands linked into the fence, standing on tiptoes and peering across the space within.

Large lights, currently switched off, stood around the flat expanse between buildings. A few tools lay discarded on the ground. It seemed if there were any archeologists here today, they were off somewhere on a break. Blocks were tumbled here and there, some with labels affixed to the piles with numbers scrawled on them. Over to one side sat a stack of crates. Jack was just about to turn away, see what else he could see, when something about the crates snagged his attention. He leaned in closer to see. He couldn't be sure at this distance, but on the side of one of the crates was stamped a symbol—and the design looked like something he knew only too well.

"Where are the people?" said Billie.

"They are probably working on another section today," said Hervé. He was looking through the fence, an expression almost like longing on his face.

Jack took the opportunity to tap Billie on the shoulder and get her attention. He gestured toward the stacked crates with his chin. She looked over in that direction, narrowed her eyes, and shook her head. Jack traced a quick circle in the air. Billie took his meaning immediately and turned back, narrowing her eyes and leaning in a little closer. When she turned back to face him, her mouth was half open and she was nodding slowly. He had been right. The symbol stamped on the side of the boxes was a snake eating its own tail.

"Dammit," he breathed. He tried to ignore the slight chill the realization brought. It was the same symbol that had crawled through his dreams when he'd been dealing with Outreach back in the Locality, the same symbol that had worked as the key to that case.

"Did you want to know something, Mr. Stinson?" asked Hervé.

"Um, yes," said Jack slowly. "I couldn't help noticing that there's a design on those boxes over there. Does it mean anything?"

Hervé looked where he was pointing. "Oh, that. No, it is nothing to do with the site. Part of the work here is funded by a corporation. One of those big companies. The university only has so many resources. It relies on external funding for some of the work. Some of the equipment is provided by this corporation and they ship it in using those crates. It's just the transport company symbol."

"You don't know which corporation it is?" asked Jack.

Hervé's big round face looked troubled for a moment. "No," he said. "I don't pay much attention to such things. Why do you ask?"

"Just interested," said Jack. If he had anything to do with the site proper, then he'd have to know something like that. It wasn't worth pushing it right now. Hervé really might not know, but Jack had some idea. Unless he was way off the mark, his old friends Outreach Industries had some sort of involvement. There was no way that could be a good thing.

He glanced at Billie again. She returned the look flatly, showing no reaction apart from a slight narrowing of her eyes. He nodded and changed the focus.

"And what's over there?"

Again Hervé looked where he was pointing. Large sheets covered an uneven shape.

"Ahh, that. Yes. That area is very interesting. This particular cluster had a central platform that looked like it was some meeting area, or a commemorative device. We can only speculate as to its purpose. There were some interesting artifacts found there, still intact. Of course most of them have been removed now for further study, back to the university."

"Artifacts? Like what?"

"I was lucky enough to see some of them. They were like stelae. You know, like stones or tablets with carvings or designs on them. They were held in position, set into platforms beneath." He illustrated with his hands.

"So they were stones?"

"No, like stone tablets, but they were made of some sort of metal. The floor was very interesting too. There were designs, pointing to these things. Some of the team postulated that they were maps. They were like no map that anyone had seen though. The same researchers said the artifacts themselves were keys. Of course, there were others who disagreed. I myself would like to think that it was possible. Imagine it. Maps that point to the location of an alien race. Just think . . ." His face got a faraway expression and just then, Billie's attention seemed to drift off into the same place.

Jack couldn't share the feeling. The pointer to Outreach's involvement was still working somewhere deep in his guts.

Hervé walked them through several more sections of the City of Trees, but apart from the fenced-off place where the work was taking place, there was a vast empty sameness to the buildings. All of them were hollow; either their contents had been looted or they had simply deteriorated over the passage of the years. He glanced inside as many of the entrances as he could in the hope of finding an object, something left behind that he could use as a dream prompt, searching for the stored impressions and energies that might prompt his visionary state. Vast echoing chamber after vast echoing chamber revealed nothing more than dust or rubble.

Hervé glanced up at the sky and then at his timepiece. "We should be heading back," he said.

Jack glanced at his own, suddenly realizing that they'd been here for almost four full hours. He nodded. Billie looked slightly disappointed.

Hervé led them through the ordered grid, back toward the parking area. Jack could feel the buildings stretching up around him, like some bizarre petrified forest. He was missing something, but it hadn't come to him yet.

On the way back to the Mandala Country Club, Billie rode up front, chatting merrily with Hervé about archeology, about work he'd done on the site, about what he thought had happened to the aliens. Jack only paid them half a mind. He was more interested in what he might be missing. He watched the site out of the back window as they approached the mountain path. The City of Trees. Hervé had said that the buildings were probably clad with something slightly reflective. It would have shone from a distance. Jack tried to correlate the dream image with what he was seeing behind him, but it just didn't match. He narrowed his eyes, attempting to blur the image, trying to overlay what he remembered from his dream; then suddenly he realized what it was, why the match had been so hard to make. The City of Trees was only half a city. What lay stretched out behind them was the bottom half.

"Yes," he breathed to himself. They weren't clusters of four buildings. Each grouping was the base of one entire building. They were partial pictures of the vast structures that had been in the city in his dreams, but they were missing the central spire. Cathedral trees. Cathedral buildings. It was as if some giant hand had taken a vast knife and simply sliced off the city's entire top half. What sort of power could do that? He sat staring, trying to come to terms with the enormity of what he was thinking. It was contextual. There was no reason that the archeological team would think of them as anything other than individual buildings. No pictures.

No graphical representations, or so Hervé had said. The only thing that had given Jack the clue was the dream.

He watched the city all the way until it disappeared from sight behind the craggy rocks they climbed, and then he turned slowly back to face the road ahead. He wasn't really seeing it though. The city, buzzing with shiny silver shapes, floated before him in his thoughts.

Just before the Country Club came into view, Billie turned to Hervé and said something that brought Jack back with a snap.

"Can I see that place close up—the one with the maps?"

Jack frowned. Hervé slowed the vehicle and turned to look at her, chewing at his bottom lip.

"We're not supposed to allow access to the central area. That place is strictly out of bounds to visitors."

"Oh, but why?" said Billie. "I really, really want to see it. It's just so interesting."

Jack could see what she was up to, and he bit his lip and let her continue. Maybe this was the opportunity he needed. Hervé was saying nothing, clearly considering. At last he answered.

"Yes," he said. "Why not? But you have to promise me that you won't tell anyone. We should go tomorrow, if we're going to do it. You seem really interested in the site, and you know, I like that. I cannot see what harm it would do."

"Oh, thank you, thank you," said Billie, bouncing up and down on her seat.

Jack leaned forward. "We really appreciate this, Hervé. When tomorrow?"

Hervé glanced back at him. "I'm afraid I can only take your niece, Mr. Stinson. It would be too difficult otherwise. Sometime very early in the morning. Say seven o'clock. I will be there to pick her up."

Jack sat back, not entirely comfortable. He wasn't sure that he liked the idea of Billie going off with this man alone. He cleared his throat.

"Um, why can't I go too?"

"It would be far too difficult. If we're found there, it would be easy enough to explain Susan's presence. I might get into a little trouble, but nothing like if I took an adult in there. Other guides in the past have been found on the site in the secure area, having been paid to take visitors in, out of the normal tour routes. They were very quickly dismissed."

Jack considered. "Perhaps you would like to talk about a consideration . . ."

Hervé lifted a hand. "No, that's not necessary. I am perfectly happy to do this for Susan. I appreciate her hunger for knowledge. It is something I admire in someone so young. We have to look after our growing minds, encourage their enthusiasm. But you have to understand, I can only do it for her."

Jack leaned back again. "Okay."

Hervé left them at the parking area. He waited till they climbed out of the transport and then stood grinning.

"It is certainly a lot to take in, is it not, Mr. Stinson. I hope you have found today's expedition worthwhile. I know it is sometimes too vast for the imagination to come to terms with. You were very quiet on the way back. Not like Susan here." He chuckled. "I am sure that some questions might come to you when you've had time to truly absorb everything you have seen. Quite often, people require more than one visit to really appreciate the site. If you wish another excursion,

I am here for you and ready. Just book through your room system."

He reached down a hand and ruffled Billie's hair. "I am sure Susan here would like to see the city again in more detail, eh?"

Billie nodded at him and smiled. Jack noted her reaction wryly. If he'd tried to do that, Billie would have torn his hand off.

Hervé glanced around, checking there was no one else in earshot. "I'll see you at seven in the morning," he said quietly. "Make sure you're awake and ready, Susan." He gave her a big wink, then clambered back into the vehicle and drove away.

Jack stood looking at her. "Are you going to be okay?" he asked her.

"Uh-huh," she said.

"I'm not sure I am," he said slowly. "What do we know about this guy, Hervé?"

"He's fine," she said.

"Hmmm."

"Well, what do you want?" she said, staring up at him. "Do you want to find out stuff about this place or not?"

"Yeah, you're right, of course. And it was good thinking. I just don't know if I'm entirely happy."

Later, after they'd eaten, Jack sat down at the table, wanting to talk through what he'd been thinking. He was still not comfortable about the following morning and the discomfort was niggling at him.

"Well," he said to Billie, "you seemed to get on pretty well with our guide." Jack surprised himself, hearing the touch of resentment in his words.

"So? He was nice." She grabbed a chair and sat down facing him.

"Looked like it was a little bit more than that."

She ran her finger back and forth over the glass surface. "What do you want?" she said. "You said you wanted to find out as much as we could, didn't you?"

"I guess."

"Well, that's what I was doing." She looked across at him defiantly, daring him to say that it was anything else.

He shrugged. "Okay. I've just never seen you like that."

She shrugged back. He didn't want to get into a debate about it. He was feeling tired. The whole time difference thing seemed to be getting to him. The shorter day. The even shorter night. He couldn't be feeling possessive about Billie's attentions, could he? Not really. And if she did come up with something in the morning, then it would all be worth it.

"Listen, I've been thinking about the site. You know, I don't think they have the whole picture about the place. The stuff I've seen in the dreams, the things he was saying about the coverings on the buildings. I think, somehow, there was some great disaster. Maybe a war or something. The city should have something at the top." He tried to illustrate with his hands. "I think that's why all the buildings seem to be broken off."

Billie got a faraway look as she processed what he was saying.

"Now, if what Hervé was saying about some sort of a key to a map was right, I can see why someone would want the artifact. That's going to make it pretty valuable. Whether it turns out to be of any use or not, somebody's going to think it leads to something. You don't deliver a set of directions to take you nowhere, do you?"

Billie was running her finger across the table again.

"What is it?" he said.

"Aliens." She looked up at him again. "Imagine being able to find aliens."

He looked at her, frowning, taking in what she was saying.

"Hey, you're right," he said finally. "It's going to be valuable for that reason even more so. It's not just a map taking you to a particular place. It's like a treasure map. Lost civilization. Alien culture. Who knows what could be there? That's got to be worth a lot to someone, doesn't it?"

"Uh-huh."

Shit. Things were suddenly falling into place. It was obvious why someone like Outreach Industries would be interested. Technology, new science, who could say? Even being the first to make alien contact might be enough. He could understand other parties being interested too. Where there was a hint of some major payoff, greed was going to pull them all in like scavengers. "Yeah, it's big. Bigger than I thought. It still doesn't explain this Talbot guy and Bridgett Farrell, does it? Okay, he deals in antiques, he comes from Utrecht where the university is located, so maybe he's got the access. Maybe he takes one of these things and tries to sell it on the open market. Maybe he's even got someone inside the university. All that works. But where does our Ms. Farrell come into the picture? I don't get it. I'm starting to get the feeling that there's more than one player involved here."

Billie tapped her temple with one finger, a wry grimace in place.

"Yeah, yeah. I know," said Jack. "Anyway, if you can find out more tomorrow morning, that's really going to help. One thing . . . if you can manage to pick up anything, a piece of broken tablet or anything like that, it's going to help. I need something to work off."

She grimaced at that, but said nothing.

"Come on, Billie. What is it now?"

She just shook her head and then walked out of the room. He ignored the gesture and watched her leave. Yeah, yeah. Very smart, Jack. He had to get over this habit of treating her like an idiot. A moment later, her bedroom door closed.

He'd had enough for one day too. He headed for his own room to try and get some sleep.

The next morning he was up early, still feeling nervous about the whole solo trip out to the site. He was sure Billie could look after herself, and he had no real reason to question Hervé's motivations, but all the same, he didn't feel comfortable about it. He kept flashing back to images of the type of predator who used to hang around the parts of Old back in the Locality.

Billie emerged, dressed for the expedition, looking smug.

"What is it?" he said.

She planted her hands on her hips. "Well, when you were asleep last night, I did something . . ."

"Okay . . ."

"I got into the hotel system."

Jack stopped what he was doing and turned to face her properly. "Really? What did you find?"

"Nothing. I was looking for that woman or Carl Talbot, but there was no trace. The records were pretty tight too. It took some time to get into them. They've got a lot of security."

"Mmmm, that's interesting," said Jack. "Still, a place like this, they're going to want to be discreet. Half their business is going to be from people who don't want to announce they're here. Particularly these days when it's easier to get out to Mandala. The rich and famous tend to like their privacy."

"Uh-huh," said Billie.

"Well, good work, anyway. I wish I'd thought of that." He was just about to cross and give her shoulder a congratulatory squeeze, when any further conversation was interrupted by a door announcement. Hervé had arrived. Jack quickly walked over to Billie and squeezed her shoulder anyway.

"You be careful out there with him," he said.

She looked up at him, then set her lips in a tight line, moved out from under his hand, and walked out to answer the door.

"We're going," she called.

"Okay," said Jack, not feeling particularly okay about it at all.

Jack spent the next hour pacing. After a while, he settled a little. Billie could look after herself. He had to keep telling himself that anyway. He wasn't achieving anything at all wearing tracks in the floor. Hopefully Billie would come back with something that he could use, but he thought he might as well take the opportunity of her absence to do a bit of checking on his own. There was no point doing any more probing on the hotel systems, though; what took Billie minutes would have taken him hours, so he finished getting dressed and wandered up to reception.

Behind the desk stood an unfamiliar face. That was just as well. He walked over and placed his hands on the top of the desk and leaned forward slightly.

"Good morning," he said.

The desk clerk smiled. "Good morning, Mr. Stinson. How can I help you?"

Oh, these people were good. He couldn't remember having seen this guy before at all. "Yes," he said. "I just had a brief query."

The clerk looked at him attentively. One of the other guests, a middle-aged woman, walked past carrying a towel, clearly heading for the pool. Jack cleared his throat, waiting till she was out of earshot before continuing.

"I must say, I'm very impressed with the place," he said.

The smiling clerk nodded. "I'm glad, Mr. Stinson. We like to keep our guests happy."

"The country club was recommended to me by a couple of friends. I was just wondering when the last time they stayed here was. I couldn't recall offhand."

The clerk's eyes narrowed slightly, though the smile stayed in place. "I'd like to help you, Mr. Stinson, but you must understand, we are not permitted to release guest records. It's one of the features of the service we provide here at the Mandala Country Club."

"Yes, yes, of course," said Jack. "Perhaps you might recall them, that's all. I don't have to know exact dates precisely, but I'd appreciate it. I couldn't remember which one of my friends made the recommendation and I wanted to thank them without looking like an idiot for forgetting."

"Yes, Mr. Stinson. Of course, I understand."

Jack nodded. "It was either Bridgett Farrell or Carl Talbot. Perhaps you remember them."

There was a slight frown as the clerk processed, and then he shook his head. "I'm sorry. Neither of those names is familiar. I have a pretty good memory of our guests and I'm afraid those names don't mean anything to me."

"Hmmm," said Jack. "Bridgett Farrell. About so

high . . . He illustrated with his hand. "Slightly reddish brown hair. Very petite. Carl Talbot. A few inches shorter than me, dark hair, olive complexion."

The clerk's narrowed eyes were becoming narrower. He shook his head. "No, I'm sorry."

Jack shrugged. "Oh, well. It doesn't matter," he said. "Thanks anyway."

He turned away from the desk and headed for the doors. He could feel the clerk's gaze on him all the way down the path until he'd passed around the building's corner and out of sight. Hmmm, maybe it hadn't been that smart after all, but he'd had to try.

He spent the rest of the morning flicking through the hotel information channels and half glancing at the newsfeeds, but it was just displacement activity and he knew it. What was really on his mind was Billie's expedition to the site.

About an hour later she appeared, looking flushed and slightly out of breath. He quickly stood, subjecting her to a quick assessment before asking, "Are you okay?"

She frowned. "Of course I am." Just as quickly, the frown disappeared. "It was great, Jack. I wish you could have seen it. There was this open area, and it had designs and patterns all over it. Hervé explained to me what they were, or what they thought they were. It was like some giant key. And anyway, this thing was round, and flat, but there were ridges leading into the center and then pointing out and these sort of stands made of rock. Each one of them was supposed to have a metal bit fixed on the top, but they've only found a couple of them. They don't know what happened to the others. And then when we looked at them—"

Jack held up a hand. "Whoa. Slow down a bit. It's too much, Billie."

She blinked a couple of times, then took a deep breath. "But you should have seen it . . ."

"Yeah, I know. I wish I could have. Come on. Come and sit down and tell me all about it . . . slowly."

She nodded and headed for a chair. Jack took a seat opposite and leaned forward, waiting. She took a moment to gather her thoughts.

"Like I said, there was this circle in the middle and there were designs all over it, but they were pretty faded, really old. You couldn't see what they were in some places."

"Hmmm, nothing lying around?"

The touch of a frown before she answered. "No, it was all clean. Anyway, these lines went out from the center, came back in, and then pointed out to these . . . like . . ." She gestured with her hands. "Little mounds, but flat at the sides. And they had these teeth at the top. No, that's wrong. You could see where these pieces of metal used to go. Most of the lines pointed to one in the middle."

"So what did Hervé say they were?" asked Jack.

"He thought that everything pointed to them, so they were significant things. He said they weren't sure, but they did think they were maps. It was really interesting."

"Hmmm," said Jack, leaning back and tapping on the table. "Well, we're not getting very far, are we?"

Jack had one more thing he wanted to do before they left. The dreams still hadn't been back and he thought there had to be something, anything, he could get from the site, something he could use. He arranged another trip out to the City of Trees, departing mid-

morning. Billie was perfectly happy with that idea.
Again Hervé was there to meet them, and as he and
Billie had the previous day, they drove out to the
site, only this time, again, Billie sat up front, with
Jack perched in the back watching them. She and
Hervé chatted away, seeming to have forged quite a
bond during their little excursion, leaving Jack to
think.

He was mulling over the best approach when they
reached the parking area and Hervé led the way down
into the site proper. He was going to take them on a
different route today, just to break up the sameness of
it all, but Hervé warned them both that there wouldn't
be much more to see. The point was to drink in the
majesty, to take away an unforgettable experience that
they would treasure for the rest of their lives. Jack decided it was far wiser to keep his theories to himself
for the moment. Revealing anything about his dream
images, about the ideas they'd prompted, would seem
just a little strange, and he didn't want to divert the
matter at hand by getting into some sort of speculative
discussion. He doubted it was something that Mr. Stinson would bother with either.

As they trailed through between the buildings, Jack
looked for his opportunity. Billie had dashed ahead,
and Hervé was walking at a leisurely pace, his arms
thrust out, swinging from side to side, perhaps in an
attempt to counterbalance his bulk.

When Billie was far enough ahead and conveniently
out of earshot, Jack called Hervé to a stop.

"Listen, Hervé," he said. "You've worked on the
sites themselves."

"Yes, Mr. Stinson. How can I help you?"

"Well, I've heard about small things going missing.
Little objects that might not be missed."

Hervé looked into his face, blinked a couple of times, then chewed at his bottom lip. "I am not sure what you are saying, Mr. Stinson."

Jack glanced in Billie's direction. "Well, the girl, you know. I just thought it might be nice to get her something that she could keep as a souvenir. Something she can treasure, to take the memory away with her."

Hervé frowned. "I'm still not quite sure I understand."

"Oh, come on, Hervé," said Jack. "You know. You've worked on the site. How hard would it be to get a little piece of something? For a price, of course."

Hervé physically stepped back. The frown got deeper. "I think perhaps I don't want to understand what you are saying, Mr. Stinson. I don't know what you think of me, but I am an archeologist. Do you not understand the importance of this site? And you are suggesting . . . . No. I am disappointed, Mr. Stinson. Very disappointed." He shook his head. "I will forget we had this conversation." He turned and walked away, following the direction that Billie had taken.

"Shit," said Jack to himself. That had not gone at all like he expected. Students were always poor, looking for a bit of extra income. He was working here to supplement what he was doing, after all. Damn.

The rest of the morning was spent in silence. Hervé did not talk to him again, though the conversation between him and Billie flowed freely. When he drove them back, it was as if Jack did not exist. He let them off at the hotel parking area and drove the transport away, only pausing to say good-bye to Billie.

"What happened?" asked Billie as they walked down to the cabin to get ready to leave.

Jack told her about the conversation. She simply

sighed and opened the door, stepping back to let him in. As he stepped inside, she muttered something behind his back.

"*What*, Billie?" he said, turning to face her.

"Nothing. Forget it," she said, stepping past him and into the room beyond.

Twelve

They left Mandala on schedule, departing in much the same style as they'd arrived. All the while Jack was carrying serious doubts about what he'd spent to get them there. What he could have done with those funds . . . . And now they had to go back to Yorkstone and find something else to make up the difference. The prospects weren't looking good.

Sure, he'd gotten at least a sense of what he was dealing with out of the trip, the importance of the artifact, its potential—and Billie certainly had her own set of positives, but he couldn't help wondering if it had all been worth it. Choices. It was all about choices. Whether he'd been prompted by a dream or not, he'd chosen to listen, and therefore, he was responsible. The whole thing was weighing on him so much most of the way back that he even forgot to be nervous through the jumps. Billie, on the other hand, seemed unusually happy. She spent most of the trip buried in pictures and notes on her handipad. Jack looked over her shoulder a couple of times, but it was all Mandala and the City of Trees. He still failed to understand the level of fascination she had with the place.

They reached Yorkstone in the early hours of the morning. The travel, the time difference, everything was just making Jack feel drained and empty. And he was empty. Nothing inside was giving him the clues he needed. He didn't want to think about the possibilities of what that might mean. Was he losing his abilities? Or maybe they were just becoming more selective about when they manifested. It was starting to become a real concern. What the hell was he going to do if they dried up completely?

Putting the feelings down to tiredness, he decided he'd leave that for when he'd gotten some rest and worked himself back into time zone. Better to think about things with at least a partially clear head.

Back at the apartment, he dumped the bags in the living room and headed straight for bed, leaving Billie to look after herself. He gave one last look as he closed the door, but she was curled up on the end of the couch. There was a suspicion growing in the back of his mind that he didn't really want to deal with. What if it was Billie who was affecting his abilities? What if it was her presence that was responsible for the apparent dampening of his extra senses? He paused, watching her for a couple of moments before finally closing the door. It couldn't be Billie. He'd dreamed, he'd found stuff. There was no reason she could be affecting him. He'd be better equipped to think about all of it after a good night's sleep.

Jack rose late. There was no sign of Billie yet either. He was halfway through brewing a coffee when he remembered that he hadn't even bothered to check messages when they'd gotten in. He wasn't expecting anything apart from one, and that was more like dreading it—the call he didn't want to happen—Morrish or Laduce. They'd only been gone just over three days. What could possibly have happened in the meantime?

He wandered into the living room, carrying his coffee, and called up the system.

There were two messages.

He settled himself on the couch, cupping his mug in both hands, and asked the system to play.

The first was a face he didn't recognize. "Mr. Stein. This is Christian Landerman. I know you don't know me—"

"Pause," said Jack. He studied the face. The man had snowy white hair. His face was slightly ruddy, high cheekbones, thin with a sharp chin and nose. The eyes were gray. No, he was right. Jack didn't know him. He looked hard though, hard in the way that didn't countenance compromise.

"Continue," he said.

"—but I believe you have made the acquaintance of one of my employees. He informs me that you have an item that belongs to him. I would appreciate it if you could get in touch with me at the Excelsior Hotel. Again, my name is Christian Landerman."

"Stop," said Jack. He didn't know what this Christian Landerman was talking about. He placed his mug down on the table. He wasn't in time zone yet and he wasn't thinking straight. His thoughts were dragging themselves sluggishly through his slowly waking consciousness.

"Play again."

He sat forward and watched the message, looking for hints. The fittings certainly looked like the Excelsior. Perhaps he was talking about Talbot. But that couldn't be right. If this man was Talbot's employer, then Landerman had no idea that Talbot was dead. But then Talbot could hardly have told him that Jack had anything. It still didn't make sense.

"Play next," he said.

Landerman's face appeared on the wall again. "Mr. Stein. Perhaps you didn't receive my previous message. I would appreciate it if you could contact me. I am staying at the Excelsior. Christian Landerman."

He looked at the time stamp. The messages were a day apart, and in the second one, Landerman had looked mildly pissed off. Jack reached for his coffee again. He needed some caffeine in his system before he decided what he was going to do.

By the time he'd finished the cup, Billie had emerged.

"Billie, I think you want to see this. Something interesting."

She humphed at him and headed for the kitchen. Okay, he could wait. He followed her in to get himself another coffee. She was making breakfast, slopping from cabinet to fridge to drawer, clattering around, her pajamas rumpled and her hair back to a tangle. This was the Billie he was used to. He grabbed his coffee and left her to it.

While he was waiting, he watched both messages again. There was someone in the background in the second one whom he hadn't noticed before, just a shape, nothing he could clearly identify.

Billie had clearly chosen to finish her breakfast in the kitchen. The time zone change seemed to be hitting her harder than Jack. Finally she joined him, wiping her mouth with the back of one hand and scrunching up her hair with the fingers of another.

"What is it?"

"Watch this," he said, and replayed the messages. She watched them and shook her head, semiscowling.

"Okay, I need to know who this guy Landerman is."

She shrugged.

"Well?" he said.

"Well what?"

"Can you do it?"

"I guess," she said grudgingly. She pushed herself from the couch and headed off into her room. She was in a bad way.

She'd jump into the shower now, so he decided to take the opportunity to call Landerman while she wasn't in view.

"Call Excelsior Hotel."

The desk program greeted him. He was getting a little tired of this particular hotel.

"Could I speak to one of your guests, please? Christian Landerman."

He half expected to get the same runaround as last time he called, or even to hear that Landerman had checked out. He was half disappointed when the program put him through to the room.

"This is Landerman." The same severe face took over the wall. He was wearing a deep green silk robe of some sort; at least it looked like silk.

"Jack Stein."

"Ahhhh, Mr. Stein. So good of you to get back to me. I was starting to give up hope."

"Well, Mr. Landerman. Sorry about the delay. I've been out of town for a couple of days. I must say, your message intrigued me, though I have to be honest. You said something about an employee, about an item. I'm sorry, but I can't say I know what you were referring to."

Landerman laughed. "Poor Larkin. He is a little forgettable sometimes, I must admit. What it must be to go through life and make such little impression on people."

Jack frowned. "Larkin?"

"Oh, yes," said Landerman. "He was not impressed

when he returned from your meeting. Not at all impressed. I believe you took something from him. A gun, perhaps?"

"Oh, damn. I'm sorry." Jack had completely forgotten about the little man across the street.

Landerman waved his hand. "No, no. Nothing to be sorry about. I'm sure you were perfectly within your rights. It's important to protect what's yours, no? Though Larkin is still not very happy with your . . . rough treatment of him. Naturally he feels offended. Suffice it to say he does want his property back. Guns are expensive things, Mr. Stein. And I too would appreciate it should you be inclined to return it. No recriminations, of course. Unfortunate things happen from time to time, and it is good when we are in a position to make amends. So, would you be prepared to return the weapon in question?"

Jack nodded. "I can't see why not."

"Good, good. So I can expect you when, Mr. Stein?"

"Let's say in about an hour or so. Would that suit?"

"Perfect," said Landerman, and smiled. He steepled his fingers in front and gave a little smile with his tight thin-lipped mouth. There was nothing pleasant about the smile. "I'll be here. End," said Landerman. The wall blanked.

Jack hadn't even been close enough to form a real impression, but he knew he didn't like this guy already. He considered, waiting.

It took a little while for Billie to emerge again.

"Listen, Billie, I'm going up to see this Landerman guy. Remember our little friend across the road with the gun? He works for Landerman."

She stood in the doorway with crossed arms.

"Well, can I have some money before you go?"

"What for?" he said.

"I need to buy some stuff."

"What sort of stuff? Haven't we bought enough?"

She screwed up her face. "Just *stuff*, Jack."

"Ohhh," he said. Having a young woman—because that's what she was becoming—in his charge sometimes had its disadvantages. There really was some stuff that he didn't want to think about. With a slight grimace, he dragged out his handipad and transferred some funds into the home system where they could both access them. Repressing the urge to clear his throat, he kept his attention focused on the handipad and spoke.

"That should be enough. Take what you need."

He stood, grabbed his coat—the old coat—replaced the handipad in its pocket, then tried to remember where he'd put the small ugly gun. Billie waved her hand in the direction of the shelves.

"Oh, yeah," he said. He reached up to the top shelf, felt around, and located the gun, giving it a quick look before shoving it in his other pocket. "And Billie?"

"Uh-huh."

"When you can. Stuff on this Landerman guy." Anything to change the subject.

She nodded and disappeared back into her room. Okay, let her take her own time. He left the apartment, leaving her to get on with things as she would.

He felt strange walking up to the Excelsior yet again, especially so soon after Mandala. It was like some weird form of déjà vu, but with another high-end hotel. He was immensely conscious of the weight of the gun in his left pocket as he strode into the now-familiar lobby. Yet another new face was behind the front desk. He wondered exactly how many real staff this place employed. It was nice to be able to afford it.

"Hello, my name's Jack Stein. I'm here to see one of your guests, Mr. Landerman. I believe I'm expected."

"Of course, Mr. Stein. Mr. Landerman says you should go straight up. If you go over to the right, the elevators will take you up. Mr. Landerman has suite eight two five. Eighth floor."

Yep. That figured. Top floor. Right on the roof of the world.

He nodded and wandered over to the elevator. At his approach the doors whisked silently open, and he stepped into mirrored and paneled shine, smelling deeply of polish. He knew the scent was fake, piped in to give the impression, but it had the desired effect anyway.

"Eight," he said.

There was barely any sensation of movement as the doors slid shut and the elevator began its ascent. At the eighth floor, the doors slid silently open. He stepped into a broad corridor, plush pale carpet, retro, gold-striped wallpaper in a pale yellow. Large vases of lilies sat on tables at either end of the corridor. Their heavy scent hit him as soon as he stepped out. On the wall opposite, small arrows pointed the direction, picked out in gold. He got his bearings and headed down the corridor. Three doors down was suite 825. He stood for a moment outside the door, seeing if he could get an impression. After a couple of seconds, he sighed and knocked.

The door swung open and Landerman's voice spoke from within. "Come in, Mr. Stein."

Jack entered, stepping into a wide, richly carpeted living area. There were couches, cream and gold, chairs, a couple of low tables in what looked like deep mahogany. Landerman sat in one of the high-backed chairs, dressed in the same green silk robe he had worn in the call. Two white roses, one on each shoulder, were woven into the design. In front of Landerman on a low table sat a silver tea service. Jack suddenly became aware that it wasn't a robe Landerman was wearing, but some sort of coat, over a highnecked shirt and straight black trousers.

The door closed behind him. The next instant, Jack felt something hard and round shoved into his back. He stiffened, looking accusingly across at his host while hands patted him down, found the weapon in his left pocket, and wrenched it free. He lifted his hands. The hard object pushed into the small of his back, painfully, shoving him forward.

Landerman chuckled. "Mere precautions, Mr. Stein. You understand."

Jack clamped his jaw shut and took a half step forward. Again he was shoved. Jack had had enough. He took a quick step to the left, spun, and chopped down with one hand. The gun that had been pressing into his back fell to the floor, the sound muffled by the thick carpeting. The little guy with the brown jacket stood looking at him wide-eyed, sudden fury growing on his face. Before he could do anything else, Jack grabbed the little man's other hand, holding the gun taken from Jack's pocket, and twisted hard. That too fell to the floor. Jack grabbed a handful of shirt and slapped the guy hard.

"I don't appreciate having guns pointed at me," he said. "I would have thought you'd have learned by now."

The man, Larkin, had fallen back against the doorway, pale shock written all over his face. Jack stooped, quickly scooped up the pair of weapons and, dangling them from each hand, crossed to the low table and placed them down. He looked back as Larkin emitted a low growl and took a step forward.

Landerman, giving another chuckle, waved him back. "No, Larkin. Mr. Stein is right. It was very rude of us. That's no way to treat a guest."

Larkin, his pale face written with fury, stood where he was, fists bunched at his sides. Jack turned away from him dismissively, looking down at the weapons on the table. The other one was large, much nastier than the smaller weapon he had previously removed.

"So, Mr. Landerman, is that it?" said Jack. "Or is our business here done? If it is, I'll be going." Jack wanted to test the boundaries. And despite his little performance, he really *was* annoyed.

Landerman nodded slowly. "I apologize for the circumstances, Mr. Stein. I would like to talk to you. Will you sit? Take tea with me?"

"What about clown boy there?" He glanced over at Larkin who stood where he was, fists still bunched, a muscle working at the side of his jaw.

"Larkin, leave us, will you?" said Landerman.

Larkin looked from one to the other of them, his eyes widening again, and then stalked from the room, only pausing to shoot a glare of complete hate in Jack's direction. Jack waited until the door was closed.

"So," he said.

Landerman waved at a chair. "Please, sit, Mr. Stein. It is far better to discuss our business in comfort, don't you think? Now, can I offer you tea, or would you prefer something else."

Really, Jack could have done with a coffee, but he pulled out a chair and sat. He couldn't understand why people insisted on drinking tea. He guessed he could put up with it. "Yes, tea will be fine."

He waited while Landerman made a performance of setting out the cups, pouring the tea, and then asking whether Jack wanted anything with it. Jack shook his head and took the proffered cup.

"Yes, very wise," said Landerman. "I always just prefer to have a little slice of lemon with my tea. It enhances the flavor rather than dulling it."

"Uh-huh," said Jack. "But that's not why you got me up here, is it? We're not here to talk about the aesthetics of tea."

Landerman chuckled again. The chuckle was starting to annoy Jack too.

"No, of course, you're right," said Landerman. "I wanted you here to have the opportunity to discuss a matter of some importance."

"Go on."

Landerman paused to take a sip at his cup, closing his eyes and breathing deeply of the vapors before continuing. He placed his cup back down and then fixed Jack with a penetrating look. Beneath the mannered façade, Landerman was clearly a man who knew precisely what he wanted.

"I understand that Larkin is not the only one of my employees that you've had dealings with recently."

Jack gave a slight frown. "I'm not sure . . ."

"Oh, but I'm sure you are, Mr. Stein. A woman. Slightly reddish brown hair, petite. Well presented. I am sure you know who I mean." His gaze was unwavering.

Jack did know who he meant, and his mind was racing. Landerman was telling the truth, and Bridgett Farrell did work for him, or there was another possibility—Landerman might be setting him up, just as a way to get to Farrell. There was enough about the man to make Jack suspicious.

"Okay, say I do know this woman you're talking about. You need to give me a little more than that. I don't know you, Mr. Landerman. I don't know anything about you."

Landerman slowly placed his cup and saucer down on the table, then sat back, linking his fingers in front of him. He paused for a moment, tapping his forefingers together, and then finally spoke. He looked less than amused.

"Two of my people came to Yorkstone to retrieve a particular item for me. Now, this item is very, um, shall we say, significant to me. Unfortunately, I have had difficulty contacting either of them. One is the woman I was talking about. The other is a man."

Jack nodded slowly. "So far so good . . ."

"I see," said Landerman. "All right. The item is something of great age, an antique, you would call it. Now, from what I understand, you were contacted by the woman to assist her efforts to retrieve the item."

"And the man?"

"He seems to have disappeared completely. The last contact I had was from Danuta, a mere few days ago. I decided that it was necessary to come to Yorkstone myself and find out what had happened."

Jack frowned. "Danuta?"

"Yes, that's her name. Danuta Galvin."

Jack sat back. "Okay, Mr. Landerman, you seem to have things right up until a point. But I don't know any Danuta Galvin."

"Oh, dear." He chuckled. "And what name is she using this time? Carlotta perhaps? Or might it be Bridgett?"

Jack sighed. "Yeah. Bridgett. Bridgett Farrell."

Thirteen

Landerman poured himself another tea, took his time placing the slice of lemon in the cup, carefully selecting which one he wanted, and then gestured with the pot in Jack's direction. Jack lifted his hand.

"No, thanks."

Landerman nodded, lifted his cup and saucer and sat back, fixing Jack with that penetrating stare. Jack didn't mind the slight respite in the interplay; he was thinking hard.

"So, you understand my problem, Mr. Stein."

"No, I'm not sure I do," said Jack.

Landerman tilted his head a little to one side and then chuckled. "Well, well, Mr. Stein. I think perhaps you do. I send a couple of people to this nice enough little city to do something for me. Both of them disappear. I know one of them at least has contacted you. What am I supposed to think?"

Jack wasn't quite sure how much to reveal. Not yet.

Landerman continued. "I think it would only be right that you tell me what Danuta, or Bridgett, as you know her, discussed with you. Otherwise, I might start to become suspicious."

Jack glanced down at the weapons still lying casually on the table. Landerman followed his gaze.

"And yes, Mr. Stein. There are implications."

Jack came to a decision very rapidly. There was no way he could keep track of the little guy, Larkin, twenty-four hours a day and have any hope of working the case, and who knew what the so-called implications might be, especially with Billie around. He had no idea how far Landerman might be prepared to go.

He cleared his throat. "All right, Landerman. Bridgett Farrell hired me. She hired me to find this artifact. Or at least she hired me to find who she thought had taken it."

"And who might that have been?"

"Carl Talbot."

There was a flicker of interest in Landerman's eyes. "Really?"

"Uh-huh. Really. But I'm afraid I've got some news for you. Talbot's dead."

Landerman placed his cup and saucer back down on the table once again. "Is he now?" he said, for once not looking at Jack. "That is most unfortunate."

Slowly the cold, probing gaze lifted again. "And what might you know about that, Mr. Stein?"

"Not a hell of a lot," said Jack, returning the gaze just as pointedly. He looked at the weaponry again, then across at the door that Larkin had disappeared through. "I thought you might know something about it."

Landerman pressed his lips together; then a moment later, his face relaxed and he gave that low annoying chuckle. "Oh, Mr. Stein. Very good. Yes, very good. But no. That is not the answer. Not at all. So, you see, we seem to be no further on than when you first arrived. And what of Ms. Farrell?"

"I haven't heard from her for a few days. I don't know where she is."

Landerman linked his fingers again, obviously considering. "Interesting. Well, we both seem to have a problem then. Let me see if we can't address that. I have a proposition for you."

"Okaaaaay," said Jack slowly.

"Well, I find myself with this dilemma, and I think you might just be able to help with it. It is clear to me that Danuta is looking to profit from the transaction with you. She clearly knows the full value of the item we are seeking. Obviously, when we commissioned her and Talbot to find it, her little mind started scheming again. Let me suggest something that might serve both of us better than the current unfortunate circumstances. We are businessmen, Mr. Stein. Let us do business."

"Go on."

"Let me propose this to you. You were looking for Talbot, but instead, you change the emphasis of your search. You continue to look for the item. Instead of working for Danuta, you work for me. I am prepared to offer you double whatever she was paying you."

It made a kind of sense, but there was still a lot about Landerman that he didn't like. It was nothing to do with his extended senses. He just didn't like the guy, or his little sidekick. If he refused the offer, there might be consequences that he didn't want to think about right now. Regardless, there was another consideration—if he took the case, it would go some way to recouping some of the losses he'd accrued over the last few days.

"Okay. I'm listening. She was paying me fifteen hundred a day and expenses. You're saying you'll match that . . . double?"

There wasn't even a flicker. "Of course."

"Oh, and there was more. She said that there'd be a reward for the object's retrieval."

Landerman nodded. "Whatever it was, I'll double it too."

Jack glanced quickly around the room. It looked like Landerman could afford it, but not even a moment's hesitation? He must want this thing pretty badly.

"I don't buy it, Landerman. Why's this thing so important to you?"

"That's nothing you need to worry about, Mr. Stein. Nothing at all."

Jack shrugged. "Yeah, whatever."

"So, I take it we have a deal."

Jack nodded. "Yeah."

"Very good. Larkin?" he called. "Will you come in here?"

The little man entered from the adjoining room, shooting a look of undisguised hate in Jack's direction. He stood there in the doorway saying nothing.

"Mr. Stein here is now working for us. You will please show him the courtesy of any of our people."

Larkin's eyes narrowed and Landerman continued. "I would like you to accompany Mr. Stein when next he goes looking."

Jack stood. "Now wait a minute. What I do, I do my way. I don't need some useless little piece of baggage hanging around to get in my way. Forget it. I don't need a sidekick. Especially not this one."

Larkin took a half step forward, but Landerman waved him back.

"As you will, Mr. Stein. It doesn't matter, Larkin. Let us trust Mr. Stein to do things his own way."

Jack nodded, satisfied. "Oh, and one more thing, Mr. Landerman."

"Mmmm?"

"You might want your boy here to grow up a little bit before you let him run around playing with toys that are too big for him. He might just get hurt." Jack reached down and pocketed the larger of the two weapons. Somehow, he had the feeling he might be needing one around. He looked deliberately at Larkin as he did so.

Larkin's eyes widened and Jack could see the fury and desperation working in his face, but the little man didn't make a move. Jack smiled sweetly, then looked back at Landerman.

"I guess you're not going to be checking out?"

"No, Mr. Stein. We will be here."

"Okay. I know where to get in touch with you then. And if that's it . . . ?"

Landerman nodded.

"Good. I'll see myself out."

Outside the door, Jack pulled the gun out of his pocket and stared down at it. Why the hell had he taken it? He hated guns. And this one was a high ratio energy weapon, guaranteed to take a good chunk out of someone at a distance. He hated to think what it might do close up. The damned thing wasn't his sort of thing at all. Sure, he knew enough about weapons from his time in the military, but even then he'd tried to avoid them. The more you obviously carried a gun, the more you were likely to get shot at. He'd learned that on more than one occasion. During his time in the military, it was luck that had kept him going rather than a weapon. The gun was just the sort of thing he'd expect of someone like Larkin though. Little man, big gun. With a shake of his head, he buried it back in his pocket and turned toward the elevator. He kept his hands in his pockets all the way down to the street, unconsciously fingering the thing as he thought about the encounter.

Landerman was weird. Clearly a man used to power and someone with resources, but the little game he played all the way through his visit was almost too much for Jack to deal with. The little verbal flourishes, the chuckles, the circumlocution.

And as for Larkin . . . he didn't know what it was. Jack didn't know why he'd acted the way he did toward the guy. Sure, part of it was performance, something designed to deliver a message to Landerman, but there was more. He really did feel the aggression. Maybe he was just seeking a target for his frustrations. Anyway, as far as he could tell, Larkin was insignificant. He just jumped to his master's tune.

He wandered out of the hotel's front doors and scratched his head. He just couldn't see why everybody seemed to be placing such value on this metal tablet. It was an artifact, okay, some chunk of alien metal. Rarity generally upped the value of things, but there had to be much more than simply wanting to own it. As he walked toward the shuttle stop, he thought about the treasure map aspect, but that didn't really make sense either. Sure, it was a nice theory, but a treasure map only meant something if you had a good idea there was some treasure there.

What did they expect to find? As far as he knew, nobody else suspected what he did about the City of Trees. Some great force had simply sheared off the top of an entire vast city, destroyed it completely. There was no rubble or anything. Even if they did find these supposed aliens, who was to say what the results would be? They could be hostile. If the aliens had the power it looked like they had, it could be disastrous. He shrugged. There were just too many what-ifs involved. Way too many. All that really mattered right now was that he had another case—well, the same case—and it was going to pay, unless Landerman and his little henchman pulled a disappearing act as well. He could worry about the other parts of it later. All he knew now was that if he was going to find this artifact, then he had to find the Farrell woman again, or Danuta Galvin as she was called. Funny, he couldn't really think of her as a Danuta. Somehow, the name Bridgett suited her.

Danuta. He rolled the name around on his tongue a couple of times testing it, but it still didn't feel any more comfortable.

When he got back to the apartment, Billie was huddled on the couch, her arms wrapped around a cushion in front of her, the wallscreen wide open on some text.

"Hey," he said.

She looked up at him and then returned to looking at whatever was on the screen.

"Well, aren't you going to ask me what happened?"

She gave a little shrug. "I guess."

Jack sat and dug the gun out from his pocket, placing it carefully down on the table, waiting for her to turn her attention back to him.

"What are you looking at?" he asked her, finally.

Again a little shrug. "Some archeology stuff." She pulled the cushion tighter against her chest.

"How come?"

She took a little while to answer. "Because I like it."

"Okay. Did you manage to find anything on this Landerman?"

She glanced at him, then looked back to the screen. "Nuh-uh. Not yet."

Jack watched her for a little while, but he decided not to push it.

"Okay, well, when you're ready."

She nodded.

"So," he said. "Our little friend from across the road with the gun works for Landerman. His name's Larkin. I don't think he's important, just an annoyance. And guess what . . . he had another gun. Well, he used to have it."

She merely glanced at the weapon.

"Landerman's everything you'd expect. Money, definitely, and an attitude that says he's used to authority. Real boss man, that one."

Jack rubbed at the back of his neck. "I've got something more for you to find out too," he said. "Our lady friend, Bridgett Farrell . . . well, that's only one of her names. She goes by at least one other. Her real name is Danuta Galvin, according to Landerman, and according to him she also works for him—or did. The case is back on. Landerman hired me to find the artifact. If we can track down the Farrell woman, or Galvin, or whatever she wants to call herself, then I think it's going to lead us to where the artifact is. I'm going to need your help for that, Billie."

She turned slowly to look at him. "And what's happened to you?" she said.

"What do you mean?"

"Where are these 'talents' of yours? What's happened to the great Jack Stein? How come I've got to do everything?"

Jack sighed. "I don't know, Billie. I don't know. It would have helped if I'd been able to bring something back from Mandala other than bits of rock. Luck just seems to have been working against me this time. I can't seem to get anything solid. That's why I need you to do the research."

"Hervé told me what you said."

There was a long pause while Jack thought.

"Yeah, and . . . I told you about it too."

"He wasn't very happy."

"Yeah, I could see that. What's wrong, Billie? What did you expect me to do? It seemed like the perfect opportunity, don't you think?"

She shrugged.

"So what else did Hervé tell you?"

"He thinks the City of Trees is one of the most important archeological sites ever. They think it's going to lead them to lots of stuff. He said it was really important to keep everything that they could until they worked out what the things mean."

"Okay. I can see why this guy would be excited about it, but it's only a few rocks and lumps of metal, isn't it? Sorry, but I just can't get excited about some old ruin, whether there's supposed to be aliens or not. And of course he'd want to keep it. I mean, that's what he's studying. This guy's just some student."

"Nuh-uh," said Billie. "Well, kind of."

"What do you mean?"

"Hervé isn't just a student. He's Dr. Antille. He was leading part of the research team."

Jack frowned. "Well, what the hell was he doing acting as our guide then?"

Billie shrugged. "He likes to do that in his off time. He likes telling people how important the site is. He wants the message to get out about what they're doing there."

Apparently, some of the enthusiasm had rubbed off on Billie. He tugged at his lower lip. "Hmmm, that's interesting." He didn't quite know what else to say about it. "So, did he tell you anything else we might be able to use?"

She pressed her lips into a thin line and shook her head.

Okay, wrong approach.

"Listen, Billie. I know you like this stuff, that's fine. But we need to think about the case. You were the one pushing me to get something to start with and now that I've got something, I need you to help me. Is that okay?"

She nodded, slowly, reluctantly.

"Good. Now, I'll wait until you're ready, but we need to find out about Landerman and Danuta Galvin. Then I can do some work. And you never know, this might turn out the right way. I don't particularly like Landerman and there's something weird about what he's doing. I just have a gut feeling that we're in this for a reason. So," he said, slapping his thighs. "I'm going to leave you to it and when you're ready, just do the stuff you're good at for me. Okay? I'm going to be in the office doing a bit of my own research."

He waited for any further reaction from her, but there was none.

"Okay," he said, pausing only to retrieve the gun from the table and shove it up on one of the upper shelves. "I'll talk to you later to find out what you've come up with."

In the meantime, Jack spent his time in the office scanning through notes on Mandala. He couldn't quite see what Billie's fascination with the whole thing was. She'd always been quick to seize things and run with them, but this was somehow different. When he finally emerged from the office, thinking, for once, about something to eat, she didn't appear to have made any headway either. He got her to call up the directories and order whatever she wanted. She seemed happy with that, though still a little withdrawn. She said barely a word to him as she worked through the listings and made her choice. When the food arrived—Chinese—they ate in silence, and then Billie announced she was going to bed, leaving Jack to sit there staring after her retreating back. He had no idea what had gotten into her. It didn't take much for him to say the wrong thing these days, apparently.

He cleared away the containers and dropped them into the recycling unit in the kitchen, then headed back into the living room to take a seat on the couch. He spent some time flicking through the vid channels one after the other, trying to find something that would hold his attention. Yorkstone programming was pretty bland. Finally, he found something that was almost watchable and settled back, his brain on auto. After an hour or so, he started to drift.

He was standing in front of the City of Trees, only it wasn't the ruins, but the whole version. Shiny silver shapes whipped between the spires. The sky, green-tinged, was clear, bright, the light making him squint. Each structure with its central spire reflected the light around them, shining. There was movement between the structures too. He was too far away to make out any detail, but things drifted and raced in between the large legs of the buildings. An ozone smell caught in his nostrils.

"You see this?" said someone beside him.

Jack turned. There stood Hervé, pointing out across the plain. He wasn't wearing his hotel uniform, but some sort of simple one-piece white garment that fell to his knees, straight down from his vast belly. Simple sandals were on his feet.

"What am I supposed to see?" asked Jack.

Hervé slowly lowered his arm. "You must understand. This is what it was. Before."

"Before what?"

"We do not know. Perhaps we will find out soon."

Jack looked back at the city. There, near the foot, small figures moved. He could tell they were figures now. He strained to see the detail, but it was still too far away.

In the next instant, he and Hervé were close to the city. Hervé had something held under one arm. Jack peered closer. It was the metal tablet. Herve's arm was looped around it so that the detailed surface was facing toward Jack.

"You see?" said Hervé.

"No, dammit, I don't." There was something he was forgetting. He turned slowly, seeking. Everything had slowed. He was moving through a thick atmosphere, pushing, slowing his reactions.

Something was standing in front of them.

It was one of the silver tripod things. A tripod that wasn't a tripod because it had four legs. The top section tilted down toward them. It was as if it was looking at them, but there was nothing to look with. The top surface of the central cylinder was blank, smooth and silver. The thing tilted up again.

Without any sense of arrival, there was another. And then another. One by one, more of the things appeared around them, tilting at the top and then straightening. They were encircled. Hervé looked around the circle and gave a big grin. Jack couldn't see what he was so happy about. What Jack felt was . . . was . . . He was afraid. These things, these alien, living pieces of equipment, were encircling the both of them and there was no way Jack could know what they wanted. He couldn't read them. He couldn't feel them. The chill grew inside. A sense of panic was starting to well up from deep within him.

"What is it, Hervé?" he asked, trying to control the reaction.

Hervé turned to look at Jack, then tilted his head questioningly. "They—" He swept his hand in a wide arc—"are why we are here."

Jack shook his head, trying without success to ignore the alien creatures, the shining silvery spires. "Why am I here?"

Hervé held the tablet forward, tracing the symbols with the end of his finger. "This is the way," he said as if pointing out directions on a map. "This is the way across the sky."

Jack shook his head. His frustration rose in anger and burst out in shouted words. "I don't get it! Don't you see? I don't get it!"

"You will," said Hervé, gently.

They all disappeared. Jack was whipped up, ever up, into stars and blackness.

Fourteen

The dream nagged at him throughout the morning, the images floating up, trying to tell him something, a constant distraction. And still he was getting no nearer to finding Bridgett Farrell. He was totally reliant upon Billie, just in the way he'd been reliant upon his own sense in the past to tell him when something wasn't right. His experiences over the last couple of years, particularly that last case in the Locality, had taught him he needed to use his head a little more, but he was failing in that respect. Instead of supplementing his senses with thought, he was taking the easy way out and relying on her. And now something appeared amiss with Billie, but he had no idea what it was. Everything seemed to be going wrong.

Billie emerged from her room finally, but then it was only briefly, only to go to the kitchen, clatter around in there for a few minutes, and then disappear back inside. He waited, but she didn't come out again.

What was wrong with her? At first he had thought it might be hormonal, but it had to be more than that. He went over to her door and knocked gently.

"Billie?"

Silence.

"Billie, come on, we need to talk."

After a couple of seconds, the door slowly opened. "What about?" she said, one hand still on the door.

"Come on. Come out here and talk to me."

She screwed up her face, but took her hand from the door and pushed past him into the living room. She stood in the room's center, waiting for him impatiently.

"Sit down, will you?" he told her, and took a seat himself. She sat on the edge of the couch as if eager to get back to her own room as quickly as possible.

He watched her carefully, but she was reluctant to meet his gaze. "What's going on, Billie?" he said finally.

"What?"

"You know what. There's something wrong. Something's upset you. Are you going to tell me, or not?"

She worked her jaw, and then shook her head. "Nuh-uh."

"Jesus, Billie. Come on. What is it?"

She rocked back and forward almost imperceptibly, her jaw still working. Finally she turned her face to look at him.

"You don't care, Jack."

He frowned. "I'm sorry. I don't know what you mean."

"You do know. Billie find this. Billie do that. Billie find out about her. Billie research that. Billie rig the system. What about what I want to do? You're using me for what you want. That's all. You're the same."

He frowned. "Of course I'm the same. Is there something wrong with that?"

"No, that's not what I mean. The same as them back in the Locality, back in Old. You just use me for what you want. You don't care about what I feel."

She pulled her knees up, wrapped her arms around

them and glared across at him, daring him to deny what she was saying.

And what she was saying stabbed through him like a frozen knife. He stared back at her. How could she believe that? How could she even say it? Slowly he closed his mouth, then stood, rubbing at the back of his neck, having difficulty meeting her eyes. "Billie, you can't believe that."

She looked away.

Jack didn't know what to say. He stood where he was, staring across at her hunched posture, at her tight jaw. She couldn't really believe that, could she? He shook his head and walked back into his office, leaving her sitting there. Even after all this time, he really didn't know how to deal with her. He crossed to the window and stared out at the street, considering. Was she right? He'd prefer to think that she wasn't, but where in the hell had all that stuff come from?

Out there, standing opposite the apartment block, stood a familiar figure, casually leaning against a tree. Jack growled deep in his throat. Larkin. The little bastard hadn't learned. Well, maybe it was time he did learn. And Jack was just in the mood right now to deliver the lesson. He tore his gaze away from the window and headed back into the living room, half prepared to grab the gun he'd taken with him from Landerman's hotel room. Billie was still sitting on the couch where he'd left her and he stopped, his shoulders slumping. Larkin could wait.

Slowly he walked across and stood in front of her, then kneeled. He reached out and took one of her hands.

"Billie, look at me."

She shook her head.

"Come on, Billie."

Slowly she turned her face; her eyes were moist, but there were no tears. Her jaw was set tightly. He still was having difficulty meeting her gaze.

"Billie, you can't believe that stuff you said. Not really. I care about you a lot. You've got to know that. You don't know how special you are."

"Yeah," she said. "Daddy's special girl." The words came out dripping venom. Jack felt the chill strike deep within him.

"You know damned well that's not what I was saying."

She pulled her hand away.

"Jesus, Billie. Give me a chance. Have I ever asked you to do anything you didn't want to? Haven't I always thought about you in the things we've done? What do you want me to do?"

"Look at someone else except yourself, Jack."

She pushed past him, off the couch, and raced across to her bedroom. The door shut a moment later.

Jack got slowly to his feet. He didn't get it. He just didn't get it. He stared at Billie's door, not knowing what he could do to solve it.

He screwed up his face, spun on his heel, and headed for the door. Well, at least he could solve one thing . . .

It took him only moments to reach the elevator and descend to the street. As he headed out the building's front doors, Larkin saw him coming, clearly recognizing the fury on Jack's face and in his gait. The little man was gone in a shot, disappearing rapidly up the street, not even giving Jack the chance to cross and confront him.

Jack stood in front of the building, growling, impotent with his frustration. He wasn't going to charge up the street after the little man. With set jaw, he turned back and reentered the building.

When Billie emerged again, Jack was a bit nervous about how he should handle it. If he was too nice, too gentle, then she was bound to think it was just a performance because of what she'd said. If he behaved normally, she'd think that whatever she'd said had gone in one ear and out the other. Instead, he said nothing.

He needn't have bothered.

"Jack, I found something." She seemed quite excited. She jumped up on the couch and called up the wallscreen. "It wasn't easy. I didn't know what I was looking for."

"What have you got?" he asked, crossing behind the couch and placing his hands on its back, leaning forward to look at the screen. It was an old newsfeed item. There was a picture of Landerman.

"Okay, that's him all right."

Philanthropist and politician Christian Landerman today spearheaded the first introduction of the anti-immigration bill to government. Jack frowned. Philanthropist? Politician? Okay, the second made sense. He read further. *Chairman of the Progress Party.* What the hell was that? He was still shaking his head over the philanthropist bit.

"Hmm, he didn't strike me as the type. So, where's this from?"

"Utrecht Newsnet."

"And let me guess . . . he's based out of Balance City."

Billie nodded. "I did some more follow-up, cross-referencing with the Progress Party of Utrecht. Landerman comes up quite a lot. There's also some other stuff about donations to the university."

He looked at her sidelong. It was as if their previous conversation had never taken place. Okay, that would keep for now.

"Anything on Danuta Galvin?"

"Nuh-uh. Nothing."

"What about Talbot?"

She shook her head.

He crossed from behind the couch and took a seat, steepling his fingers in front of himself as he thought. "Okay, it's a start, and it's good, Billie, but I think we need some more. I still don't get this philanthropist bit. And you know . . . anti-immigration legislation isn't the sort of thing that goes with that image either. Donations to a university . . . yeah, I can see that, but not unless he was getting something out of it. So what the hell does he want with this artifact?"

"Maybe he just wants it," said Billie.

"Maybe . . . but I don't see it. This is the sort of guy who has some reason for doing things. He's involved in politics for a start, and don't forget, I've met the guy. I didn't get any sense of warning from him, nothing edgy, but there was something about him. Something not very nice at all. You get these rich people who collect things just so they can have them and so no one else can, but there's got to be more to it than that."

He got up and started pacing. "Jesus, I hate politicians."

"Jack?"

He paused in his circuit of the room. "Yeah?"

"What do you want me to find out?"

Jack rubbed his chin and walked slowly back to the chair. "I'm not too sure, Billie. I've been having dreams about this . . . ."

"And?"

Jack took a few minutes describing the progression of dreams about the City of Trees and Hervé. "And so," he said, "I think somehow this artifact is more important than we think. What do you say?"

She nodded slowly. "Why would Outreach want it?"

"What?"

"Outreach. That was them at the City of Trees, wasn't it?"

"Yeah . . ." Jack rubbed his chin again. Outreach involvement just couldn't be good, but so far, there was nothing that showed they were really involved in any way apart from shifting a bunch of crates and equipment around.

"Okay, here's what we need. Landerman is involved with the university somehow and that has to be the source of the artifact, so there has to be some contact there, otherwise it's simply been stolen. See if you can find any reports of thefts from the University of Balance City. Anything as big as that has to make a splash. See if you can't find out any more about Landerman's involvement with the university too. There's still something I don't get though. How the hell is our Bridgett Farrell involved? Carl Talbot worked for Landerman, and we know that Farrell, or Galvin, or whatever she calls herself worked for him too, or so he says. Maybe Talbot did have the artifact. Maybe she had it. The question is, where is it now? We have to assume that whoever killed Talbot has the artifact. That leaves both Farrell and Landerman out of the equation."

"So, you need to find someone else," said Billie.

"Yeah," said Jack, and sighed. "But then why has Ms. Farrell disappeared? It doesn't make sense. Unless she's afraid of what Landerman might do to her for losing the thing in the first place. Nope. I don't like it. It just doesn't *feel* right."

"What about Outreach?"

"What about them?"

"Could they be the other person?"

Jack considered the possibility, turning it over in his mind.

"Okay, add one more thing to the list. Probe the university link some more. See if you can find anything solid on Outreach. We know these guys though. They're big and they're careful. Anything like donations or things like that are going to be clean, aren't they? But there might be something there. Some slipup. You're good enough to find something, Billie."

She looked across the room at him, her gaze analytical. Then she sighed.

"What?"

"You didn't have to say that."

Jack bit his lip. "Yeah, I know, but I did say it, didn't I? And guess what, Billie? I meant it. Is that okay?"

She took a second to respond, and then she nodded. But there was still no smile to go with the nod.

Later that day Jack was still worried about her, and he was still wondering what had prompted the whole scene that morning. What did he know about girls as they grew up? Maybe it was only a phase, but still it was something that had him concerned. He really did rely on her, and if their relationship was going to suddenly start deteriorating, now was not the time for that to happen. They had the chance to make something here, maybe go somewhere, a new environment that might be better for her. Maybe he could do something about her sudden interest in archeology. Or perhaps that was just a phase too. He didn't know. All the same, there was guilt there, though it wasn't a guilt he could really pin down. He'd done the right thing getting her out of the Locality, but did that mean he was still doing the right thing?

Come on, Stein, he thought to himself, there were more immediate things to think about right now, like the case.

At least the dreams were telling him something. That meant that it wasn't his relationship with Billie that was responsible for restricting his natural abilities. It too had to be the environment. Yorkstone was sterile. He stared out at the clean natural-looking street. Well, there was one small positive; Larkin seemed to have gone for the time being. The guy was lucky for now. Next time, Jack was really going to deliver his message and make sure it stuck.

Billie had decided to do the work in her room, and until she came up with something, Jack was at a loose end. He wandered out of the office and headed for her door. Again he knocked. This time she was quicker to respond.

"I'm going out for a while," he said. "You going to be okay?"

"Uh-huh," she said. She looked fine.

"Okay." He left her there and wandered out of the apartment and out onto the street, heading off to find a bar—something he hadn't felt like doing for a long time—and now he had a fair idea of what lay nearby. This time it wasn't going to be the Keg, either.

He found a place on one of the main streets. It looked discreet, nothing flashy, and he wandered inside. Unlike the police bar, it used all the standard programmed furnishings you'd expect in a place like this. He wandered up to the bar and ordered a scotch. By his third, he was deep in thoughts about what the hell he was doing, and what the hell he was doing with Billie too. He just didn't know if he was doing the wrong thing.

Leaving the Locality had been a relief and he'd felt justified, as if he was doing the right thing with Billie. Yorkstone was a *good* environment—a nice place for Billie to grow up. After all she'd been through back there, he needed to give her some sort of stable environment where she could mature properly without any real further potential for harm. In a sense though, that was avoiding things. Avoiding his own life. Was he just using Billie as an excuse? The thought of her leaving him just didn't enter into it. Somehow, they belonged together. He couldn't even think about her going somewhere else away from him. Then again, who was Jack Stein to offer a young girl a life? She needed to be with a family, with a normal, stable environment. The problem was, Billie wasn't a normal, stable kid. She'd seen a lot, done a lot—more than some adults had seen and done. Besides which, she'd attached to him. Was it wrong what he'd done, the attachment that had formed? He didn't really know.

Four scotches later, he'd gotten no closer to resolving the conflicting thoughts running through his brain. He shook his head, pursed his lips, and then tossed back the remains of his drink and signaled for another. It arrived in front of him and he turned the glass around and around on the bar before lifting it and taking another big swallow. He wasn't going to find any answers in the bottom of a glass, but by now, he didn't really care.

When he finally staggered back to the apartment, much later, Billie was already asleep. Jack went straight to bed, somewhat the worse for wear. His sleep was deep and dreamless.

Fifteen

Everything had changed so much since he and Billie had left—no, more like escaped—the Locality together. Jack had cleaned up his act, and as a result, last night's session had left him feeling like crap. He wandered into the bathroom and rummaged around in the cabinet, looking for something he could use. There was a time when he would just slap on a patch to get through whatever it was that was affecting him . . . *whatever* it was. Nothing. Just a few stray analgesic patches. He had no idea how long they'd been there. He couldn't even remember getting them. Peeling one free with a sigh, he applied it to his neck and smoothed it into place. At least it might do something about the headache.

He finished getting himself up for the day, and two extra-strong coffees later and with the analgesic patch kicking in, he was starting to feel like something that almost resembled humanity. Billie would be occupied for a while, doing her searches and scans, and she would work better if he was out of the way. Until she came up with something, or something else happened, Jack was at a loose end. There was nothing he could do, particularly, until she made some progress with her work. He could use the time for thinking, but he thought it might be better if he got out of the apartment and went somewhere else. Occasionally, that was just the sort of prompt he needed to get his inner sense working again—a decent change of scenery.

Making sure Billie was up, he announced that he was going out. She shrugged and said nothing. Jack filed her reaction away, intending to chew it over later. There was still something not right between them, but now was not the time to deal with it. He just had to let her get on with things. The moment would happen when it was right. Jack wanted to go somewhere where he could find open space, uncluttered. Somewhere he could think. Maybe he was just looking for excuses, but at least it was something to do.

Once outside, he walked unhurriedly up the street, strolling, heading for the shuttle stop. Time to put his observational faculties to work, or at least attempt to kick-start them again. In a way, things were too easy here in Yorkstone. There was none of the grit and struggle to be found back in the Locality, no hard edge to keep you sharp.

He boarded the shuttle, glancing around at its other occupants and the interior, assessing, before taking up his usual spot. Clean, pale green seats. Slick white interior. Soothing. Smooth, padded handholds and railing colored in neutral gray. Advertising was even kept to a minimum. Maybe that was the difference between Yorkstone and the Locality. The Locality had deep corporate roots, whereas Yorkstone had grown from a sense of shared community. The origins walked through the unconscious mind, shaping the way people acted and interacted. The Locality was all about profit. Yorkstone, on the other hand, was all about having a life, a clean, safe, family life. His fellow passengers showed that. Over to one side sat a large woman. Plump and jolly. Sensible shoes. Decked out in florals. She carried a bag with her. Further down the compartment was a man with a kid. They were watching the outside together and passing the occasional comment to each other with a smile and a look which spoke of clear bonding. There was nothing untoward there. Clean and healthy. Jack wondered briefly if he and Billie looked like that to the casual observer. He turned to watch the passing streets and plazas as they traveled slowly past.

Alighting near a small paved park, Jack strolled over to take in the trees and the empty uncluttered space. He found a bench to one side and wandered over, sitting, crossing his legs and leaning his head back to look up through the clear ceiling panels. Far above clouds drifted over, white and scattered. The sky was clear, blue. It was nothing like the green tinge that had been there floating through his dreams over the past few days. He watched the clouds as they sailed past, thinking. It was funny; without the work Outreach had done on the drive, there was no way anyone could have even contemplated what Jack thought they were considering. A few years ago, there could have been no conception of traveling such enormous distances on the hope that something might just be there. The supposed alien world would have just been another interesting conjecture with no hope of reaching it. Technology surrounded you and you absorbed it. It informed your decisions and choices, without even having to consider them, and at the same time, it shifted your boundaries. Each new innovation that became a part of their lives changed everyone's expectations. Within the space of a couple of years, people, not everyone, but at least a select few, were suddenly considering seeking out an alien civilization as if it were the most natural thing in the world. He shook his head, rubbing gently at his throat with one hand. And who knew what might happen if those people succeeded. He knew what they were like, what drove them.

Choices. He had a few options now too. The problem was, he didn't particularly like some of the choices that came so naturally. Yorkstone wasn't right. He just knew it was this oh-so-pleasant place that was limiting him, limiting what he could get involved in. And if he couldn't get the cases, then he wouldn't have the income needed to support them both. The problem was, the sort of events that turned into cases for Jack happened in places that had a true underbelly—places where that hard edge was a normal part of everyday life. They'd left the Locality because of that very thing. He'd wanted to get Billie out, away from it, and that's why they were here in the first place. Maybe what he should be doing was thinking about finding some alternative arrangement for Billie.

He grimaced. No, he didn't even want to think about that. He had a responsibility. He'd dragged her out of the place; it was his duty to make sure she was okay and he didn't need anybody else's help to do that. She was such a weird kid anyway. He doubted she'd settle well with anyone else. She needed someone like Jack, someone who could understand how and why she was the way she was. Maybe that was just rationalization, but it felt right.

He sighed and leaned forward, propping his elbows on his knees, and stared down at the paving, tracing the lines with his gaze. Lines. Just like the lines in his dream, leading off into the distance. There was something he was missing about this whole thing—apart from Bridgett Farrell. Why would she take off like that? The only thing he could think of was that she thought she was in danger. That was if nothing had happened to her too, and he had to consider that as a real possibility. Well, if she turned up dead, he was sure Morrish and his partner would be the first to let him know. He could just see Laduce's face now.

Jack stood, stretching, easing some of the kinks out of his back, and walked slowly around the small low-walled space. This was getting him nowhere. It seemed like his little excursion was in vain. All he was doing was turning things over and over in his head, no sensations, no insights, nothing useful. He might as well get back to the apartment and try and do some real work, see if Billie had come up with anything. He took one last look up at the sky before heading off to the shuttle stop that would take him back home. It was all very well acting on things, but if fate didn't start lending a helping hand soon, Jack was going to be in trouble, and Billie with him. The thought gave him pause. It shouldn't be up to the fates to lend a hand, should it? But that's what it was like. Just sometimes, you could simply sit back and things would eventually fall into place. Jack grimaced. Maybe that was part of the problem, that expectation. It was about time he stopped expecting things and took events into his own hands.

Sixteen

"Answer," said Jack.

Bridgett Farrell's face bled into view, dominating his office wall. She wore a high-collared demure dark suit. Her hair was immaculately done, but the jewelry was missing. She looked into his office from the screen, waiting. The slight touch of her tongue between her lips came a moment later. Jack felt a sudden drop in his stomach, but pushed it aside. This woman really was something. For a moment he was lost for words. He struggled for a moment, trying to get a grip.

"Jack," she said, when it was clear he wasn't going to say anything. "I need to see you."

Jack considered. "Yeah," he said. "Well, that's going to be a little hard, isn't it, if I don't know how to find you. Where are you?"

"Can't I come there?"

Jack turned away from the screen. "I don't think that's a very good idea, Ms. Farrell. I think this place is possibly being watched." It was time to put things back on his terms. He turned quickly back to the wall, watching the frown as it vanished from her face. She was still playing at trying to manipulate him, giving him what she thought he wanted to see.

"Who? Who is watching you?"

"That's not important right now. Let's just say I need to know where you are. I'll come to you. We can't do it any other way."

There was a quick nervous glance to the side, then the thing with her tongue again. "Can I trust you, Jack?"

Was there someone there with her? The thought made him feel uncomfortable. He shoved his hands in his trouser pockets and leaned back on the desk. "You hired me, didn't you?"

"I just need to know that it's safe. You must understand that."

"Yeah, I just might at that, but I think you've got some explaining to do, Ms. Farrell."

She frowned, but just as quickly regained her composure, the mask slipping back into place. "Listen, Jack, I know it might seem strange, but I was afraid. I was afraid for my safety, afraid for my life."

"Yeah, that's fine, Ms. Farrell, but I've got to know I can trust you too. So where are you?"

There was a long pause. "All right," she said finally with a brief sigh. She pressed her lower lip between her teeth before speaking. "I'm staying at the Barclay Apartments. In Taylor. Do you know them?"

Taylor was far closer to the port end of Yorkstone, far less salubrious than her previous accommodations at the Excelsior. "No, but I can find them. I'll be there in about an hour. Make sure you're there this time, if you want my help."

"I'm not going anywhere."

"Okay, what apartment?"

"Fifteen."

He nodded and cut the connection.

He stayed where he was, leaning back on the desk for a couple of minutes while he thought about what he was going to say to her, how much of his dealings with Landerman he wanted to reveal. He pushed himself off the desk, headed for the living room, and grabbed his coat. Billie was there.

"I'm going out," he said.

"Yeah, I know."

Jack rolled his eyes. "You've been doing it again, haven't you?"

She just shrugged.

"Well, we might just get a few answers this time. You got anything more for me?"

"Not yet."

"Okay, well, keep at it. I'll be back in a while. And keep an eye out for that guy, Larkin. I don't want him hanging around. Call me if he shows up. I don't think he got the message last time."

The apartment block was a simple affair. Jack stood out on the street trying to feel it before entering. He scanned the street in both directions, but there was nothing to pluck at his internal alarms. He shook his head. This case was weird. He hoped to hell he really wasn't losing his abilities. Sure, he was still dreaming, but there was still something missing. Who was to say his internal alarms were even working? Perhaps what he was going through was just a temporary lapse, but it was having a healthy attempt at unsettling him all the same.

"Come on, Stein," he muttered to himself. "This is simple."

Shrugging his coat around his shoulders, he entered the building. There was no lock on the outer door.

There was no need for entry systems in Yorkstone, no matter where you were. He located the elevator and pressed for the first floor. Apartment 15 was at the street end of the building. Again he paused outside the door, trying to get some sense of what awaited him inside. Nothing. He knocked.

Bridgett Farrell—he still couldn't think of her as Danuta Galvin—peered out of a slim crack and then stepped back to let him in. He scanned the room as soon as he was inside. Simple but adequate furnishing. A couple of windows looked out over the street. He stepped over toward them and looked out. A few pedestrians walked past, but that was about it. A city transport whirred by. Jack turned back to look at her, gesturing at the window.

"Curtain," she said, and the windows went half dark.

She stepped across to him and touched his arm. "Thank you for coming," she said. "I've been so scared."

Jack looked down at her face. She was looking up at him with those big, wide blue eyes, but he wasn't buying any of it. He couldn't afford to. He stepped back, biting his lip.

"You'd better start talking, Ms. Farrell, or is that what I should call you? Maybe I should call you something else."

She turned away from him. "Jack. I'm sorry. You're right. I haven't been entirely honest with you."

"Damned right you haven't." Jack crossed to a chair and sat, crossing his legs. "Right now would be a good time to start. If we're going to keep working together, then you'd better start telling me the truth."

She turned back to face him and stood beside another chair, resting one hand on its back. As she started speaking, she ran her palm gently back and forth across the top of the chair. "What can I say? Things have changed. I told you I was afraid. Well, I am. Very afraid."

"Why don't you sit down, cut the crap, and tell me what's going on. You want me to help you, you're going to have to do better than this."

She pressed her lips together, nodded, and sat primly on the edge of the seat. She folded her hands in her lap. No gloves this time. Jack tore his gaze away from the hands and looked back to her face.

"I'm afraid something terrible has happened to Carl and I'm afraid the same thing is going to happen to me."

"And what makes you think that? Perhaps it's because Christian Landerman's in town. Is that it? Is that why you skipped so quickly?"

Her pale hand drifted up to touch her pale throat and then to rest lightly on her chest as if she was gathering her thoughts. Landerman's name didn't seem to have flustered her at all. She was ice cool.

"Yes, you're right," she said slowly. "I was working for Landerman. When the artifact went missing, I was afraid of what he might do to me. The only option I had was to stay out of sight and try to get it back again. That's why I need your help, Jack. Landerman is someone you don't want to cross."

"Yeah, well, something has happened to Talbot, but I don't think Landerman had anything to do with it."

She stood and turned away so he couldn't see her face. "What do you mean, something's happened?"

"Talbot's dead. Somebody killed him."

He was waiting for something, some reaction, a

slight stiffening of the shoulders, but there was nothing. She wasn't giving anything away. Perhaps she already knew it; perhaps she didn't. A moment later, she turned.

"See," she said. "See what I told you? And I could be next. You have to help me. If we can find the artifact, then I can get it to Landerman and it will be over."

"Will it?" said Jack carefully.

She slowly sat again. "Yes, I think so."

It was Jack's turn to stand. He started pacing as he thought. "Who else could be involved in this, Ms. Farrell? It just doesn't make sense that Landerman would have Talbot killed. Otherwise he'd be gone, the artifact with him. But Landerman's here. That means he hasn't gotten what he came for, unless the artifact's not the only thing." He looked at her pointedly. She was watching him as he paced, but the comment didn't draw any reaction either.

"Come on. There has to be something you're not telling me. Who else is involved?"

She bit her lip and shook her head.

"Dammit," he cursed. "How long have you been working for Landerman?"

"About a year and a half."

"Well, you have to know something about his operation. This politician, this *philanthropist*. What did you do for him, Ms. Galvin? Give me something about him."

Even the use of her real name didn't faze her. Maybe she hadn't noticed but he doubted that. "We, Carl and myself, we used to locate and acquire things for him. He's a collector."

"Acquiring things. Yeah, I can understand that about Talbot. That's his business, but why you?"

"Sometimes the acquisition requires skills that Carl did not have."

Jack stopped his pacing. "Like what?"

"I don't need to go into that, Mr. Stein. Let's just say we worked best as a team."

"Hmmm. It's a funny sort of team if he goes off without you, taking the object you're meant to get together."

She remained silent.

Jack slowly shook his head. "All right. I'm not entirely happy, but I'll help you."

"You can be sure I'll make it worth your while."

Jack nodded. "Oh, you can be sure of that. I've got something I want to check first, and when I've done that, I'll be back. Next time I come, I expect you to be straight with me. I'm really not happy yet. Know that."

"I can help to make you happy, Jack. I'm sure I can. You just tell me what you want." She ran the tip of her finger over her lower lip, let her fingers trail over her chin and down her neck, then slowly looked up at him. Despite himself, his breath caught.

"Damn, you really are a piece of work," said Jack, narrowing his eyes and shaking his head. "I'll be in touch. Don't go anywhere. I'll let myself out."

There was an idea forming in the back of his head as he headed for the shuttle stop. What he'd told her had been true. He did want to check something out. Somewhere, somehow, there had to be a clue to Talbot and who had killed him, something the police might have missed. He needed to get back to the apartment, check whether Billie had come up with anything else he could use, and then check with Morrish. Time to call in another favor. If his guts were telling him anything, he thought he might be able to pay that favor back in more ways than one. Meanwhile, he was still annoyed that he'd had nothing to work with right from the start. Something about this case had to start falling into place soon. He didn't know quite how far his relationship with Morrish would stretch, but he was about to find out.

Billie was waiting for him when he got back.

"I found something, Jack." She was clearly pleased with herself.

"Yeah, and I have some stuff to tell you. But you first," he aid.

She didn't even bother calling up the wallscreen. "That thing on Utrecht, the Progress Party . . ."

"Yeah, what about it?"

"A couple of articles were talking about links to something else called the Sons of Utrecht."

"Huh. And what's that?"

"It's an extremist group. Anyway, that's what the articles called them. They're talking about wiping out the underclasses. Getting rid of any social welfare. They believe that for humanity to progress, they have to get rid of anything that holds it back. They say things in society that are bad for progress will simply self-destruct if they let them."

Jack got rid of his coat and sat, waiting for her to continue. "Is there more?"

She nodded enthusiastically. "It started on Utrecht about twenty years ago. There have always been links to Utrecht government, but everyone always denied it. Some of the stuff talked about closed back rooms full of rich old men and women trying to change the way the world worked. One of the pieces said something about attempts to ban the group. Christian Landerman's name was there a few times. They were politics newsfeeds, but there has to be something there, doesn't there? It's all a couple of years old now. I tried to find anything else, but there was nothing after that. It all went quiet."

Jack considered. Things like this movement had existed throughout history, but what was it about Utrecht in particular? What was it about any place that fostered such a movement?

"Yeah, that could be Landerman, all right," said Jack finally. "But it doesn't say anything about why he might want this artifact. It gives me a good idea of who I'm dealing with though, and that's a start."

"And what about Bridgett Farrell?" said Billie.

"Yeah, well. That's another story. She was just like she was before, only worse. There's absolutely no way she's giving me the whole story. I think you were right about her, you know."

He ignored her sudden smug look.

"So what are you going to do now?" she asked.

Jack ran his fingers back through his hair and grimaced. "I've got an idea, but I'm going to need to talk to Morrish."

"The police?" Billie paled.

"Yeah, I know. But Morrish is okay, I think. The problem is, I haven't had anything solid to work with. Sure, I've had some dreams, but that isn't enough, is it? I need something—an object, something I can feel. At the moment we're running blind, Billie."

She nodded her understanding.

"Okay, I'm going to call him. You wait out here. I know you're probably going to listen in anyway, so you can get rid of that pout. We can talk some more when I'm done."

She gave him a sly half grin and bundled herself up on the couch. Jack headed for his office.

"Call Morrish," he said.

"Yorkstone Police," the desk program said a moment later.

A couple of seconds more and Morrish's face was on the wall, looking slightly surprised.

"Stein. What can I do for you?"

Jack leaned back in his chair. "Jim, how are you doing? Have you gotten anywhere on that Talbot case?"

Morrish grimaced. "Not a thing. It's a dead end. How about you?"

"Well . . ." said Jack. "I have a couple of things that might prove useful, but I've got a proposition for you. If you help me out, I might be able to return the favor and help you."

"Come on, Jack. What are you saying?"

Jack made a show of playing with the nail on one finger, then slowly looked up. "I need some details on Talbot."

There was a quick narrowing of Morrish's eyes and then a frown. "You know better than that."

"Hey, Jim, listen. If you want this case to go into the bottomless file, that's nothing to me. I just thought we could help each other out here."

Morrish scratched his head. "Dammit, Stein. You're pushing it."

"Look, with what I'm working on right now, I promise you it will be worth your while. I just need something from you to make it happen."

"So, what is it that's so damned important?"

Jack folded his hands in front of him on the desk and leaned forward. "I can't give anything to you yet . . . and yeah, I know. I just need to know if you found anything with Talbot, some personal possession . . . I don't know . . . a picture, a pen, something solid that he might have handled more than once, anything at all."

There was a long pause as Morrish considered; then he leaned in closer to the screen. "You know, Stein. You'll have my job. But okay, there was something. We've got his handipad, but I can't let you have that. There were a couple of appointments listed in it though. There was one with a dealer here, another which we checked out, but there was one that made no sense at all. Alan Dean. Next Wednesday. No place, just the name. The name's not in any of our records and we've drawn a blank. We did some extensive database searches but there's no record of anyone called Alan Dean. Apart from that . . . nothing. I don't know if that's going to be any use to you."

"That's great," said Jack. "I really appreciate it, Jim. I promise you, this is going to be worth your while."

"Hmm," said Morrish. "Against my better judgment."

"Are you sure there's nothing of Talbot's I might get hold of? Just something small. You know the way I work. If there was just something of his . . ."

"Now you're pushing it too far, Stein. I've given you what I could. That's it." He shook his head.

Jack spread his hands, placatingly. "No, okay. That's fine. I'll do what I can for you, Jim. It's going to take me a few days, but I'll be in touch. I promise you."

Morrish was still shaking his head. "We'll see."

"Yeah, we will. Thanks again," said Jack.

He cut the connection and wandered out into the living room. The wallscreen was just blanking as he entered. Billie looked up at him. Jack was suddenly glad that he didn't have any really private conversations to have over the home system.

"So, did you get that?" he asked her.

"Uh-huh. Alan Dean."

"Well, you know what that means."

"Uh-huh. If the police didn't find it in their systems, I'm going to have to look in some other places. It might take a while." She shrugged.

"Take whatever time you need," he told her. "It's not much, but it might be something."

"Uh-huh."

He left her there and went into his office, seeking something to occupy himself in the meantime. He called up the wallscreen, preparing to put up anything he had already, just to focus, to find any links that he could, prompted or unprompted, he couldn't really care which. All he had from Morrish was another name to add to the list. One by one, he added the names.

Carl Talbot.
Bridgett Farrell.
Larkin.
Christian Landerman.
Outreach Industries.
University.
Hervé Antille.

He stared at the last one for a while, wondering why he'd put it up there, but he knew it was right. His dreams kept showing their guide right in the center of things. Okay, Antille needed to be there.

Alan Dean.

He stared at that name for a while, but it couldn't mean anything apart from being linked to Talbot. Okay, so that meant there were two groups.

Carl Talbot	Hervé Antille
Bridgett Farrell	University
Christian Landerman	Outreach Industries
Alan Dean	

He wasn't convinced yet that Outreach had anything to do with this, apart from their involvement at the City of Trees. If they were, he needed something a lot more solid to link them in. He didn't even bother drawing lines between the groups. There was slight linkage between both Landerman and Outreach and the University of Balance City, but it wasn't anything concrete enough to tie it to the whole artifact thing. He sat plucking at his lip, staring at the names. No, nothing was coming. With a sigh he cleared down the wall, not even bothering to save it. Even his old routines didn't seem to be working at the moment. He linked his fingers behind his neck and stared up at the ceiling, not that any inspiration was going to come from that direction.

He was just about to suggest to Billie that they go out, just to clear the air, when she appeared in the office doorway.

"I found it, Jack!"

He sat up quickly. "What?"

"Alan Dean. It's not a person."

"Huh?"

She crossed to the desk and sat down. "It's a ship. It's an old-style freighter, the slow way."

"How?" he said to her.

She gave a little shrug. "Easy really. I cross-referenced

stuff we were working on. Carl Talbot did import/
export and stuff, right?"

Jack nodded slowly.

"Well, he has to use something to carry things from
one place to another. The fast ships are more expensive. If things don't have to get there in a hurry, you
send them the old way, right? Most of the old ships are
independent. A lot of them might not be able to afford
the new drives. Anyway, the *Alan Dean* is due here
next Wednesday afternoon."

"Here?"

"Well, the spaceport."

"Damn," said Jack. No wonder the police hadn't
found it. It wasn't the sort of thing they'd be looking
for. "Good work, Billie. Damn."

He linked his fingers in front of him, thinking rapidly. So they'd found "Alan Dean," but that didn't get
them any closer to working out what the link was. Unless . . . perhaps Carl Talbot was going to meet this
freighter and have the artifact transported back to
Utrecht, or somewhere else that Landerman had interests. Landerman didn't necessarily need to know how
Talbot went about things; hence it probably made
sense that he'd turn up in Yorkstone to work out what
Talbot was up to. He might have no idea about the
Alan Dean. That still didn't explain how the artifact got
to Yorkstone in the first place.

Billie was looking at him expectantly.

"I still don't get it," he said to her. "There's something about all of this that doesn't make any sense. I
think there's only one person who's going to be able to
help solve this little puzzle for us."

"Uh-huh," she said.

"And I think I'm going to be paying her a visit—"

He glanced at the wall display—"first thing in the morning. What do you feel like doing tonight?"

She grinned at him then. Okay. It seemed like they were making progress.

Seventeen

Later that evening they got back from the entertainment center, the requisite diversion to Molly's done with and a big smile plastered across Billie's face. Jack had barely watched the movie. He still preferred the older stuff, the stuff with real actors, but Billie seemed to have enjoyed it—some space action adventure full of explosions and noisy special effects. They churned these things out one after the other these days. The main interest he had in it was that the jump drive had featured heavily as part of the plot line. It was funny how quickly media seemed to grab on to things and run with them. It had been a diversion though, and that was the main thing.

Just before she went to bed, Billie turned to him at her bedroom doorway and bit her lip. "Thanks, Jack," she said.

"Hey, it was fun," he said. "Sleep well, huh?"

She nodded and disappeared inside.

Jack went to his own bed, but sleep was an age coming. He spent a long time staring at the ceiling, thinking.

When sleep finally did come, he slipped into dreamstate almost immediately.

*   *   *

He was back on Mandala, standing on the open grasses. The sky was bright. He looked around himself. There was no sign of the City of Trees. His awareness of where he was, that he was in fact in dreamstate, told him that this was no ordinary dream though. He searched for clues. The buzzing sound was back in the air, and the sharp electrical tang slipped barely imperceptibly upon the slight breeze.

Two figures walked over the rise toward him, but they stopped at a distance. One was Hervé. The other was Carl Talbot—the ruined Carl Talbot.

"Take this," said Hervé. "This is what you wanted."

Though they were still some distance away, Jack could hear every word. That was a little strange, as the breeze was blowing away from, rather than toward him.

Hervé shifted the metal tablet from beneath his arm and held it out for Talbot to look at.

"Here, here, and here," said Hervé. "Here is the path. These are the keys."

With some difficulty Talbot took the tablet with his remaining arm, and then placed it carefully at his feet. He dug about in his coat pocket and came up with a handful of something. Hervé held out both his hands, cupped in front of him, and Talbot held his fist above, trickling a handful of shining, glittering stones into Herve's hands. Jack knew they were gemstones. Diamonds probably.

"'Ere," said Talbot through his ruined lips. "'Ayment in full."

The figures and the tablet suddenly weren't there anymore.

Jack left the ground, whipping up and up, further through the air, the flat plain receding beneath him.

The world became an insignificant pebble in a dark gray field. Jack floated in emptiness.

Clang.

He closed his eyes and gritted his teeth. Not again.

Clang.

He opened his eyes again. Above him was a solid metal vault, picked out with large designs, but this time it was different. One by one, the motifs were glowing, then fading, in some sort of sequence, heading off toward the far distance. And as he watched, the illumination drew him, dragging him along beneath the metal canopy, pulling him forward, faster and faster. Faster and faster he sped, whipping beneath the solid sky, the wind whistling about him. And then there was no wind. There was nothing. He was floating again in a gray featureless void.

But no. There was something there. Almost fading into the background, there was a shape—a small round shape. As he concentrated, he moved toward it, closer and closer, at first slowly, and then picking up speed.

It was a planet.

It was impossible to judge the size at this distance, but he had the innate feeling that the world was large. It was brown, tinged with red. Broader olive patches crawled across the surface like mold. It turned slowly before him. There were clouds, thin ochre-colored wisps trailing around the form.

He sped down to the surface as it grew larger and larger, completely taking over his field of vision.

He was standing on another plain. This had no grass. It was flat, gray-brown rock. Off to one side, there were the shiny cathedral trees. Straight ahead was the City of Trees—the complete undamaged one from his earlier dreams. No, wait. It wasn't the City of

Trees. It was larger, spreading for miles and miles. He looked behind him and there was another similar stretch of clustered buildings. Definitely a city. A silvery shape zipped past above him, quickly disappearing into the distance of the other city, and then another. He tracked it overhead and behind him, whipping around to try and follow it.

When he turned back, there was movement on the field ahead. Some kind of flatbed transport bore one of the glistening alien creatures. Its four legs were planted firmly on the flat expanse. One of the creature's petals—he could think of them in no other way—was folded down, touching the vehicle's front. Passenger and transport cruised slowly past. He watched it as it grew smaller and smaller, apparently also heading for the other city. How the hell did the things see? He could see nothing that looked like eyes. Perhaps they didn't see at all. Perhaps they perceived in different ways. The creature, if creature it was, ignored him completely.

Then he was alone, awake, and groping for his handipad.

No matter which way he looked at it, he couldn't help feeling that this Bridgett Farrell was setting him up for something—though what, he didn't know. Jack stood watching the apartment block from the other side of the street. He didn't like the fact that people continued trying to take him for a fool, and Farrell was no exception, but he was going to see this thing through to its conclusion. The only way to find out was to play it through. He also half expected to see Landerman's sidekick showing up somewhere, even here, but since that brief glimpse out his office window, there'd been no sign. There'd been no further

contact from Landerman himself either, another thing
that gave him pause. Bridgett Farrell. What had made
her contact him in the first place? That was one piece
of the puzzle that just wouldn't slot into place. He
shook his head. Deciding he was as ready as he would
ever be, he strode across the street and toward the
building entrance. Time for some answers.

Farrell let him in after his first knock, as if she'd
been waiting for him. Jack took a quick look around
what he could see of the apartment as he walked past
her into the room, but it seemed little different from
the last time he was there. He didn't know what he expected—maybe some sign that she'd had visitors or
something.

She followed him into the room, toying with a simple necklace around her throat. Again, she was wearing a dark, well-cut suit, a different one, and a simple
white blouse. Just briefly, Jack wondered where she
had room to put all the clothes and where they came
from. He'd seen no sign of luggage.

"What can I do for you, Jack? Have you some news
for me?"

He said nothing, crossing to a chair and sitting, fixing her with a flat stare.

"What is it?" she said.

"I think you've got some explaining to do, Ms.
Farrell."

She frowned slightly and took up a position at the
end of the couch, sitting upright, leaning a little forward, her fingers never leaving the silvery strand
around her neck. She was wearing something . . . rich,
exotic, and Jack caught a hint of it even from where
he sat.

"Explaining about what?"

Jack pursed his lips, maintaining his flat stare for a couple of seconds before continuing.

"So, where shall we start?" he said. "Shall we start with your relationship with Talbot? Or perhaps with your relationship to Landerman? I don't really care. Or maybe we should talk about this family heirloom. That's what you called it, wasn't it? No, I'm sorry. Every time I talk to you, the truth changes a little. I need you to tell me what's going on."

She gave a little sigh and dropped her gaze. "Yes, of course, you're right, Jack. But you have to understand. I was afraid. I'm even more scared now, after what's happened to Carl."

She didn't seem very scared.

She looked up again. "What do you want to know, Jack?"

The gaze was clearly supposed to melt him, and it was not without its impact, but right now she had another thing coming if she thought it was going to throw him off his path. He was really starting to appreciate what was going on beneath the surface with this woman, but he just couldn't afford to let himself be sidetracked.

"Right, you can start with Talbot. What were you two to each other?"

She gave the briefest of nods. "Carl and I worked together. You know he dealt in antiquities, other items of rarity. Well, sometimes they were difficult to acquire and a little more persuasion was needed. Sometimes too, it was necessary to have them transported not as a regular consignment, if you know what I mean. That's where I came in. We worked together for over a year, and yes, before you ask, it became a little more than work. We finally decided that it was getting in the way of business though, and we cooled that part off."

He pushed aside the slight, irrational touch of jealousy he was feeling. He'd guessed exactly as much. "How much more? You seemed pretty cut up about his murder . . . ." He didn't even need to force the sarcasm.

"Yes, I know," she said without a moment's hesitation. "This is sometimes a dangerous business, Mr. Stein. It has its risks. We were aware of those. We always had been. Sometimes the prize is far greater than the risk. Of course I was upset, but I'm not a little girl."

He noted how she'd neatly avoided actually answering his question. Jack leaned forward, his elbows on his knees. "And you have no idea who might have killed Carl and taken the artifact."

She gave a slight shake of her head, her mouth held tightly closed.

"Okay, then . . . so why does Landerman want this thing so badly? It looks to me like his interest is a little more than that of a simple collector. And before you start spinning me a tale, I know about the artifact. I know what it is. I've been to Mandala."

"Y-you've been to Mandala?" For once he'd really caught her off guard. He suppressed a self-satisfied smile.

"That's right. And very educational it was too."

She sighed then. At last, Jack seemed to be getting through some of that carefully constructed exterior. Progress.

"All right. No, it wasn't an heirloom. It was just another item, an item that Landerman wanted to acquire. It came from the university, but you probably know that already. Landerman believes it's a map key that will lead to the location of an alien home-world. He's hoping to be able to use that to further his own ends." She shrugged. "How true that might be, I don't care. All I care is that the price is right. Carl and I took delivery, and realizing the potential worth of it, we decided to turn the process into an open market. We know there is definitely interest in the object from other quarters. We decided to play the advantage."

"It came from the university? How?" Something about his dream was nagging at him.

She shook her head slightly. "Carl had contacts there. Someone called Antillie or Andie or something."

Jack nodded slowly, filing the information away. Was it really Hervé? Maybe Antille was a common name on Utrecht, but he didn't think so. He'd follow that particular piece of information later.

"Okay, now we're getting somewhere. I don't get it though. What benefit does Landerman hope to gain?"

She gave a short, unamused laugh. "Oh, you should hear him when he gets on his favorite bandwagon. Advancement of the human species. Superiority. It's laughable really. He thinks that this might lead them to the aliens and they can steal a march on the opposition with the technology he hopes to get from them. Who knows? I don't know whether he hopes to steal it from them or buy it or what. Perhaps he thinks they have things that he and his blessed Sons of Utrecht can use. He really is a pain. But he's a very rich pain, Jack. If the price is right, you can ignore a multitude of short-comings."

"All right . . ." Jack rubbed his chin, considering. "What's he paying you?"

She looked away.

"Oh, come on," said Jack. "You may as well tell me."

"Five hundred thousand," she said quietly.

Jack whistled. "Damn. No wonder you're eager to get hold of it. So what's the story with Talbot?"

"After we came here—this place was a good venue, the Excelsior, nice neutral ground in which to conduct the bidding process—Carl had a couple of conversations with Landerman. He started getting cold feet about what he started to call 'betraying' Landerman. I think that was just a story though, to cover up what he was really up to. I thought he might be setting up the auction and inviting Landerman to the party. And then he disappeared. I suspected he wanted to cut me out of the deal entirely. That's why I wanted him found."

"Oh, yeah. I bet you did."

Jack stood and started pacing. She sat where she was, watching him, not saying anything, just letting him work things through. Finally he stopped.

"And that's the whole story?"

"Well, almost," she said. "Of course, after his conversations with Carl, Landerman obviously wasn't very happy. In an auction, he'd end up having to pay more, and besides, he'd contracted Carl in the first place to get it. Carl had broken the deal. And then Landerman turned up here. Here in Yorkstone. Naturally, knowing the man and knowing how he operates, I decided it was wiser not to be in close proximity to him. I've had the proof that that was the right decision. Look what happened to Carl."

"If Landerman had Carl killed, what's he still doing here?" said Jack. "He'd have the artifact. There'd be no reason for him to stay."

She shook her head. "I'm not saying it was Landerman. It could be any interested party. All I'm saying is that this is very dangerous. I know Landerman; I know what he's like. He's just as dangerous as any of them."

"Why didn't you just take off then?"

She stood and crossed to stand right in front of him. "Think about it, Jack. Five hundred thousand, and that's just the starting price." She reached out to touch his arm. "You can have a part of that. With Carl out of the way, the field's open. Help me get the artifact. Think of the possibilities. We could be a team." She lowered her voice. "I'm sure we'd make a wonderful team, Jack."

He reached down and covered her hand with his, leaning closer. Her other hand came up, resting flat against the center of his chest. He gave a slight intake of breath as he read the signal. She was playing him again. Carefully, deliberately, he removed her hand from his arm. He turned away from her and stepped over to the window, looking out onto the street below, mulling over what she'd been saying. Finally he turned back to look at her.

"Well, if Landerman hasn't got the artifact, and it wasn't with Carl, then where is it? I think there's something missing."

"All right," she said. "We don't know who has it, but that's what you do, Jack. You can find that out."

"But you're still not telling me everything, are you, Ms. Farrell?"

She gave a little frown. "I don't know what you mean."

"Oh, I think you do. You want to tell me about the *Alan Dean*?"

She blanched. Quickly she turned away so that he couldn't see her face. "I'm not sure I know what—"

"Oh, yes, you do," said Jack. "The *Alan Dean* is a freighter. You know that. Talbot had it listed for Wednesday, which is tomorrow. Unless it was last Wednesday. Somehow I don't think so though, or you wouldn't still be here. Do you want to tell me what's going on?"

She sighed and crossed back to the couch, looking across at him as though she were a naughty girl. He stood where he was, returning the look with a flat stare.

"Yes, you're right," she said finally. "It's due tomorrow. The captain is a contact of ours, does the occasional job for us. Sensitive stuff, for a fee. The *Alan Dean* is carrying the artifact."

He wasn't expecting that. "It's carrying . . . Then what's . . . ?" He shook his head. Suddenly it made sense, but then it didn't make sense. He shook his head again and took a couple of steps toward her. "Why the hell am I looking for an artifact that you know damned well isn't here? In fact, you know exactly where it is. Dammit. You have all along. What's this all about, Ms. Farrell? What are you playing at?" He narrowed his eyes, feeling his jaw tensing with the realization of exactly how much she'd been manipulating him, and getting away with it.

She sighed. "All right, Jack. Yes, I know where it is. With the new jump capability, most of the focus is on the newer ships. People forget about ships that travel the old way. Cargo freighters, that sort of thing, are beneath the scrutiny of many officials. We had to get the artifact off Utrecht and away. That was already the plan as soon as we had acquired it.

Yorkstone is close enough to the spaceport to be a convenient pickup location. It also happened to be an ideal venue for holding an auction. It's neutral.

None of the major players have interests here. For that reason, Yorkstone is often used to host such transactions.

"We just had to come here and wait for the artifact to show up. After a couple of weeks, some of the heat of the investigation relating to its initial disappearance would have cooled and the artifact would have made its way here as we intended. Then we could be free to do with it what we wanted. We didn't need to hand it over to Landerman. We didn't need to hand it over to anyone in particular unless the price was right. We'd be free to have the auction, with Landerman far enough away for it not to matter. Somehow, though, Landerman had gotten hints of what we intended."

She paused, thinking, and shook her head.

"I think perhaps Carl had set him up ready for it. Either that, or he wanted to deal with Landerman direct and cut me out of the picture. Then Landerman showed up here, unexpectedly. Nothing had been arranged. Nothing. As a result, I had to find somewhere to lie low for a while until the *Alan Dean* showed up."

"Yeah," said Jack, scratching the back of his neck. "I still don't get it though. Why hire me in the first place?"

She blinked a couple of times. Jack picked it for what it was. Her mind was racing, trying to come up with something plausible to feed him.

"No, really, Carl *had* disappeared, and I needed to know if something had happened to him or whether he was just pulling another scam on me. I really did want him found. I knew about the *Alan Dean* from him. For all I knew, that could have been a story to keep me off the scent while he made his own arrangements to pick up the item and keep me out of the deal, knowing

Carl. It wouldn't have been impossible. He'd do something just like that. But now he's dead and the artifact hasn't shown up."

"So, where the hell is it?" said Jack.

She sighed. "I can only believe that it is truly with the captain of the *Alan Dean*; otherwise it would have shown up and I would have heard about it. I'm still going to need you, Jack. With Landerman here, I'm going to need you to pick up the package—as far as I know, the captain doesn't know what he's carrying—and then bring it to me. I would be recognized. I don't know how many of his people Landerman has here. I don't know how many places he's having watched. He's aware of Carl's methods. I would think that the port would be a logical place for him to apply his attention. You have to help me, Jack. You pick up the item, and we can share the profits. Think about it."

Her desperate need was starting to filter through. But it was more than need; it was simple greed starting to spark in her eyes. Jack was starting to have suspicions about what had actually happened to Talbot, but he was going to keep them to himself for now. He crossed back to the chair and sat.

"Okay, that makes a kind of sense, but there's still one problem. Landerman knows me. That little sidekick of his, Larkin, knows me. What do you suggest we do about that?"

"You look like you can handle yourself, Jack."

"That's not quite the point, is it?"

She tapped at her cheek rapidly with her fingers and then moved them to cover her lips. After a moment's thought, she spoke. "No, but listen. I can't believe Carl would have told Landerman about the freighter. Landerman might suspect—Carl had moved things around like that before—and he might be having the port watched, but he wouldn't know which ship and when, would he? All you have to do is get to the port and rendezvous with the captain, discreetly. I'm sure you're used to being discreet."

"Hmmm," said Jack. She was forgetting one thing. If he could find out about the *Alan Dean*, then so could Landerman. Especially a man of his apparent resources. She seemed not to have considered that possibility, but he wasn't going to mention that now. He wanted this to play out properly.

"So you'll do it, Jack?"

"Yeah, I'll do it."

She made to stand and cross to him, but he waved her down. "What's the captain's name?"

"Gourley."

"Is there a first name?"

She shook her head. "Just Captain Gourley."

"And what time tomorrow? Do you know?"

"It's due to berth around four thirty."

Jack nodded slowly. "Okay." He stood. "I'll be in touch. Stay where you are. I'll see myself out."

"You won't be sorry, Jack."

"Yeah, we'll see."

As he reached the door, he turned. "Oh, there is one last thing. You talked about other interests. Do you know anything more about that? Who might be involved? Have you got any details?"

"Yes. Carl spoke about a couple of people. I think they represent corporations. There was one called Antony Vasche. And another called Van Stuben or something. A strange name. As far as those other interests go, I'm sure I can arrange to get the word out. The artifact will generate its own interest. We can be sure of that. I know how these things work, Jack."

"Van Stuben? Not Van der Stegen, by any chance . . ."

"Yes, that could have been the name."

"Hunh," said Jack. Imagine that. He paused at the door before leaving, thinking that over, and taking the opportunity to have one last long look at Danuta Galvin before he departed.

Eighteen

It was funny, but now, thinking about it, there really were some strange linkages. If Outreach hadn't made the breakthrough in the drive technology, allowing for almost instantaneous travel through the vast interstellar distances, then the artifact would probably have no meaning at all. There's no point wanting to travel somewhere if you don't have the means to travel. If the tablet did indeed point to an alien homeworld, then who knew how far it was, how long it would take with conventional travel? One thing leads to another. He wondered briefly who this other player was. The name Antony Vasche wasn't familiar, but then there was no reason for it to be. He was likely a negotiator for another corporate player wanting to get in on the act, for, no matter which way you looked at it, you'd have to have the resources to mount that sort of expedition. Visiting an alien homeworld. Yeah, right. Well, not Jack Stein. At least nowhere but in his dreams. He had trouble enough coming to terms with the things found in there without something not only truly alien, but real as well.

Jack wandered down to the shuttle stop. There was one there in moments, and as he boarded, he was deep in thought.

Hearing the name Van der Stegen again after so long came as a bit of a surprise. He thought he'd done with that family when they'd left the Locality. He had suspected Outreach Industries were involved, but there had been nothing else to link them and certainly not to link the man himself to the operation. Sure, they were involved at the site on Mandala, but that could have been something as simple as merely supplying the transport to get equipment back and forth between Utrecht and Mandala. Apart from his gut feeling, there'd been nothing to tie them in at all. But now that it came down to it, the artifact was something that *would* interest Van der Stegen, and he would have the resources to make use of what it purported to be. That sort of obscure knowledge would be something that Van der Stegen would find really attractive. Since Jack's involvement with the whole mining crew disappearance, and the subsequent revelations about the drive technology, he'd had nothing to do with Outreach. That was one thing about the Locality that he didn't miss—their corporate fingerprint all over their lives. And now it looked like there were links to Yorkstone too, despite the surface appearance. Outreach Industries. Things just moved in circles. Around and around.

He looked out the shuttle window at the passing buildings and streets and tugged gently at his lower lip. No, this place didn't have the taint of Outreach Industries. This was just events conspiring again to make the links. He was reading too much into it.

So, he'd have to get to the port in time for docking tomorrow and find this Captain Gourley, hopefully relieve him of the artifact, and then work out what to do with it. He was damned sure that he wouldn't be playing Bridgett Farrell's game. He wasn't sure he wanted to play along with Landerman either. And he sure as hell wanted nothing further to do with Outreach. The big problem was, he was faced with a wealth of choices, and none of them was particularly attractive. The other thing was that he couldn't trust the Farrell woman as far as he could throw her. Dammit. Sometimes it was almost enough to make him think that fate didn't like him very much.

He left the shuttle and headed for the apartment, keeping one eye out for Larkin, but the building entrances and streets were clear. Back at the apartment, Billie was waiting for him.

"So?" she said.

Jack dumped his coat and headed for the kitchen to make himself a coffee, his head still ticking. "Yeah," he said. "She was the same as ever. Worse maybe. The whole *Alan Dean* thing was great though, Billie. It really helped."

"Come on, Jack. Tell me."

"Yeah, give me a couple of minutes to get this coffee and then I'll sit down and tell you. Not so fast."

He took his time with the coffee, then headed back into the living room where she waited for him impatiently. He sat and took a couple of sips before starting. Billie looked like she was going to burst.

Slowly, he recounted the meeting with Bridgett Farrell, only pausing to answer questions as Billie fired them at him.

"So, I need to meet this freighter, hook up with Captain Gourley and try and retrieve the item."

"Uh-huh. And then what?" said Billie.

Jack grimaced slightly. "That, I haven't worked out yet. There are just too many people involved. I'm sort of hoping that the artifact itself might give me some clues. It's about time I started having something decent to work with."

"What do you mean you don't know?"

He shrugged. "Just what I say."

She was glowering at him. "What's wrong?" he said.

"It belongs to the university."

Again he shrugged. "Well, it did. It doesn't anymore."

She narrowed her eyes. "How can you say that? This is important." She shook her head. "Nuh-uh. It has to go back. We have to take it back."

"Oh, come on, Billie. We've dealt with stuff that's been stolen before. Why this now?"

"It's just important, that's all. You should have heard Hervé talk about all that stuff. The City of Trees and everything. You were too interested in your stupid case to understand what he was saying. It doesn't belong to you, Jack."

He narrowed his eyes back at her. She was really starting to annoy him now. "Dammit, Billie. It's out of my control. You know who's playing with this stuff. If it gets taken back, it'll just get stolen again. And I could tell you a thing or two about your precious Hervé, too."

"What do you mean by that?" She'd crossed her arms and was sitting in her defiant stance, back straight, jaw thrust out.

He sighed. "Nothing. It doesn't matter."

"But it *does* matter," she said.

"No. Forget it."

She growled at him, got to her feet and stomped off into her room. A second later the door shut, hard.

Dammit. Apparently he'd put his foot in it again.

* * *

The next morning Billie was still sulking, being precious with her conversation. Jack really didn't have time for her little performances. He needed to make sure he was ready for his rendezvous with the *Alan Dean*. Bridgett Farrell had been right about one thing—knowing Landerman and the sorts of things he was involved in, it was a fair assumption that he'd have someone watching the port, especially if he wanted to get hold of the artifact so badly.

He pulled on his coat, patting his pockets to make sure he had his handipad. He was about to head for the door when he had another thought. If Landerman truly did have someone there, then he'd better go prepared, and there was only one logical extra precaution to take. He reached up to the top shelf and retrieved the weapon he'd acquired from where he'd left it. He held it in his hand, looking at it with distaste for a few seconds. The thing was heavy. Nasty. But it would do the job if he needed it. He just hoped he wouldn't. He shoved it away in his pocket, feeling the unfamiliar weight dragging his coat on one side. He really ought to have a proper holster, but he wasn't going to make a habit of carrying the thing, so he could do without for now.

As he left the living room, Billie was pointedly ignoring him. He gave a little shake of his head and left her to it. Hopefully by the time he got back, she might have gotten over it and her mood as well.

Out on the street, he walked quickly to the shuttle stop. As he clambered aboard, he thought it funny that he would be going back to the port so soon after their little trip to Mandala. Sometimes, things just seemed to work in clusters.

The trip uptown was uneventful, and he entered the Yorkstone port area with a brooding sense of déjà vu, only this time he wasn't carrying luggage. Dammit. He should have thought to bring the smaller travel bag with him, something to stow the item out of sight when he finally got hold of it. It was too late now to go back and get it.

The ground transport to the spaceport was empty. He sat alone, watching the empty landscape pass by, looking at Yorkstone's track where it had chewed up the ground in its progress. Farther back, regrowth was starting to occur, but the whole process took years of recovery. Sometimes the city tracks remained barren for years afterwards, after the city builders had leached the ground of everything they could use.

The transport crossed a ridge, and there, revealed, lay the ocean and the spaceport spread out below him. Navigational requirements meant the complex needed to be a fixed structure so they'd have one identifiable place to aim for. They shipped in raw materials for the structures to renew themselves and maintain further growth. The port itself was a cluster of domed structures, spreading from a central hub into various terminals. Passengers arrived and left from the southern area. To the north of the complex lay the commercial and transport areas. Well separated from the rest lay a drab, unmarked dome, the home of a small military unit. Even from this distance, Jack could see the colored flickering of the passenger terminals as displays and advertisements flashed across the internal dome surfaces.

The ground transport dropped him at the passenger terminal, and he took a few moments to get his bearings. He had to go through the main concourse, right through the shopping area, and up a connecting tunnel. The port itself serviced not only spaceflight, but domestic passenger transports as well, connecting flights to the larger cities. For some reason this afternoon was busy, and the domestic gates were crowded with arriving and departing passengers. It could be a good thing or a bad thing, thought Jack. He'd either be lost in the crowd, or there'd be lots of people to see him. He really did need something to carry the artifact in, or he'd stand out like a sore thumb. He grimaced and looked around. What he needed was something he could buy that needed a bag, but was light and disposable. Nobody, but nobody, was just going to give him a bag.

Wait. This was a port. They had to have a travel accessories store somewhere. He located an information pillar and punched up directions. Yes, there was one, but it was over in the far end of the terminal. There was nothing else for it. He strode quickly in that direction, keeping an eye out for anything that might be closer and could possibly serve the purpose. As he walked he kept his hands shoved deep in his pockets. Another thought quickly came to him. He hoped to hell there wasn't a security check between the passenger and freight terminals; otherwise he'd be forced to get rid of the gun. Maybe more than that . . . he'd have to explain the artifact on the way back. He just didn't want to have to do that at all. Stupid, Stein. He should have thought it through better.

At the other end of the concourse, he spotted the small accessories shop and walked quickly over to it. He wandered around the displays, but there was nothing there that seemed even slightly appropriate. There was a wall panel over to one side, and he headed for that instead. A couple of taps and he found just what he was looking for, a small black flight bag with a detachable strap. It didn't cost too much either. He punched up the order, took his handipad and made payment, then reached into the delivery slot and dug out the bag. It was neatly folded, light. He uncoiled the strap, attached it to the clips, and put it over his shoulder. He then had another thought and reached down into the bag, running his hand around the inside so that any visible folds were cleared away. That was better. Making sure there was no one to see him do it, he reached into his pocket and surreptitiously transferred the gun into the bag, then sealed it shut. He still hadn't worked out what he'd do if it came down to a search, but he'd deal with that if it happened.

The walk to the cargo berth took him a good twenty minutes. The spaceport hadn't thought to install moving walkways in the connecting tunnels. He guessed anyone coming this way would be traveling on one of those small square beeping transports.

As he approached the entrance arches to the cargo areas, he was starting to feel nervous about the gun carried hidden in the bag by his side. He needn't have worried though; it was straight-through access, no security, no checks. It made sense really. The port was far enough away from any city that it would take a real effort to get out here. You'd only really make that effort if you had some real business out here. The cargo section was set out in a wide arc, with loading docks stretching out like teeth from a wheel. Jack stood in the entranceway, looking for some indication of what lay where. There were no signs, nothing. He walked slowly along the dock, seeking clues. A few ships sat off in the distance out through the half-shell entrance. In closer was some company hauler, big, shiny and new. The ships further out were none so grand. His footsteps echoed as he walked and the smell of machines and something else, probably fuel, tinged the underdome space. He glanced up at the flat dome surface, gray, strangely reminiscent of the flat solid sky in his dreams. There had to be some way to get out to the ships, but there didn't look like there was any form of transport in evidence. Maybe this place was only staffed when they were loading or unloading, or when a ship was due in, because right now, there wasn't a single sign of life.

"Dammit," he muttered.

"Can I help you?" The voice came from above and behind him at the same time.

"What?" Jack turned around and around, but there was no sign of anyone.

"Can I help you?"

Jack shook his head. There was no pinning down the source of the voice. "Yeah, maybe. I'm looking for the *Alan Dean.*"

"Of course. Behind you."

That was stupid. The ship wasn't . . . he turned slowly. What before had apparently been blank wall was now completely clear from about waist height up. Two men sat there in port uniforms sitting at a desk. One of them held a mug, and the other one sat back with another mug sitting on the desk in front of him. The one not holding the mug waved him closer.

"Over there, toward the left. It's the old brown hauler, slightly beaten up. It'll be a bit of a walk though. All the transports are currently out. I'm not sure if there's anyone out there though. He's been down a while. It should be safe to go out there now if you want to. There's nothing else due in today."

That would explain the lack of activity. And of course, there were no transports. Great. Just what he needed—more walking. "But the *Alan Dean* was due in about four thirty, wasn't it?"

"Yeah, came in a couple of hours early."

And he'd wasted time fiddling around in the accessories shop.

"Okay. Thanks," said Jack.

"No problem. Do you want me to page the ship for you, see if anyone's out there?"

That was the last thing Jack wanted. He didn't want anyone warning the captain he was coming. "No, thanks. I'll be fine. Wish me a pleasant walk, guys."

The man who had spoken grinned and the other raised his mug in salute. The wall went blank again. With a knowing nod and a wry smile, Jack headed for the nearest stairway to the ground. Yeah, let them laugh. A job like that, you had to get your entertainment where you could find it.

It *was* a long walk out, and by the time Jack neared the ship, he was grumbling. At least he'd headed for the right ship. There it was, *Alan Dean* in letters as battered as the old tub itself. He stood looking along its length for a couple of minutes, wondering how much business this Captain Gourley actually got. A hatch toward the front sat open. Okay, that was a good sign. It looked like the good captain was in residence.

Jack headed for the stairs leading up to the hatch. They creaked as he put his foot on the bottom one and groaned as his full weight followed. They didn't feel very solid at all and shook with each step. At the top he stepped quickly inside the lock, trusting more to the battered hull than the steps themselves. Inside the lock, the ship reeked of unwashed human stuck in a confined space for too long. He wrinkled his nose and tried to breathe through his mouth as he stepped inside properly. He stopped and listened—there was no noise, not even the sound of circulating air, but that much should have been evident. Captain Gourley clearly ran things lean.

He was just about to head for the front when something made him stop. A sudden chill worked in his guts. Reaching down slowly to the bag, as quietly as he could, he unsealed it and felt around for the gun. He lifted it out slowly, looking first one way up the corridor, then down the other. Still there was no sound, no sense of movement. Frowning, senses on alert, he took one silent step toward the ship's front, followed by another. Closer to the very front, something else struck him. It was the vaguest scent. A smell, familiar.

"Oh, shit," he whispered under his breath. Blood.

He held the weapon at the ready and moved closer to the door. There were smears on the door's edge. Quickly he ducked his head around the frame. The space beyond was a chaos of disorder. His brief glance hadn't been enough to get any proper impression, but there was no one living in there at least. Slowly he moved his face around the door. It was where the captain spent his time. There were bits and pieces of clothing, junk, food, everything. There was blood on the floor as well. Not a lot, but there was blood. There was no sign of anything that looked vaguely like the artifact. He looked beyond the room, but there was nothing farther forward.

Jack came back and stared at the blood. What had happened here? Someone had been wounded. No sign of the artifact. No sign of any body. No sign of Captain Gourley. He walked the length of the ship, through the stinking disorder, looking for some other clue to what had taken place, but there was nothing apart from more mess and disorder.

He headed back up to the captain's living quarters

and gingerly started shifting some of the mess around, looking for the artifact or anything else that might prove useful. After a while of fruitless searching, he realized that it was pointless. He might as well give up.

Dammit. He had to assume that the artifact was gone. Whoever had done this already had it.

Nineteen

All the way back to Yorkstone, Jack was cursing himself. If only he hadn't wasted time in the port. If only he'd been there earlier. It was all "if only," and he knew there wasn't a damned thing he could do about it, but it still rankled. In the shuttle back down from Yorkstone's port to the apartment, it was no better. He got a couple of suspicious looks from fellow passengers as he muttered to himself under his breath, but he ignored them. Now he had to work out who the hell had taken the thing. And what had happened to the captain, anyway? The most likely suspect was one of Landerman's people, possibly even Larkin himself, but there was nothing there apart from blood to tell him that. He wouldn't put it past any of the Outreach crew either. It was just as likely that they could have arranged it. Well, one thing he knew for sure; it wasn't Bridgett Farrell. At least he didn't think it was. She had seemed reluctant to leave her apartment, but then that could have been bluff as well, knowing her. Just some performance meant to convince him that she was an innocent victim. As he left the shuttle, he was no closer to an answer, and he was cursing his missing senses again as well. Missing . . . well, he hoped it was more like dormant. He really should have had some warning.

More "should haves." He growled to himself as he walked toward the apartment.

He was bouncing on his heels all the way up in the elevator, desperate for a coffee, anything to take his mind briefly away from the problem. Already, he could see the look on Billie's face. You've screwed up again, Jack. What are you going to do about it, Jack?

Stepping out of the elevator, something snagged him like a cold hook grabbing the middle of his abdomen. Jack stopped where he was, waiting, sensing, extending his perceptions. No, he wasn't imagining it; the feeling was definitely there. Carefully, he reached down into the bag and pulled out the gun. He stood just outside the elevator, hesitating. What if it was Billie? What if something had happened to her?

"Dammit, Stein. No more 'what ifs,'" he said quietly. Step by careful step, he headed down the corridor and toward the apartment door. He stood there for a couple of seconds, listening, sensing, seeing if there was anything further to hold on to. But nothing . . . just the cold hard chill nestled in his gut.

The door was locked. He hissed with exasperation.

"Open," he said, but it remained firmly sealed. "Billie, are you in there? Open up."

He leaned on the wall beside the door, the gun held upright, ready, waiting.

Still nothing.

"Billie. Dammit!"

Gritting his teeth, transferring his grip on the weapon, he reached out with his left hand and physically knocked, rapping sharply on the door. He was just about to knock again when it opened a crack, and a sliver of Billie's face peered out.

"Are you alone?" she said, looking past him through the narrow opening.

"Shit, Billie. What is it? Let me in!"

She opened the door a touch wider and poked her head out, looking both ways up the hallway, and then pulled back, opening the door only wide enough for him to slip inside.

"Come on," she said through closed teeth when he hesitated. "Quick!"

He stepped past her and she shut the door. "Lock."

Jack turned on her. "Dammit, Billie, what is it? We've talked about this before. You can't just lock me out."

Instead of answering, she waved for him to follow, her face a pale brushstroke in the dim light of the entranceway.

Frowning now, Jack followed as she led the way into the living room. She stood in the room's center, waiting for him, her head tilted toward the couch. She wasn't alone.

Lying there on the couch was a man, unshaven, rumpled clothes, a thick old spacer's jacket and a broad dark stain across his chest. His face was gray, his breathing shallow. Jack knew the dark stain was blood. There was no issue worrying about some guy bleeding all over the couch. The couch had already consumed most of it and would be done with it soon.

"Shit," said Jack. Forget about how he managed to get here—what the hell was he doing here? This had to be Captain Gourley. He sure as hell wasn't some stray resident of Yorkstone. Jack wasn't sure if the guy was conscious, but he didn't look very good at all. Slowly he lowered the gun, tossed it on the chair, and undraped the bag from his shoulder, dumping it as well.

"How long's he been here?" said Jack, looking down at him distastefully.

"About an hour," said Billie, still looking pale. She was holding up pretty well considering.

Damn. Jack didn't want to touch him. He didn't really know quite what to do about him.

"Did he say anything?"

Billie gave a little shrug. "Just your name, then he sort of collapsed inside. I had to help him to the couch." She waved over to one side. "He had that with him."

There was a bundle lying on one of the chairs, wrapped in greasy gray cloth. Jack merely glanced at it. He crossed to the couch and squatted down. The man's breathing really was barely there. Reaching out a hand, he prodded at one dirty shoulder. There was a brief flutter of the eyelids, but no other reaction. Jack shook a little harder.

The captain gave a deep, shuddering intake of breath. It sounded wet. His eyes struggled open, and he peered at Jack with a half-focused gaze.

"Jack Stein?" he rasped, the words barely comprehensible.

"Yeah, I'm Jack. What are you doing here?"

"Danuta. Danuta Galvin." He gasped, gave another deep moist, labored breath, and his eyes went wide. A long slow exhalation, then nothing. Jack shook the shoulder again, and then gingerly withdrew his hand. The captain's eyes were staring. His chest wasn't moving at all.

"Oh shit," said Jack, and stood quickly. He knew what had just happened. He should really feel for a pulse or something. Hesitantly he reached out his fingers to the man's still-warm neck, but there was nothing. Jesus, he hated dead people. He hated dead people in his living room even more. And when they had just become dead . . . .

"We've got a problem, Billie," he said slowly.

"What?" she said, frowning.

"Our friend here has just died, I think."

"Jack, do something." She had her arms wrapped tightly around herself.

Jack reached for the man's wrist and felt for a pulse, but it was absent there, as well. There was a hole from which the stain across his chest spread, and gingerly, Jack lifted the shirt and looked beneath. It was ugly. He swallowed. He'd seen wounds like that before in his stint in the military. Cardiac massage didn't look like it was an option; the hole was right over where his heart would be.

"Dammit, there's nothing to do."

She glanced from the dirty body on the couch to his face and back again. "Well, cover him up then. He's looking at me."

"Yeah, shit, you're right." He quickly disappeared into his bedroom, dragged a cover back with him and draped it across the couch, hiding their visitor from view.

Only then did Jack cross to the other chair and look at the bundle lying there. He knew damned well what *that* was. Crouching down in front of it, he reached out and carefully started to unwrap the bundle, expecting at any moment to be assailed by a rush of images. If this thing was what he believed it to be, he had to be careful. Who knew what energies it might contain? One fold of greasy cloth after one fold of greasy cloth, and still nothing. He grimaced. The final fold lay obscuring what Jack knew lay beneath, and tentatively he pulled back the cloth. There sat the artifact. It was lighter in color than he'd imagined. He crouched there looking at it, still reluctant to touch it. Already it had been the cause of two deaths as far as he knew, possibly more. Who knew what power was trapped within the object, or even what kind of power. He had no idea what might be left by an ancient alien race.

Pressing against a small part of his bottom lip with his teeth, Jack gingerly reach out with a couple of fingers. His fingers merely brushed the surface and he pulled them back quickly. Nothing. Giving a slight frown, he reached out again, this time making firmer contact with the designs on the object's upper surface. Again, there was nothing. He wasn't getting a single impression from this thing. The frown growing deeper, he took hold of the thing and lifted it away from the dirty cloth. It was light—far lighter than it looked. He hefted it in one hand, then turned it over, inspecting it from each side. It looked exactly like the sketches and images he'd seen so far. The back surface had a slight bubbling in the gray-black metallic material, as if it had been molten stone, suddenly solidified. He traced his fingers over the surface, feeling the slight pock marks, then turned it over again to inspect the surface. Strange that he was getting absolutely nothing from it. Very strange.

"Jack."

He turned to look at Billie, who was still standing with her arms wrapped around herself, looking pale and worried.

"Hmmm? What is it?"

"What about that?" she said, gesturing with her head toward the couch.

He chewed at his bottom lip. "Yeah, you're right," he said, giving a little shake of his head. "I have to think." And he did. Yet another problem he hadn't been expecting. He looked back down at the artifact. Okay, whatever he did, he didn't want this around to prompt questions from someone like Laduce. "Hang on a second," he told her.

Jack disappeared into his office after wrapping the artifact back in its cloth, carrying the bundle with him. He shoved it in a small cupboard to one side, then returned to the living room, rubbing his hands against each other, then on the back of his trousers, trying to get rid of the greasy feeling left by the cloth.

"What have you done with it?" Billie said.

"Out of the way, for now," he answered. "There's something weird about it though," he added thoughtfully. "But we can think about that later. At the moment, you're right; we need to deal with our friend here, before he starts to stink the place up."

She wrinkled her nose and looked away.

"Okay," he said. "I think I know what to do."

He turned to the wall and took a deep breath, holding it for a second before proceeding. "Call Police," he said. He glanced at Billie. She was staring at him. He nodded at her while the connection was established. He knew what he was doing. At least he thought he did. She crossed to one of the chairs, clearly not reassured in the least.

Jack asked for Morrish and was immediately thankful that the investigator still seemed to be there. The big pudgy face took shape on the wall.

"Morrish, I've got something for you," said Jack.

"What is it, Stein?" He was obviously smarting a little from their last conversation. "What is it you need this time?"

"No, Jim, listen," said Jack. "I think you need to get over here. Bring your partner with you."

Morrish looked doubtful. "Look, you've got to give me some reason to go traipsing over to your place. It better be good."

"Oh, it's good all right," Jack said. "Remember Alan Dean? It's not a person. But I'll explain more about that when you get here."

Morrish frowned slightly. "You need to do better than that."

"Oh, I think this will be good enough." He stepped back and pulled the cover back briefly from the body on the couch.

Morrish's eyes widened slightly. "Is that what I think it is?"

Jack nodded, dropping the cover back into place.

"Yeah, I think that's good enough," said Morrish. "We'll be over right away."

Jack cut the connection.

Billie and he spent the next twenty minutes sitting in silence, occasionally glancing in the direction of the couch, no words necessary between them. She was still clearly disturbed, not that Jack could blame her. He wasn't feeling too comfortable himself. Despite the apartment's systems, the atmosphere was starting to become a little questionable. Finally, the door announced an arrival. Jack jumped up from his chair and headed for the door. It was Morrish, and as Jack had asked, he'd brought his partner, Laduce. The narrow-faced investigator was already glaring at him and Jack shrugged inwardly. Let Laduce think what he wanted. The guy didn't have to like him.

"What have you got for us, Stein?" said Morrish.

Jack gestured them both inside with his head and led them into the living room. "So?" said Morrish.

Without saying anything, Jack crossed, pulled back the cover from the body on the couch, and stood back. Morrish stood where he was, fingering his chin. Laduce stepped forward, craning around his partner's bulk for a better look.

"What is it about you, Stein?" said Laduce.

"What do you mean?"

"Well, it looks like around you, people keep on ending up dead. What have you got to say about that?"

Morrish waved at his partner for quiet. "Who is he? Do you know?" said Morrish.

Billie was sitting there, not moving. She suddenly got up from her chair and disappeared into her bedroom. Jack watched her go, waiting before speaking. The investigators seemed barely to have registered her presence. That was good.

"This," said Jack, "is the captain of the *Alan Dean*."

"Huh?" said Morrish. "The *Alan Dean*'s a ship?"

"Yeah. It's out at the spaceport now."

Morrish leaned forward, peering closer at the dead man. "Mmm, nasty. Projectile weapon." He tilted his head to one side. "Dead enough, by the looks of things." He stepped forward and reached down to feel for a pulse. "Still warm." He nodded and closed the captain's eyes. "Yep. He's dead."

"So what's he doing in your apartment, Stein?" said Laduce.

"Not a hell of a lot, Laduce. He's dead."

Laduce narrowed his eyes and took a step toward Jack. "Don't get smart with me, Stein."

Laduce took another step, but Morrish waved him back.

"It does look kind of funny, Jack, you have to admit. You know, first the name *Alan Dean* comes up, and then this guy ends up dead in your apartment. You're looking for a guy called Carl Talbot, the next thing he winds up dead. It's a bit more than coincidence, don't you think?"

"Listen, I can't help how things happen. I called you, didn't I?"

"That doesn't mean anything, Stein. Maybe you want to confess," said Laduce.

"Confess to what, Investigator?" said Jack, barely able to restrain the sneer threatening to creep over his face and into his words. "This guy turns up at my apartment, he winds up dead, and I call you. What more do you want?"

Morrish was still rubbing his chin, looking at the body. He looked at Jack sidelong. "You've still got to admit, it's a bit suspicious, Jack. After our little talk, and now this." He tilted his head in the corpse's direction. "He hasn't been dead long. He's in your apartment. What are we supposed to think? What was he doing here? How did he wind up dead?"

"He got shot, is how. That's pretty obvious," said Jack. "As to who shot him, I don't know. That happened before he got here."

"Is that right," said Laduce, and was quickly across the space between them, patting him down. "Where is it?" he said."

"Where's what?" said Jack.

"The weapon, Stein," Laduce growled into his face. Jack just rolled his eyes.

Laduce glanced around quickly and the next moment was over by the chair, looking down and nodding. "Well, what have we here?"

Jack felt a sinking feeling as he remembered the gun. With everything else, he'd simply forgotten about it. Laduce reached down, lifting the weapon triumphantly with one finger hooked through the trigger guard. "Well, well, well."

Morrish looked at Jack accusingly. "You want to explain that?" he said.

Jack sighed. "Look at the thing, Morrish, then look at our friend on the couch. That thing would make a hole the size of a fist. It's not a projectile weapon, is it? *That's* not what killed him. What do you want?"

Laduce peered at the gun from either side, holding it out from him, then curled his lip.

"He's right, Steve," said Morrish.

"Yeah, well, we'll be keeping this," said Laduce. He wrapped it in a handkerchief and shoved it in his pocket. "It doesn't explain why you have it in the first place."

"Come on, Laduce," said Jack. "It won't do you any good."

Laduce just looked smug. Well, let him have his tiny victories . . . for the moment.

"Okay, Stein," said Morrish. "If you didn't shoot him, who did?"

Jack shook his head. "Don't know. If I did, we'd be a lot closer to working this whole thing out, now wouldn't we? He just turned up here."

"If that's the case, what was he doing here? What did he want with you, Stein? Why here?"

"He came here looking for me, to deliver . . . a message."

"Which was . . . ?"

"Can't tell you that."

Morrish pressed his lips together. "Come on, Jack. You have to do better than that this time."

"I can't tell you," said Jack, shaking his head. "He was dead before he could say anything."

"You're expecting us to believe that this guy turns up on your doorstep and dies without saying a single word."

Jack rubbed at the back of his head. "I wasn't here."

That stopped them for a moment. They glanced at each other, and then back at Jack, waiting.

There was nothing for it. Jack sighed to himself. "Billie, will you come out here, please?"

A moment later, Billie emerged at her bedroom doorway, looking distinctly nervous. She brushed at her hair, looking from one policeman to the other.

"I was out when the captain turned up. You were here. He didn't say anything, did he?"

Billie looked at Jack, then back to the other two men, not saying anything.

"We'll ask the questions, Stein," said Laduce. "Well?" he said to Billie.

Billie merely shrugged.

"Come on, little girl. Tell us what the man said."

There was the slightest narrowing of Billie's eyes at the "little girl" but thankfully she restrained herself. "He didn't say anything," she said. "He came, asked for Uncle Jack, then fell over. I helped get him to the couch."

Morrish spoke then in a much gentler voice. "And your Uncle Jack wasn't here then."

Billie shrugged. "Nuh-uh."

"When did he come in?"

"Maybe half an hour after. I don't know."

"And this man said nothing."

Billie was glancing at the body as she spoke, looking troubled.

"Listen, Morrish," said Jack. "You've heard what you needed to. Does she have to stay?"

"No, no. You're right. Thank you, Billie," said Morrish.

Billie quickly slipped away again, back into her room.

Jack looked from Morrish to Laduce, waiting. "Okay, Stein," said Morrish finally. "And you have no idea who might have done this?"

"No," said Jack with finality. "How many times do I have to tell you? We can go over the same things all night if you want, but it won't get us anywhere."

"Okay, well, we should do something about the body, I suppose," said Morrish. "Steve, make the call, will you?"

Laduce grudgingly pulled out his handipad and did as he was asked. There was nothing left to do but wait for City Services.

Jack crossed and sat on the arm of one of the chairs. "You might want to get out to the spaceport," he said. "The *Alan Dean*'s out there, as far as I know. There might be something out there that can tell you what happened."

Laduce and Morrish glanced at each other again, simply standing there, looking ill at ease.

"Yeah. Maybe," said Morrish.

"Don't think you've got away with anything, Stein," said Laduce.

"Jesus, Laduce. Give it a rest. I'm on your side."

Laduce just looked sour.

"And while you're at it, you can give me my gun back."

Laduce shook his head. "It's evidence. Until we've determined for certain that this is not the weapon used in the shooting, it remains with us. You'll get it back when we've finished the investigation."

Jack pursed his lips and shook his head. He knew there was no point arguing it. Laduce was determined to make things as difficult as possible, even though he knew full well the energy weapon had had nothing to do with the captain's shooting.

For half an hour more, they waited in uncomfortable silence. City Services came, dressed in their pale green uniforms, carried out the body, and that was that. Jack followed them out and closed the door after them. He headed into his office and watched out the window while the green-uniformed pair loaded the body into the back of their vehicle, closed the door, and took off up the street. Jack shook his head and went back into the living room to face the hostile glare of Laduce and the more sheepish expression of Morrish.

"Well, gentlemen," said Jack. "That's about it. I'll see you out."

Morrish nodded.

"Don't think about going anywhere, Stein," said Laduce.

Jack grimaced. At least the guy could come up with something original. "If I manage to discover anything else, I'll let you know," he said to Morrish as he saw them to the door. He wandered back into the living room, giving the couch a dubious glance, then took up position on one of the chairs.

"Billie, you can come out now," he called. "They've gone."

Twenty

After a while Billie emerged properly from her room, but every time she wandered past the couch, she glanced at it suspiciously, and refused to go anywhere near it. A few moments later, she disappeared back inside the private space of her bedroom. Normally, by now, she should have been back to dominate the living room, taking over every bit of available space with whatever she was working on, sprawled on the couch and relegating Jack back to his office. He thought about disturbing her, seeing if she wanted to talk about what had happened. He was just about to cross to her door, when he shook his head. No, it was probably better to leave it for now. And besides, he still had something to do. Something big.

He walked slowly into his office, head bowed, considering. It was strange that there'd been nothing from the artifact. And it was continuing to trouble him. Digging the bundle out from where he'd put it, he dropped it on the desk and stood staring at it. Okay, now to find out what was with this thing. Once more, he unwrapped the cloth, eased it from beneath the metal, and dropped it to one side. Once more, he reached out his fingers and traced them over the strange symbols on the artifact's upper surface. Nothing.

It was blank. If something was as old as this was supposed to be, then by rights he should be getting some impression, at least some sensation from his upper abdomen telling him the object had existed, but even that was strangely lacking. He stood back again and frowned. Plucking at his lower lip briefly, he had another thought and stepped toward the desk again.

Slowly, gently, Jack ran his fingers over the top surface, then over the edges and along the sides, his senses alert, looking for the slightest twinge. Blankness. He turned it over and proceeded to do the same thing with the lower, slightly bubbled surface. It was inert.

He stood considering. Okay, maybe it was because of what the thing was made of. Maybe this strange metal denied the accumulation of the type of energy he worked with. That was one plausible explanation. Could alien energies affect the human psyche? But then that didn't make sense either. Plenty of people had handled this thing. Stepping around the other side of the desk, he rummaged around, looking for something. Ah, there it was. He knew he kept a knife in there somewhere. He lifted it out and opened it, looking at the short blade, considering, and then leaned over the artifact. It was only the underneath. Pressing the very tip of the knife to the surface, he applied gentle pressure. He sucked in his breath. The knife tip had gone in slightly. Quickly he lifted it away. As he watched, the tiny mark he'd made faded and disappeared. No, that couldn't be right. He leaned forward and scored a line with the knife tip, a long scratch in the undersurface, applying even, heavy pressure. It left a visible mark. And then—it took a little longer—but as he watched, the same thing happened. What had been a visible scratch a moment before quickly faded.

"Shit," he said. If this object had lasted for all that time unaffected by the elements, by the passage of time, he just shouldn't be able to mark it with an ordinary knife. Or maybe that was the way it worked. Maybe it repaired itself, fixed itself. The problem was, it reminded him of something else, something that was all around him. There was a real suspicion starting to grow in his mind.

"Dark," he said. Time to try one more thing to test it out. The windows opaqued and the lights dropped. He carried the artifact over to the sleep couch and stripped off his shirt and trousers, draping them carefully over the stand he had programmed just for that purpose. Well, this time he had something to work with, so he was going to work. Moving the artifact to the side, he lay back on the couch, then carefully lifted the light metal tablet and placed it on his chest. He reached up, feeling for the inducer pads, applied them to his temples, then linked his fingers above the artifact, holding it in place in the center of his chest.

"Begin."

The waves pulsed through him, starting to work at his consciousness, pushing him down, further, further. The object was cold and smooth against his skin, resisting the warmth of his flesh.

Darkness. Waves. Lapping against his thoughts. Deeper still.

He was back on Mandala. At least he thought it was Mandala. The brightness of the sky made him wince. An open featureless plain stretched around him. The sky was right. The plain looked right, just as it had before in the dreams. He turned slowly, looking for some indication that he was not misreading the location. Flexing his fingers, he realized suddenly that he was no longer holding the artifact. Okay, that was bizarre. Usually, if he used a physical object as a dream prompt, it would come with him into the dreamscape, guiding him. Sometimes larger, sometimes smaller, there was normally a dream representation of what was giving him the cues.

Jack concentrated, slightly disconcerted by this absence. He tried to will the artifact into existence, holding his hands in front of him, visualizing its appearance between them. After a while he gave up. That wasn't going to happen. He looked around again, searching, but the empty expanse of plain still stretched around him, nothing breaking up the smooth, rolling ground.

Jack muttered. Even the dreams were starting to fail him. He picked a direction at random and started walking. He walked and he walked. It seemed like he crossed miles, but still the landscape stayed the same. Slight rises and dips in the ground were the only thing to break up the continuing sameness. Eventually he stopped. This was getting him nowhere.

"Where are you going, Jack?"

He turned slowly, toward the sound of the voice. It had come from directly behind him. It was Talbot—the "before" Talbot.

"Well, it looks like I'm going nowhere fast," said Jack. He gave himself a quick frown. What had made him say that?

Talbot threw back his head and laughed. It was a deep belly laugh that shook his entire frame.

"What?" said Jack.

Talbot struggled to regain control, looking as if he was going to burst into laughter again. "Oh, that's good, Jack. Oh, that's so good. Nowhere fast."

Jack shook his head. "I don't get it."

Talbot turned and started wandering away. Jack could hear him talking to himself, saying "Nowhere fast" over and over and shaking his head, occasionally chuckling. And then, Talbot was gone. He was alone again on the empty plain.

Jack turned and started walking again. For some reason, he knew he had to walk. The ground started to rise in front of him. Step after step he climbed the gentle slope, and as he traveled the angle grew steeper. Finally he stopped. Nowhere fast. This was getting him nowhere fast too.

Quickly the sky darkened, the light slipping away, not like a sunset, but as though someone had slowly turned a dimmer across the landscape. He glanced up. A black sky was peppered with stars. He half expected this to turn into a flying dream again, but it didn't. Talbot's laughter came again from somewhere in the distance.

He concentrated on the artifact again, seeing if he could force the dream into some sort of shape that made sense. The darkness grew darker. No. That wasn't what he wanted.

But then he was somewhere else. The realization came to him slowly. The darkness had made the transition imperceptible. He was in a room. Featureless. Four walls. A ceiling. Low light. There were noises coming from an adjoining room. Jack reached out one hand, feeling for a door, and found it. Carefully he opened it and looked out. A wide, dimly illuminated space stretched out in front of him. Long benches stretched across the wide room, a lab or something, and bits and pieces of things lay scattered across the surfaces. The space was windowless, and what meager lighting there was, was directed down over the benches. The objects lying scattered in seemingly random order across the bench tops were just that—objects. He couldn't tell what they were.

He poked his head farther through the doorway. He was about to walk over and start inspecting these things, when something else caught his attention.

Over in one corner, there was more light. One of the benches was brightly illuminated by some lamps. A couple of large machines sat in the corner next to the illuminated space. In front of the bench stood a familiar rotund figure, dressed in a white coat. Hervé Antille.

"So fast, these new ships," said Hervé. He turned to face Jack, breaking into a wide smile. "So fast. They really can go nowhere fast." He threw back his head and laughed. "Nowhere fast." He tapped the side of his nose with one finger, then beckoned Jack closer.

Taking the cue, Jack crossed between the benches and moved up to stand in front of Hervé. Hervé looked him up and down, still grinning. "Yes, very good," he said. He waved his hands at the two large machines. "Wonderful what you can do these days," he said. "What would you like? A bag? Some luggage?" He threw back his head and laughed again. His belly jiggled. The laughter stopped and Hervé lowered his face, fixing Jack with a serious expression. "Anything you want," he said. He reached across to the closest machine and pulled open a door. "Here, for you," he said.

Jack stepped forward, leaning closer to look inside the open door. Inside sat the travel luggage Billie and he had taken to Mandala. Jack frowned and turned. Hervé laughed. "Anything you want," he said.

Jack shook his head.

Hervé turned back to the bench. In front of him lay the artifact. He beckoned Jack closer, and leaned over it. As Jack watched, he reached out with one hand and twisted some of the designs on its surface with his fingers. They changed, staying in the new shapes impressed upon them.

"Where do you want to go?" said Hervé. This time he was peering at Jack with narrowed eyes.

Again Jack shook his head.

"Nowhere fast," said Hervé, and laughed. "Like everyone else."

And Jack was awake.

As he peeled the pads from his temples, shifted the artifact from his chest and slowly sat up, there was more than a suspicion starting to form in his head, and the possibility amused him. "Lights," he said. He remembered the way Hervé had reacted when he'd even suggested that he acquire just the smallest thing from the site.

He looked down at the artifact and slowly smiled, running his hand over its cool hard surface. Yes, it was very good. Very good indeed. Billie was going to like it too.

He retrieved the greasy cloth from where he'd dropped it, carefully rewrapped the artifact, and slid it away out of sight. That would do for the time being. Now it was time to get some proper sleep.

Twenty-One

The next morning, Jack's mood was buoyed by the previous evening's revelation. He wandered around the kitchen humming while he got his first coffee of the day in process. His sleep had been deep, populated by dreams, but dreams that were just the normal workings of his subconscious mind, nothing to lead him down a further path of discovery. Billie wandered in looking disheveled, and stood watching him, her morning scowl firmly in place.

"So what's wrong with you?" she said.

"What do you mean?"

"Well, something must have happened. What's made you so happy?"

"Hmmm?" he said. "Oh, I think I've worked some things out. It came to me last night. Everything is not as it seems, Billie. Everything is not as it seems."

She grimaced at him and pushed past, pulling out her breakfast things. It was a bit early yet for him to drop the bombshell on her. He wanted her to be well and truly awake. He grabbed his coffee and headed into the living room, found himself a place on the couch, and waited for her to get through her morning ritual.

There was another advantage to the plan that was

starting to take shape in his head. If Outreach and Van der Stegen were truly involved in this whole mess, then making sure they didn't get the artifact either was another bonus. Any way he could frustrate their efforts was a good thing. He still hadn't forgotten what made that particular outfit tick, and there was no way he could have imagined that he'd have an opportunity to get back at them. It wasn't as if he was carrying around a grudge—it was more that they deserved to have things work against them occasionally. If he, Jack Stein, could be the one to make that happen, then that was all the better. Outreach, Landerman, all of that type deserved what they got. It had even gotten to the point now where he wasn't too worried about his fee, but he was going to make damned sure he collected, regardless of how this whole thing turned out. He sipped at his coffee, contemplating. Some ideas were starting to form, even though he hadn't quite worked out how he was going to handle all the finer points yet. He would need Billie's help, of course. Making everything believable was the key and of course, timing. Timing would be everything.

It took a while, but at last Billie seemed as if she was ready to hear what he wanted to tell her. He called her in to the living room to sit down. She avoided the couch again and instead took the chair opposite.

"After everything happened last night, I had a session, Billie."

She frowned. "What do you mean?"

"Well, I did some work with the artifact. Some dream stuff. It gave me some clues and I think I know what we have to do now."

"Uh-huh . . ."

He held his hands out, palms up, one on either side.

"How do you make someone stop wanting something?"

She shook her head.

"You give it to them." He closed his fingers into fists, then opened one hand again.

"Huh?"

"Well, Landerman wants the artifact, Farrell wants it. Probably someone else as well. All we have to do is give it to them."

Billie looked outraged. "You can't."

"Ahhh, but here's the trick," he said. "You give it to them, but you don't."

"I don't get it. You can't give it to them. It belongs at the university. You've got to send it back, Jack." There was an almost pleading tone in her voice now. "You can't let them have it."

He grinned. "That's right. And someone else has already had the same idea."

She was frowning again.

He opened his other hand. "You give it to them, but you don't give it to them." He fixed her with a steady look. "I think the artifact's a fake."

She took a couple of seconds to process that. "But how . . . ?"

"I'm not really sure. I should have gotten something big from it, but I felt nothing. That's what made me suspicious in the first place. I took it into the office and used it as a dream prompt."

"So . . ."

"And then I made a couple of connections. It was the Copy Shop that did it, finally."

She pulled her knees up, looking confused. "I still don't get it."

"I think the real artifact is still safe and sound on Utrecht at the university. Probably in the hands of Dr.

Hervé Antille. I think what we have here is a repro-
duction. A very good copy, but a copy all the same. I
have the idea that it's probably not an exact copy either. If I'm right, whoever copied it has changed something, maybe something about the pattern on the top,
something that makes it different from what it's supposed to be."

She looked into the distance, thinking. "But why
would someone do that?" she said finally.

Jack stood, breaking into a smile again. "Because
whoever did it is very clever."

Billie sighed. "Stop playing games, Jack. Just tell me."

Jack nodded. "All right. This is how I think it happened. Talbot had some contact at the university,
someone who could get him material from the site, or
at least said he could, which isn't quite the same thing.
That someone would have to be reasonably high up in
the archeological chain to have access to the proper
parts of the university. I think that that person is Hervé
Antille. You saw yourself how he was about the site,
how important he thought it was." He'd started pacing again.

"So . . ." he continued. "Whether it's Hervé or not, it
doesn't matter, but it would make sense. He keeps on
popping up in the dreams about Mandala and the artifact. So, just say it is Antille. He knows that there are
some pretty powerful people wanting to get this thing.
He knows that they have massive resources and, at
least in the case of Landerman, commitment. They
won't stop. So, how does he stop them, how does he
turn them away from wanting it?"

Her eyes widened. "He gives it to them."

"Uh-huh . . . *but* he doesn't give it to them. He gives
them something that they think is the artifact."

She was sitting up straighter on the chair now, a

look of revelation on her face. "And he makes a copy, just like they copy things at the Copy Shop."

"Sure. He has the technological resources of a university to do it. Why not? At the Copy Shop, they said they could program it to make a faithful copy of whatever it was you wanted. It would look like it, feel like it, but it wouldn't be the same. There'd be differences. The holographic logo, for example. That's a difference. That was where the dream pointed me."

"Uh-huh," said Billie, nodding her head slowly.

"So . . . how do you safeguard what you're doing? How do you make sure that the knowledge will belong to everyone if you crack the code?"

"You keep the real code and give everyone else a fake one."

Jack slapped his hands together and stopped his pacing. "Exactly!

"So, what do you think?" he said, crossing back to the chair and sitting slowly.

She was picking at the end of one fingernail, frowning. That made him nervous. He'd lost count of the number of times he'd sought some sort of validation from Billie. She had a sharp mind and had a way of cutting through the crap. She was refusing to look at him. He narrowed his eyes.

"Billie?"

"Hmmmm?" she said, still not looking at him.

"Well . . . what do you think . . . ?"

She sighed and tutted. "I don't know," she said. She shook her head. "I just don't know."

Jack frowned. How could she not see it?

Then she looked up, fixing him with a blank, uncomprehending expression.

"I don't get what you're saying," she said.

"Billie?"

She suddenly grinned. "Ha! Got you."

"Billie . . ."

"Well, it serves you right. You should have come straight out and told me."

He growled, and then despite himself, broke into a grin too.

Twenty-Two

Jack had spent the rest of the morning thinking things through. In the early afternoon, he decided it was time to put his plans into action.

"Billie, I'm going to need you to do something."

The way he'd said it had obviously alerted her. She stood with crossed arms, looking at him suspiciously.

"Okay, listen, you may not like this, but you're going to have to visit Morrish. I think you can get away with doing it where I can't. Laduce really doesn't like me, and if we're going to make this all happen, then we have to get both Morrish and Laduce to play along. You've got a better chance of being able to do it than I have."

Slumping back into a chair—she was still avoiding the couch—she looked at him, both sulky and accusatory at the same time.

"Why do I have to do it? Why can't you just call?"

"No, it's too complicated. You know that Morrish and Laduce aren't exactly the brightest pair. It may take a bit of explaining. I can trust you to do that. If I was to turn up there, Laduce would be just as likely to accuse me of conspiracy or something and lock me up again. We can't afford to take that risk. I have to be around to do this. While you're gone, I'm going to call

Landerman and Farrell and get them here. Meanwhile, before you go, I need to know if you can do something for me . . . and this is another reason why I need you to go and see Morrish. You're the one who understands how these things work, and you're the one who can explain it to them so they might have a chance of understanding."

She gave a little frown and shifted position on the chair. She didn't look comfortable. Really, what he needed to do was grow a new couch. It would take a full night for the building's programming to put it in place, but perhaps that would fix the problem. Stupid that he hadn't thought of doing it before. Anyway, that was a side issue at the moment. He licked his lips and took a breath.

"Okay, this is what I've been thinking. Is there any way you can rig the home systems so that someone outside can watch in from outside and see and hear what's happening without it being obvious from here?"

Billie got her thinking face on. He sat back and let her work at it for a moment or two. Finally, she nodded slightly, the traces of a frown still on her face as if she hadn't quite finished thinking.

"Uh-huh. I think so . . ." she said slowly. She narrowed her eyes.

"But we have to be able to control it somehow," he said.

She nodded again.

"Okay. Good. I need to get Landerman and Farrell here. It's important that Morrish gets to see what's happening. Do you understand what I mean?"

Billie pressed her lips together and shook her head. "I know what you mean, Jack," she said, impatience in her tone.

"Yeah, sorry. Of course you do. But you can do it, right? Because if we can't do it, it's not going to work."

"I said I could, didn't I?"

"All right." Jack slapped his thighs and stood. "I'll wait till you're ready to go before calling our players together. How long will it take for you to set things up? I need it to function in my office rather than the living room. I want in here to be clear."

Billie looked thoughtful. "For me, not too long. I don't know about them."

Jack paced past the couch. "Yeah, of course." He trailed his fingers across the back of the couch and Billie wrinkled her nose. Remembering, Jack quickly withdrew his hand and shoved it in his pocket. "One thing though, I don't want them to be able to gain access again once this is all over."

She nodded. "No problem."

"I'll tell you what," he said. "Why don't you get down there, and once you're sure that they're able to do what we need, then call me. I'll make the other calls then. How much time do you need here?"

She shrugged. "About half an hour. Maybe."

"Okay, well, I've got some stuff to do. I'll leave you to get on with it. Let me know when you're ready to leave."

She nodded. He left her sitting there.

He did have things to do. He wanted to compile all of his dream notes together, put them in some sort of order—maybe edit them and make them properly comprehensible. He had to make a couple of sketches too, to convey what was in the notes. There were reasons, now, and very good reasons too, that he needed to do that. He had something to do with those notes, once everything had played out.

*   *   *

Jack was sitting in his office, waiting, when his handipad announced a call and he flipped it open. It was Billie, as expected, and she looked less than impressed.

"You okay, Billie?"

"Uh-huh," she said. "They know what they have to do."

"Okay, I'll need you to stay there. I don't want this thing kicked off until they're here."

She screwed up her face, but then nodded.

"Are they treating you okay?"

She nodded again. "I guess."

"Okay, I'm going to make the calls now. I'll just call you when I'm ready. Don't answer. You'll know it's me."

She nodded and he thumbed the connection closed. He thought about that for a minute. There wasn't anyone else that was going to be calling her, was there?

Gathering his composure, he readied himself to make the call. He had to run everything in sequence. It was the only way to make sure all this came off properly. Timing was going to be everything.

He took a deep breath and got ready, facing the wall. "Call Bridgett Farrell." He gave the address.

Moments later, Bridgett Farrell's face took shape on the wall in front of him.

"Jack, what is it?" she said.

"Ah, good, you're there. Something's happened. I needed to make sure you were there."

"What is it? What's happened?"

"Just something important. Some information's come to light in the last couple of hours. I need to check something out first just to make sure, and then I'll call you back."

She looked worried. "Really. What is it?" she asked again.

"No, it's okay. Just make sure you're there. End call," he said.

Taking another steadying breath, he made sure his expression was as deadpan as possible. So far so good.

"Call Excelsior Hotel." He waited while the connection was made and the desk program came into view. "Please put me through to Christian Landerman."

"Who shall I say is calling?"

"Jack Stein."

A couple of moments, and the desk program's face was replaced by that of Landerman. Jack could see Larkin hovering in the background.

"Ahh, Mr. Stein," said Landerman. "I was starting to give up hope."

"You should never give up hope, Mr. Landerman."

Landerman chuckled. "Of course not, Stein. Of course not."

"I have something that may be of interest to you."

Landerman leaned forward, his eyes narrowing. "Really?" he said. He glanced back over his shoulder at the figure behind him and then back at the screen.

"Yes, really," said Jack.

Landerman sat back and linked his fingers before him. "So, how soon before you can be here?"

"No," said Jack.

Landerman frowned. "What do you mean, 'no'?"

"That's not the way we're going to do it."

Landerman pursed his lips, rubbing one thumb over the other. "I see." Then he chuckled. "All right, Stein, tell me what you want."

"You come here. I'll hand it over to you then. Four o'clock. You see, I can be more assured that things will go the right way if you come here. It's not that I don't trust you or your little friend, Mr. Landerman, I'd just feel more comfortable."

Again Landerman chuckled. "Oh, I can see that, Mr. Stein. Very wise of you. Very cautious. I admire such caution. I will, of course, bring my own safeguards."

"I understand," said Jack.

Landerman severed the connection.

The second part was in place. Now, just one more call to make.

Bridgett Farrell answered almost as soon as the call had gone through. She must have been waiting by the wallscreen. She looked nervous.

"What is it, Jack? Will you tell me now?" she said, her hand flat against the base of her throat.

"Yeah, I'll tell you. I had a visit last night, but I think you know that."

"Who?"

"Your Captain Gourley."

Her lips parted in an almost-sigh, the slightest exhalation. "Do you have it?"

"Yeah, I've got it."

She stood. "Oh, Jack. That's wonderful."

"Uh-huh. Not so wonderful for Gourley though."

"What do you mean?"

"He's dead. Someone shot him." He waited for the information to sink in.

She dismissed it with a wave of her hand. "What do you want to do?"

"Tell you what," he said. "You come here. I've got some things to do. I should be finished right about three forty-five. What do you say?"

"But the item?"

"It's safe for now. If you can come here, we can work out what the next steps are, together."

"Three forty-five?"

"Uh-huh."

She nodded. "End call," he said.

And part three in place. He glanced at the time display. He had about an hour and a half to script what he was going to say.

He headed for the kitchen to make a cup of coffee, feeling to make sure that he had his handipad ready so he could make the call to Billie.

When the door announced the first arrival, he was ready. He checked that it was indeed Bridgett Farrell and quickly grabbed for his handipad. Jack had set it up to call Billie at the touch of his thumb. Checking the call had gone through, he thumbed it off. He didn't want to be disturbed at all over the next hour. Heading for the door, he let her in.

"Good afternoon, Ms. Galvin," he said, for once using her proper name.

"Jack, where is it?"

He put his finger to his lips and beckoned her inside.

She glanced around the living room as soon as she was in, frowning. "Where's the little girl?" she asked.

"She's not that little," said Jack. "And she's not here anyway."

"Good. I think it's far better if we're alone."

Jack stepped back out of her way, just in case she decided she wanted to touch him again to reinforce her point. He needed his concentration intact right now, and the concept of being truly alone with Bridgett Farrell—or Danuta Galvin, whatever she wanted to call herself—was having its own effect.

"I think we should go into the office," he said.

Jack led her across to the door, then stepped back to let her enter. It was times like this that he really missed having an office separate from the place where he lived, but there was little he could do about it right now. He hoped to hell Billie had everything set up.

His client looked quickly around the office as soon as she was inside, clearly searching for the artifact.

"Where is it, Jack?" she said.

He shook his finger at her. "Not yet."

"What do you mean, not yet?" She was now looking distinctly annoyed.

"Not before I get a few answers. You may as well sit down, Ms. Galvin."

She chose a chair and sat. "And you may as well call me Danuta and drop this pretense of formality, Jack."

She put her bag down beside her on the floor and crossed her hands in her lap. Jack walked across to his own chair, framing what he was about to say carefully, watching her. He glanced at the wall display and sat. Any time now. He just had to spin this out long enough.

"I think you need to give me a couple of answers," he said. "Let's start with the *Alan Dean*, with Captain Gourley."

"What about him? He was Carl's contact. Just one among many." She shrugged.

"Come on, Danuta, he had to be more than just Talbot's contact, didn't he? He knew to come here, didn't he? How do you explain that? He wound up dead, but more than that, he wound up dead at my place. I didn't appreciate that."

She smiled. He couldn't believe she smiled. "Of course he knew where to come. I sent a message to the *Alan Dean*. I told him to expect trouble and I gave him your address. It's as simple as that."

Jack waited, but that was all the explanation she was going to give. "Yeah, well, he found trouble, didn't he?"

She blinked a couple of times. "Is that all you want to know?"

"No, there's a hell of a lot more that I want to know, Danuta. When Talbot wouldn't play, he mysteriously disappears and winds up dead. All very convenient. How long before the same thing happens to me?"

She moistened her lips and lifted one hand slowly to touch her earring, her face tilting slightly to the side. "You're wrong, Jack. You're so very wrong. We can work well together. Now we have the artifact, there's so much we can do. This is just the start. I'm going to need your help to set things up with the auction. It would be perfect. You, me, the child. It's the perfect cover. Think about it."

He simply stared at her. She could not be serious. And the fact that she'd already factored Billie into the equation almost prompted him to say something. What the hell did she think he was?

He was saved from answering. The front door announced an arrival. He glanced at the wall display.

Landerman, if it was Landerman, was about five minutes early but he seemed like the sort. Good.

"Wait here," he told her.

She sat forward. "Just let whoever it is go away. You don't have to answer."

Jack stood. "Sorry. I can't do that."

He left the office, carefully closed the door, and stepped close to the living room wall. "Show visitors," he said.

It was Landerman and Larkin all right. Jack nodded to himself. Good. Everything was working exactly to plan.

Twenty-Three

L arkin was hiding a little behind Landerman, his face averted. Landerman was dressed in something other than the green designer robe for once, a dark luxurious suit and a high-necked white top. He pulled at his cuffs as Jack opened the door, then looked up to meet Jack's eyes with a steady gaze of his own.

"Well, Mr. Stein," he chuckled. "Are we ready to do business?"

Jack stood where he was, blocking the doorway. "Yeah, as long as your little friend isn't going to pull anything funny."

Landerman lifted his hand. "Oh, you can be assured, Mr. Stein. Our friend here will behave himself, won't you, Larkin?" He stepped back out of the way.

Larkin looked back at Jack with a set face. He was sporting a deep purpling bruise around one eye, the eye almost closed, and a nasty red welt across his chin. Jack found that immensely interesting.

"Been sticking our face where it's not wanted, have we?" said Jack with a wry smile.

Larkin made to step forward, but Landerman thrust out a hand. "Now, Larkin. We have some business to conduct. As Mr. Stein says, we should do this in a civilized manner."

Jack nodded and stepped back to let them enter. He wasn't entirely comfortable having Larkin here, inside the inner sanctum, but with the current working arrangements there wasn't a lot he could do about it. Landerman stepped into the living room and looked around with a disdainful eye.

"Yeah, well," said Jack, "it might not be what you're used to, but it's what you get."

Landerman spread his hands wide. "Of course I meant no criticism, Mr. Stein."

"This way," said Jack, leading the way to the office. He opened the door and stepped through.

"We have visitors, my dear," he said.

Landerman stepped through the door with Larkin just behind. Landerman stopped, took in the room, then fixed his gaze on the woman in the chair. "Oh, dear," he said, and chuckled.

Galvin blanched. She sat there for a couple of seconds, then shot to her feet. "You bastard," she said to Jack.

"Now, now, Ms. Galvin, that's not very nice," he said to her. "I thought we could work all this out together. It was all just getting far too confusing. So many different stories, so many different people . . . some of them alive, some of them dead."

Again Landerman chuckled. Jack pointed to one of the vacant chairs, and Landerman nodded and moved across to sit. Jack waved Danuta down and, still glaring daggers at him, she slowly retook her seat. She avoided looking at Landerman at all. Jack turned to Larkin.

"And you . . . you can sit over there." He waved at the sleep couch. Larkin's eyes widened, the heavily bruised one as much as it could, and then narrowed again. He backed toward the couch, keeping his hands in his pockets and never breaking eye contact with Jack's face. Jack gave a little snort and turned away, moving around behind the desk and taking his place in his own chair.

"All right," he said. "We're all here. Now we can get down to business."

Landerman looked to Galvin and then back at Jack. "Have you got the item?"

"Uh-huh," said Jack.

Landerman glanced around the office. "I don't see it, Mr. Stein."

"Oh, it's here, all right," he said. "No goods though, until I get a few answers."

Landerman unclasped and clasped his hands again. "Very well. What is it you want to know?"

"No, I think we'll start with Danuta, if you don't mind." She was still glaring at him. He turned his attention to her. "I like this much better," he said. "Now that we're all here like one big, happy family, I think I might get something resembling the truth out of you, Ms. Galvin, or Ms. Farrell, or whatever you want to call yourself."

Landerman chuckled. Galvin just returned Jack's look without batting an eyelid. Jack glanced over at Larkin, but the little man was still perched on the edge of the couch staring across at Jack, a flat expression on his face, his jaw set.

"All right, Ms. Galvin, tell me. What was Carl Talbot to you?"

"You know this already," she said. "We worked together. We were partners."

"What else?"

"That's it. We became . . . close . . . at one time, but it didn't last long. It complicated things too much."

Jack glanced at Landerman, but the older man was

just watching serenely, his fingers still clasped in front of him, the hint of a smirk playing on his lips.

"Both of you worked for Mr. Landerman here."

"Yes, that's right."

He glanced at Landerman again, who gave a brief nod. "And you were here to pick up the artifact that Mr. Landerman had commissioned you to find for him."

She gave a brief annoyed sigh. "Yes. You know that."

"And instead, you wanted to cut Mr. Landerman out of the deal, put the artifact into open auction, sell it to the highest bidder, is that right?"

She bit her lip. "Well?" said Jack. She nodded reluctantly.

Again Landerman chuckled. "Very enterprising, Danuta. But then, of course, I knew that. Word gets out. Carl had already indicated his intentions to me."

"Mr. Landerman, please," said Jack. "I'm not done yet."

Landerman nodded and lapsed into silence.

"So, Talbot threatened to cut you out. He disappeared. You hired me to find him and the artifact. Meantime, you got in touch with Mr. Landerman here and told him you'd hired me to find Talbot. How am I doing so far?" She said nothing, so Jack continued. "However, all the time, you knew damned well the artifact was on its way here on a slow freighter. You've been playing me, you've been playing Landerman and anyone else you could find along the way including Talbot, am I right? You hired me to make sure it looked like you really didn't know where Talbot and the artifact were. I was your perfect cover."

She looked away.

"Very good, Mr. Stein," said Landerman. "It looks like you have our Danuta worked out to the finest detail."

Jack lifted his hand, slowly.

"Yeah, well, not so fast. It's your turn now. Why do you want this thing so badly? And you must want it pretty badly. What is it? It's a lump of metal. How can it be worth that much to you, Landerman?"

Again the older man chuckled. It was really beginning to get on Jack's nerves. But then Landerman's expression quickly sobered.

"I cannot expect you to understand, Mr. Stein."

Jack planted his elbows on the desk. "Try me."

"Humanity must advance, Mr. Stein. It must move forward. Those who are weak, perish. We have a duty to drive our species forward. This *thing*, as you call it, represents one chance to do that driving. Can you not imagine it? Alien technology. The chance to move above and beyond what we are. You must see that. The wealth of knowledge. Knowledge is how we move forward. Knowledge is what we become. That is what this *thing* is." There was a fire in his eyes and a fervent conviction in his voice. Jack found himself leaning back away from it.

"There is no value to be put on such an opportunity. Vast power. Vast resources. Technology we can hardly imagine. All in the right hands. We have the chance to stop our species from sliding down that path to stagnation that's inevitable if we continue in our current ways. There is no value to be put on that, Mr. Stein. And, Mr. Stein, we know whose are the right hands to do that guidance, don't we?"

"If you say so, Mr. Landerman."

He gave a low chuckle. "Oh, I do, Mr. Stein. I most certainly do."

"And I suppose that you will get absolutely nothing out of this apart from your high ideals."

Landerman steepled his fingers. "Well, of course, there will be other rewards."

"Uh-huh."

Jack glanced at Danuta Galvin. She was propped on the edge of her chair, the cool exterior no longer cool. She wore an expression of both expectation and slight fear at the same time. One hand hovered near the edge of the chair. The other was held flat on her abdomen, just above her stomach. He did a quick check on Larkin, but the little man hadn't moved. Okay, it was time to play this out.

He reached down and behind him, opened the concealed cabinet, and grasped the edge of the bundle with one hand. Damn Laduce, taking the weapon. He felt exceedingly exposed right then, his back half turned to the room, hunched back over his chair, but he had to rely on the circumstance to keep him safe. Larkin, for one, was bound to be carrying, but he just had to hope Landerman would keep him in check. Lifting the bundle out of the cabinet, Jack kept it below desk level, drawing the moment out. Landerman and Galvin both were leaning forward expectantly. Her lips were slightly parted, the tip of her tongue resting lightly on the upper one. In one motion, he hefted the bundle above the desk and dropped it. It fell in the desk's center and lay there, barely making a sound. Landerman sucked air through his teeth.

"Be careful, Mr. Stein."

"Why?" said Jack. "This thing's virtually indestructible, isn't it? Unlike some of the people who've been carrying it."

Jack withdrew his hands and sat back.

"So," he said. "There it is. There's what all the fuss is about. Who's first?"

Danuta Galvin reached out, but Landerman waved her back. "No, this is mine, I think," he said. He adjusted his position, leaning forward still further, and reached out with both hands to drag the bundle toward him, but Jack's hand shot out, keeping it in place.

"It stays there," he said. "Right in the middle where we all can see it."

Landerman gave his annoying chuckle. "Very well, Mr. Stein." He had to stretch, but using both hands, one by one, he unwrapped the concealing folds of cloth. With the last one, he gave a sharp intake of breath and then a sigh. Tentatively, he reached out, tracing his fingers across the surface. "Oh, yes," he breathed. He sat back, staring at the object, and folded his hands in front of him.

"Well, there it is," said Jack. "I think our business is just about done, Mr. Landerman. Apart, of course, from one or two problems."

Danuta Galvin shot to her feet. "No," she said. "It's not that simple, either of you. I worked for this. I worked hard for this. You don't just hand it over. No!"

In her hand she held a nasty-looking energy weapon, small, but powerful enough to take them all out. It looked like it was capable of some very ugly damage. That's why her hand had been hovering near the edge of her chair. She had her bag down there. The gun wavered between Jack and Landerman as if she wasn't sure who she should shoot first. Jack lifted his hands slowly, palms held out, showing he had nothing in them. Landerman sat where he was, chuckling.

"Ah, Danuta. Still trying to get what you can out of everything, aren't you? Don't you think it's a little late for that?"

"I *worked* for this. I'm *not* leaving empty-handed."

There was a slight click, the cocking of a weapon. Larkin was behind her, the muzzle of his gun pressed up against the back of her skull. She stiffened.

"Now, Danuta," said Landerman. "I suggest you

put that down. You know how eager Larkin is to use his little toys. I personally have never understood the fascination, but he takes great pleasure from it, and he has so little pleasure in his life."

Jack stayed where he was, saying nothing, not moving.

Slowly, slowly, Danuta Galvin lowered the hand holding her own weapon. She placed it carefully on the desk.

"There," said Landerman. "That's better. Now I suggest you sit down." He waved Larkin back. The little man took a step backward, still with his gun trained on the woman. Slowly Danuta sat, perching on the edge of the chair, folding her hands in her lap, her gaze downcast.

"You cannot do this to me, Christian," she said quietly.

"Oh, but I can, my dear. And it seems I have." He turned back to Jack. "Now, Mr. Stein, shall we conclude our business?"

Jack leaned forward, keeping one watchful eye on Larkin. "Not quite yet, Mr. Landerman. I said we had a couple of problems."

"And what might they be?"

"Well, you see, over the last couple of weeks, I've been a matter of interest for the local law enforcement authorities. That's not very good for me or for my business. Last night, I wind up with a corpse in my living room and once again, the attention of the police is focused here on me, in my place of work. That's not very good for business either. Now, sooner or later, no matter how slow they are, they're going to put two and two together and tie this whole thing in a neat little package. It wouldn't surprise me if we're all being watched."

Landerman waved his hand. "And what's that to me, Mr. Stein?"

Jack put his elbows on the desk and linked his fingers in front of him. "Don't you see? If you want to get this thing away from here, then we're going to have to give them something, or at least someone. We've got two bodies and a couple of nosy investigators who aren't going to let it drop. Do you see what I'm saying?"

Landerman's face flickered with a frown. "I see."

"So, we have to give them something. You walk out of here carrying that, and the final piece of the puzzle is going to be there in front of them." He glanced at Danuta Galvin and then at Larkin. "Now, we need to do the sums. What's the most expendable part of this equation?"

Larkin still hadn't made the connection, but Landerman clearly had. So, too, had Galvin. She had unfolded her hands and one was drifting toward the desk. Jack's hand shot out and he swept her gun from the desk so that it clattered against the wall, well out of her reach. Her face had become visibly paler.

Jack stood. He walked casually around the side of the desk, Landerman's gaze tracking him. Danuta was staring fixedly at the opposite wall, barely daring to move. Larkin's gaze flitted from one to the other of them, a slight frown creasing his forehead. He still held his gun, but his aim was starting to become uncertain.

Jack kept talking, casually. "Now, if I were you, Mr. Landerman, I know what I would think was the greatest liability, where you're going to have the most trouble. What's going to cost you the least out of this whole affair? Who is the most replaceable?"

Landerman was looking at Danuta. He shifted his gaze to Larkin, then back again. Jack kept his gaze fixed on Landerman as he took another step. Landerman's eyes narrowed.

And Jack spun. The edge of his hand came down hard on Larkin's wrist, knocking the gun to the floor. Larkin's eyes flew wide, his expression turning from nervousness to panic as Jack grabbed a handful of jacket and pushed him up against the wall. With one foot, Jack kicked the gun out of the way. He pressed hard against Larkin's chest, forcing him farther against the wall, leaning his face up close. "Who is the most expendable here, Mr. Landerman?" He locked gazes with the little man, watching the fury build. "Someone here killed the captain of the *Alan Dean*, and I have a fair bet I know who it is. Had a bit of a struggle, did we, Larkin? Put up a bit of a fight, did he?" He subjected Larkin's face to scrutiny, looking at the marked chin, the bruised eye. "He did all right for an old guy, didn't he? But then it wouldn't take much, would it? You just didn't count on him lasting long enough to make it here. Our Captain Gourley was a tough old spacer."

Jack gave him one last shove and stooped to retrieve the gun. Larkin launched himself from the wall, but Jack was ready. One quick upthrust and Jack's fist connected with Larkin's chin. He fell back against the wall, his progress halted. He slumped there, looking like a frightened deer, looking for a way out.

"So, what do you say, Landerman?"

Keeping one eye on Landerman, Jack kept Larkin's own gun trained on him.

Landerman cleared his throat and shifted uncomfortably on the chair. "I understand what you're saying, Mr. Stein, but I don't think there's any need for this. Larkin may get a little enthusiastic from time to time, but sometimes that's a worthwhile attribute in someone who works for you. No, I'm afraid I can't agree. Larkin is far too useful to me. He does what he's told, unlike some others." He shot a quick meaningful look in Galvin's direction.

"Yeah, well, that's as may be," said Jack. "But I've still got the police breathing down my neck. I'm afraid we have to do something."

Landerman looked pointedly at Galvin then. She returned the look with an expression of horror on her face. "You are not serious," she said.

Landerman looked back at Jack, raising his eyebrows.

"Yeah, well, it just might work," said Jack.

"I did not kill Captain Gourley," said Danuta, sitting straight up in her chair. "I will not take the blame."

"No, you didn't." He looked at Larkin, then down at the gun he still had in his hand. "But I'm pretty sure you know Larkin did it too, Mr. Landerman." He looked back at Larkin. "Isn't that right, Larkin? This is your gun, isn't it? And if this is the weapon that did it, then we have everything we need to pull this off."

Landerman smiled. "Then it is settled," he said. "Shall we proceed?"

Twenty-Four

Galvin leaped to her feet. "No, I will not have this," she said. "I will tell them everything. You're not going to get away with this."

She made a move toward her own weapon that still lay over on the floor. Jack hadn't forgotten it. He glanced quickly at Larkin, but the little man was in the process of struggling to his feet.

"I wouldn't do that," said Jack to Galvin, waving her down with the gun. Tentatively she retook her seat, glaring at him. Jack narrowed his eyes, giving her the tiniest shake of his head. She seemed to catch his meaning, for she relaxed ever so slightly. Oh, yeah, she was quick. Still holding the gun, he crossed back around behind the desk and retook his seat.

"Okay," he said to Landerman. "Let's do business."

Damn, he hadn't thought everything through. He couldn't use the home system from here in the office. Not now. Still, that was minor. He could use his handipad.

"Very well." Landerman reached for the artifact.

"Not quite yet, Mr. Landerman," said Jack, waving the gun meaningfully in his direction.

Landerman nodded and smiled. "Of course, Mr. Stein. Of course."

He reached into his jacket and pulled out an ornate handipad. "So," he said. "The agreed fee was double what Danuta was going to pay you. One hundred thousand, I believe."

"Plus my daily rate and expenses."

"Well, let us make it one hundred and fifty, shall we?" He opened the handipad and punched a couple of commands. Looking around, he frowned, obviously expecting the home system to be primed.

"No, wait a moment," said Jack. He dug into his own pocket with his free hand and withdrew his own more simple device and thumbed it on. "I'd prefer this not to go through the home system just yet."

"Wait," said Danuta. "You bastard, Christian. You know what you were going to pay."

Landerman chuckled. "Business is business, I'm afraid," he said. "And you seem to have taken yourself out of the transaction, my dear."

Again Jack gave her the slightest shake of his head and she sat back, clamping her lips shut.

Jack looked down at his handipad and watched as the transfer was made. One hundred and fifty thousand. Jesus. He and Billie would be eating for a while on that. Maybe more. How many Molly's meals would that buy?

"Satisfied, Mr. Stein?"

Jack snapped his handipad shut and slipped it away. "Perfectly, Mr. Landerman." He made sure not to let his expression reveal what he was feeling.

"In that case, I think Larkin and I will be leaving. It's been a pleasure doing business with you. And of course you will look after Ms. Galvin here."

"Yep. Of course."

Landerman reached down and rewrapped the artifact in the same greasy cloth it had come in, cradling it affectionately. "Get up," he said to Larkin. "Come here." He handed the bundle over, and straightening his clothing, he stood.

Jack pocketed the gun. "I'll see you out." He turned to Danuta. "You stay here." At a thought, he scooped the other weapon from the floor and slipped that away as well. He ignored Larkin's look, brushing past him to show Landerman out of the office and back out to the front door. "Good-bye, Mr. Landerman. I don't think we'll be seeing each other again."

"No, probably not, Stein, but if ever I'm in the area, I will remember you."

"Don't worry," said Jack. "That won't be necessary."

Landerman chuckled and stepped out of the apartment, Larkin hot on his heels, and Jack shut the door.

He leaned against the inside of the door, waiting a couple of seconds before going back inside. He hoped to hell Billie's fix had worked. If it hadn't, they were screwed. Still, with one hundred and fifty credits hot in his handipad, that might not be so much of an issue anymore.

Now to deal with Danuta Galvin. He headed back toward the office, fingering the gun in his pocket as he took those few remaining steps.

She was sitting where he'd left her. She looked up as he entered, her jaw set, a look of accusation on her face.

"What have you done, Jack?" she said. "Five hundred thousand. You've thrown away five hundred thousand credits."

"And what?" said Jack with a sigh. "We've gotten rid of that damned thing and you're still here in one piece. I've got a sizeable chunk sitting on my handipad. If I'd pushed for anything higher, Landerman would have become suspicious, suspected that I was working with you. Well, I thought you wanted a partnership, Danuta. You don't know what you've gotten away with. Landerman's got a surprise or two coming his way."

He sat in his chair and leaned back studying her. "What do you think Landerman would have done when he discovered that you'd delivered him a fake? And he will find out sooner or later."

"What are you talking about?" she said, a peevish tone in her voice.

"The damned thing's a fake," he said. "I expect it's going to break down eventually, but by then it will be too late. I somehow suspect your days of working for Landerman are over. You've got to look at other options."

"What do you mean, a fake?" Her eyes were wide now.

"Just what I say. I don't know what's happened to the original. For all I know it's back where it started, or someone else has taken it."

She shook her head. "But that's impossible."

"Oh, no," said Jack. "Not impossible at all. It's about time you woke up."

She bowed her head slightly and tapped a rapid staccato on her forehead with her fingertips before looking up at him again. "How do you know it's not the real thing?"

"That doesn't matter," he said, shaking his head. "All you need to know is that I do."

Her demeanor suddenly changed. Back was the Danuta Galvin he had first met, all poised and glossed innocence. "So what do you suggest, Jack?"

"Well . . . ," he said slowly. "I thought you were talking about throwing our lot in together." He paused, waiting for a reaction. When there was none, he continued. "But you see, Danuta, I have a problem there."

A flicker of a frown.

"I don't know how far I can trust you. You used to have a partner, didn't you? What happened to him?"

"I don't know, Jack. You know that."

He stood. "Oh, come on. You should know by now that I'm not an idiot. You're very smart, Danuta, but don't underestimate me. What happened? Five hundred thousand . . . was that it?" He leaned across the desk toward her. "Too much to throw away, and when it looked like he was going to cut you out of the deal, you got rid of him. Decided to run it on your own. Was that how it was?" He raised his voice a little then, snarling the words for emphasis. "And you found poor sap Jack Stein to take his place. Is that it? Needed a bit of muscle. Someone who could look after himself. Hey?"

"No, Jack, believe me," she said. "It wasn't like that." She turned her face away from him. "Yes, it may have been like that at first, but it changed. Back in that apartment when you said my name, my real name, I knew you were smarter than you were letting on. I feel something for you, Jack. You've impressed me. At first, yes, but then I saw what you were, what we could do together." She turned back to look at him. "We could be so good together, Jack. Think about it. We can have such fun together, and get rich in the process."

He held her gaze for a couple of moments, and despite himself, despite everything he knew about her, there was the briefest inner debate; then he sighed.

"Yeah, until you decide it'd be more worth your while to have me out of the picture. Would five hundred thousand be enough for you? A million? What then? Would you kill me like you killed Talbot? It all fell into place when you pulled that weapon. That's a big gun for a little woman."

She stood then, her fists bunched by her sides. "He betrayed me, Jack. He betrayed *me*. After all we'd been through, he betrayed me. *Me*. What did you expect me to do? I had no choice."

Jack straightened. "There's always a choice."

"No, there isn't. You're wrong. Look at where you are, what sort of life you have." Suddenly the coy, girl-ish demeanor dropped away. She fixed him with a steady gaze. "Sure, I've been trying to play you, Jack. The dumb private investigator, everything that goes with it. He always needs some vamp to play along, act as his foil. Isn't that the way it works? I've seen the vids too. Okay, in the beginning I might have misread you, I admit it. That was my mistake. Just stop for a minute and think though. Think of what we could have made. You, me, together. And that's just one deal. The universe is full of fools like Landerman. Rich fools with far more money than sense. Together we could have had a great future together, Jack. And the re-wards . . . With your abilities and what I know, we could have a lot of fun and do pretty damned nicely out of it too. Forget all that playacting."

Jack shook his head. "I'm sorry. I value my own life a little more than that. I trust you about as far as I can throw you, Danuta. And now," he said, "I think it's time to put this to rest. No more games. Not even this one. You're not quite as good as you think you are, Ms. Galvin."

He turned to the wall. "Morrish, you there?"

The wallscreen blossomed into life and Morrish's big pasty features took shape. "Yeah, Jack, we're here."

"Did you get Landerman?"

Morrish nodded. "Yes. We had some of our boys waiting for him when he left your place."

"And have you got enough?"

Morrish grinned. "Yeah, we've got plenty. We'll be over in a while. And I think there's someone here who'll be pleased to see you and get out of this place. She's one smart little lady, Jack."

"Yeah, she is. Okay, good. See you soon."

The display faded and Jack turned to see Danuta Galvin staring at him, her mouth open, her pale face aghast.

Jack simply smiled.

She slowly closed her mouth. "Damn you, Stein," she hissed. "You'll be sorry."

"Oh, I doubt that very much, Ms. Galvin," he said.

Twenty-Five

Once or twice Danuta Galvin sat forward, moistening her lips as if about to say something.

"Don't even think about it," Jack told her. "You've said all you have to say."

She looked aggrieved, then averted her gaze. A couple of times she glanced around the office, obviously looking for something she could make use of, seeking some avenue of escape, but there was clearly none.

Jack cleared his throat, just to break the silence.

He was about to stand up and start pacing, when the system announced an arrival.

"Who is it?" he said.

An image of Morrish and Laduce standing outside the front door appeared on the wall. Billie stood behind them.

"Wait here," said Jack. "And don't even think about moving. There's nowhere to go, Ms. Galvin."

He left the office and went to the door to let the two policemen in. As he opened the door, he was met by a big grin on Morrish's face. Laduce looked uncomfortable, but the edge seemed to have been taken off his normal hostility.

Billie pushed between the two of them and went straight in. She also pushed past Jack, heading for the living room. Who knew what was upsetting her this time?

"So, where is she?" asked Morrish.

"Or maybe she's already gone," said Laduce.

"Sorry to disappoint you, Laduce," said Jack. "Come in." He shook his head. So Laduce was still going to push it despite everything. "Through this way."

Laduce leaned in close as they stepped inside. "I tell you, Stein. You're not out of this yet. Not if I've got anything to do with it."

"Yeah, right," said Jack with a sigh and a little shake of his head. He didn't have the energy for this crap now. He was already starting to feel the effects of the adrenaline starting to fade.

He led them through to the office. Opening the door, he stood back to let them pass and followed them in. Danuta Galvin was standing by the window, her hands feeling around the edges. She quickly turned as they entered, her face becoming a mask of innocence.

"Never mind the act," said Jack. "They saw the whole thing. Every word you said, Ms. Galvin, went straight into their system."

Morrish stepped forward. "You're under arrest for the murder of Carl Talbot," he said.

She stood where she was. "I don't know what you're talking about."

"You may as well drop it," said Laduce. He turned to Jack. "Have you got the guns?"

Jack nodded and dug them out of his pocket, handing them with one hand to Laduce, who took them and turned them over one at a time, inspecting them. Laduce nodded in turn, facing back to look at Danuta.

"Yeah, with these, we've got plenty."

Laduce stepped forward and took Danuta by her

upper arm. With a sour expression she shook his hand free. "It's all right," she said. "I'm coming."

Morrish stepped forward to flank her. "Well, we'd better be going then, Ms. Galvin." He turned to wink at Jack and together, he and Laduce started escorting her to the door.

"We still might want to talk to you, Stein," said Laduce. "In fact, I'd count on it."

"Well, you know where I am," Jack responded, not even having the energy to hit him with a snappy response, and followed them to the door. He saw them out, standing waiting while they walked toward the elevator. As Morrish pressed to call it, he turned back to look at Jack.

"Thanks again," he said.

Jack gave a quick nod and touched his finger to his forehead, then closed the door. That was it. Done. Well, almost. There was still something he wanted to do, but that would keep. First he had to work out what was eating Billie and try to smooth the waters. He stood in the hallway, thinking, his hands shoved into his pockets.

Summoning his energy, he wandered into the living room, but Billie was nowhere to be seen.

"Billie?" he called.

She appeared at her door. "What?"

"So, are you going to tell me what's wrong?"

She shrugged, but her face was set with a surly expression.

"Dammit, Billie. Will you cut it out?"

She gave a heavy sigh. "It's just the same, isn't it?"

"What do you mean?" he said with a frown.

She wandered out into the living room shaking her head. "You still treat me like a little kid." She propped herself up on one of the chairs and looked at him with her jaw thrust out.

Jack turned slowly. "I'm sorry, Billie, but I don't know what you're talking about. I've never treated you like a kid. Not really. Jesus, I wouldn't know how to treat someone like a kid."

The hostility still radiated from her face, her posture. "You just don't know, do you?"

He crossed to a chair and sat. It was time they had this out. "No, dammit. I don't. Why don't you tell me?"

"You keep saying we're partners, that we work together."

"And . . ."

"You sent me to the police. You know I don't like them." She gave a half shrug.

"Yeah, and what, Billie? You knew it was the only way we could do things. What did you expect me to do? It was the only chance we had of making the whole thing work. I rely on you. So, you went to the police building. What else do you want?"

She glared at him. "For you to tell me what was going on," she said.

"Huh?"

Billie stood and wandered over to one of the shelves, trailing her finger across the edge, her head tilted slightly down so her hair obscured her expression. "You knew that woman killed Carl Talbot."

"Well, I suspected, yeah . . ."

"And you didn't tell me."

"Oh, come on, Billie. I had to make her admit to it. I couldn't just run with the supposition until I was sure. She was the one who had to confirm it to me."

"So, why didn't you tell me?" The voice was petulant.

"I don't know. In case you let anything slip to the police. I don't know. With Laduce convinced I was in on it, I couldn't afford to let anyone know what I was thinking. You might have said something." He knew it was a mistake as soon as the words were out of his mouth. Billie whirled on him, pale fury on her face.

"Is that what you think? What am I, stupid?"

Jack held up his hands. "No, no. That's not what I was saying at all. Jesus, Billie. Of course you're not stupid. Think about it. What was I supposed to do?"

She stalked over and stood in front of him. "Tell me what was going on, that's what!"

She had a point. He sighed heavily. "Look, I'm sorry. I didn't mean to cut you out of things. I just wasn't sure. This whole case has been different, Billie. I've had less to work with, less that I was sure about."

She was still standing glaring at him.

"Listen, go and sit down, will you?" She turned and walked stiffly over to one of the other chairs.

"Look, there's been a whole lot of stuff going on, with the case, with this place, with everything. I was beginning to doubt my abilities, you know? I wasn't getting any flashes, no prompts, nothing."

"But you had the dreams," she said, voice still petulant.

"Yeah, I had a few dreams, but they weren't exactly like dreams I had to work with before. They weren't giving me a hell of a lot. I had to use my head, actually think about things more. That's different, Billie. I didn't want to be wrong. You've got to understand that."

"Uh-huh. I do. That still doesn't change things."

"What do you mean?"

"You still treat me like a kid. You have to tell me stuff, Jack. You have to tell me what's going on in your head." She tapped her temple with one finger.

Jack sighed again. "It doesn't work like that, Billie," he said. "You know, I'd like to tell you what's going on, what I'm thinking about, but I want to be sure first.

I talk to you about things once I've thought them through. I need to process stuff before I start talking about it."

She blinked a couple of times, processing herself. He continued.

"Look, I tell you about as much as I can. Before you came along, I didn't talk to anyone. I worked solo. That was it. You've made a really big difference to the way I do things. You know that. But give me a break, okay? I can only do so much."

He watched her as she sat across from him, one leg jiggling up and down, her eyes narrowed.

"Look, I understand, and okay," he said. "Maybe now is not the best time to talk about all this. We will though. Right now I'm tired, and I think you're probably tired too. We've done some good things here today. I wouldn't have been able to do any of it without you. And really, we have some big things to talk about too. Like about what we do now. And yeah, maybe we have to set some ground rules between us as well."

She was chewing at her bottom lip, looking down into her lap.

He didn't really feel enthusiastic about what he was about to suggest, but he could see no other option right then. "So, what do you say," he said. "You hungry?"

She looked up at him slowly, breaking into a grudging smile.

Twenty-Six

Billie, of course, pushed for Molly's, but Jack had other ideas. It was time for a serious discussion, an adult discussion. Molly's wasn't the right venue for what he wanted to talk about. There were decisions that had to be made, but he needed to explore the boundaries of what lay between them. He suggested a restaurant uptown. Billie frowned at him.

"Why there?"

"I don't know, I thought it would be good for a change. We're sort of celebrating, don't you think? The successful conclusion of the case. Let's eat something nice. Some good, proper food. Sit in some nice surroundings. We can talk about things and take our time."

"I guess," she said grudgingly.

Jack couldn't remember the last time he'd been to a proper restaurant. Mandala didn't count. That was working. Besides, the whole country club resort thing had been so alien that it was hard to have a full appreciation of it. That was another life, somebody else's life.

"Okay, so Alexis it is." He'd seen the place, passed it a couple of times, and remembered reading something about it once. He glanced down at his clothes and then at Billie's. No, they'd be fine. Anyway, they had the funds now to do just about anything they wanted, for a while. They headed up to the shuttle stop together in silence. Jack didn't want to talk about anything till they were comfortable, had had some time to relax.

It took about half an hour to get to their destination. Standing outside Alexis, Billie looked dubious. Jack ushered her in.

"Have you a booking, sir?" A cool look down the nose, and a distinct narrowing of the eyes as he looked at Billie. This guy looked like he'd purchased a gilded sneer. Jack ignored it.

"No, but we'd like a table anyway. Somewhere quiet, thanks. And not near the kitchen, or the bathroom."

The maitre d' adjusted his collar and cleared his throat. "I can assure you, sir—"

"Save it," said Jack. "Just find us our table." He glanced at Billie, who wore a half grin. He narrowed his eyes at her and she bit her lip, still grinning.

The guy behind the desk fussed around making a show of checking reservations, but Jack could see the place was three-quarters empty. Finally, nodding, pursed lips in place, the maitre d' led them toward a table in a fairly secluded area, but well away from the window, and as per Jack's request, they were nowhere near the kitchen or the bathrooms.

The maitre d' disappeared, and a moment later a young guy came across and cleared the extra place settings. Jack looked around while the glasses and plates and cutlery were removed. The walls were done in a deep green. Proper pieces of art hung on the walls, instead of programmed displays. Over near the entrance, the maitre d' looked over in their direction, gave a visible sniff, then looked away.

Jack turned back to Billie. "So, what do you think?"

"Uh-huh," she said, looking around. She leaned back as the waiter shook out her napkin and laid it across her lap. There was no confusion; she'd definitely done this sort of thing before.

The waiter did the same for Jack. "Your serving program will be with you shortly," he said. "Enjoy." With a brief tilt of his head, he withdrew. Jack considered. It was funny how the mix of technology and tradition prevailed. The more toward the upper end of the scale you got, the more tradition overtook what was available. He guessed, not that he'd ever been in one, that in the high-end restaurants, it was all people.

Moments later, giving them a reasonable time to settle, a serving holo appeared above the table's center.

"Welcome to Alexis," it said. "I am Carla. I will be your server for this evening."

The woman's face was replaced by a menu board, but her voice continued. "While you are looking over the choices, can I get you something to drink? Or perhaps you would like to see the wine list."

"Yeah, beer for me," said Jack. "I'll think about the wine in a while. Billie?"

She ordered a cola and turned her attention back to the menu, jiggling and occasionally frowning as she scanned the options. After a suitable pause, Carla asked if they had any questions. The waiter appeared, carrying their drinks, and quickly disappeared.

They made their meal choices and Jack leaned forward, positioning his elbows on the table.

"Billie, it's time we had a serious discussion," he said finally.

She narrowed her eyes across the table, still jiggling. "What?" she said.

"Well, we need to discuss some of the things that

have been happening with us and what we're going to do about it. Don't think I'm an idiot, Billie. Something's going on and you're not telling me."

She pressed her lips together, saying nothing. Her hands were out of sight, under the table.

Jack took a sip of his drink, placed the glass down carefully, then continued. "I can't go around all the time feeling as if I've done something wrong and if you don't tell me what it is, I can't do anything about it, can I?"

She worked her jaw.

"Well?" he said.

"I said it before. You don't tell me enough. You treat me like a kid."

The waiter appeared bearing their first course, forestalling further conversation. Jack waited till he retired before answering.

"How's your soup?"

"Yeah," she said, nodding after tasting it. "Good."

He took a small taste of the terrine, closing his eyes briefly as the small piece melted and filled his mouth with flavor, rich, earthy. It had been too long. He opened his eyes again, looking across at Billie concentrating on her soup. He took another mouthful, briefly indulged in the sensation again. God, he could get used to this.

He took a deep breath, laid his utensils down, and folded his hands in front of him.

"Billie, look at me for a minute, will you?"

She too laid down her spoon and met his gaze.

"Look, you want me to stop treating you like a kid, then you've got to stop acting like one. Yeah, we work well together. Yeah, I say we're partners. But we're not going to work as partners if you keep putting on these little performances. Sulking, stamping off into your room, locking yourself away, not telling me what I'm supposed to have done. I've told you before, I rely on you for lots of things. You're so good at the stuff you do, Billie. Far better than I could possibly be. I think it's really lucky that we found each other. Maybe one of the luckiest things that's happened over the last couple of years. I just need you to work on acting like someone who really is a partner, not some little girl playing at being all adult and responsible."

She picked up her spoon and started playing with the soup, stirring it around and around, looking down at the bowl.

"What do you want, Billie? What do you really want?"

She looked up at him then, the motion with her spoon halted.

"How should I know?" she said. "How am I supposed to know what I want? I'm not some tough guy running around solving cases. I'm just a kid, Jack. I'm fourteen. That's all." Her face was threatening something, her bottom lip working as she looked at him.

"Jesus, Billie," he said, rubbing his forehead with the tips of his fingers. "I know." He shook his head. "And I'm not any better at this than you are either. How am I supposed to know?" He gave a heavy sigh. "Look at us. We're not very good, are we?"

She gave a little shake of her head.

Jack ran his fingers back through his hair as he thought about what he wanted to say next. "Listen, I want to make sure you're happy. I don't know how to do that, but I can learn. It's got to work both ways though. You've got to work with me. You have to let me know what's going on in your head as well. And I promise I'll think about it more, talk to you more about what I'm thinking. Just sometimes I have to work things through before I can put them into words. Can you understand that?"

She nodded slowly.

"But like I said," he continued, "I need you to help me out. If I'm not telling you stuff, or you *think* I'm not, then you've got to let me know. Tell me. Don't just go storming off into your room and giving me the big chill. That's not going to help anything."

Again she nodded.

"Are you happy with me, Billie?"

She narrowed her eyes, then gave a little shrug. "Uh-huh."

"Well, I'm happy with you, happy having you around. Sometimes it's not easy though, you know. We do work well together, I think. I just worry that I can't give you enough of what you need. I don't know if it's any sort of life for you. Do you understand?"

She thought about that for a moment; then her eyes widened a little bit. "You're not going to send me away? I don't want that. I don't want to go away."

"No, Billie, that's not what I'm saying." He had wondered about whether that's what she needed, about whether that was the answer to what was troubling him, but he wasn't going to tell her that now. "You're getting older," he said slowly. "I'm just not sure I can give you what you need."

Jack turned his attention back to his starter, allowing her some space to think about what he was saying. After a couple of minutes, she spoke again.

"Jack, I don't want to go anywhere else," she said.

He looked up at her, held her gaze. "Okay, good," he said. "But I want you to think about that and make sure it's what you really want. And if it turns out to be the case, you've got to promise me that you'll work at what I said."

"You too," she said back.

He nodded. "Yep."

"Now, finish your soup," he said. "It's too good to waste."

He watched her as they polished off the first course, but she seemed okay with what they'd been saying. Their waiter reappeared and cleared the plates. Jack took the opportunity to broach the other thing that had been weighing on his mind.

"There is one more thing," he said. She stopped her observation of the room and turned her face back to look at him.

"Hmm . . . ?"

"I don't think Yorkstone is the place for us, Billie. We don't fit here, really, do we?"

She shrugged. "Maybe."

"What do you mean, maybe?"

"Where are we supposed to go? It's okay here." She shrugged again.

"Well," he said, "am I right or am I wrong?"

"I suppose . . ."

"Okay," said Jack. "It's something I want you to think about too. I don't know the answer yet, but we need to come up with a solution. Cases like this last one aren't going to come up every week. Not here. Not in Yorkstone. It was just chance that made it happen here. I don't want to spend the next couple of years looking for lost dogs. I don't think you want that either."

"Maybe you should do something else."

He frowned. It was something he hadn't thought about. He wasn't sure it was something he wanted to think about. Jack Stein doing something else? It just didn't seem right.

"Is that what you really think?"

She gave a shrug in answer.

At that moment their steaks arrived, filling the space with the scent of rich sauce and well-cooked food. They looked like they were done to perfection.

"Well, maybe we've both got things to think about," said Jack. "Right now, let's just eat and enjoy."

She nodded, staring at him, but it was a long time before she broke her gaze and picked up her knife and fork.

Twenty-Seven

When they got back to the apartment, Billie at least seemed in a little better mood. Jack was thankful for that much. He felt like he'd eaten and drunk more than he had in years, overstuffed, but it was a good feeling. Jack ushered her in, trying not to catch the yawn that escaped from her mouth as they walked inside and closed the front door. They'd barely stepped into the living room when the system announced a call. Jack shrugged off his coat, frowning. It was late for anyone to be calling. It wasn't the police again though; the tone would have been different.

"Answer."

An unfamiliar face appeared on the wall, a gray corporate type, serious expression. Jack didn't recognize the face at all.

"This is Jack Stein," he said. "How can I help you?"

"Mr. Stein. Hello. You don't know me. The name's Thorpe."

Billie had taken up position on one of the armchairs and was watching suspiciously.

"So, what can I do for you, Mr. Thorpe?"

"It's a slightly delicate matter, Mr. Stein . . . I tried to call you earlier, but it appears you weren't around."

Jack sat in one of the free chairs and crossed his legs.

If it was a case and this was a potential client, he could take Jack Stein as he found him. He'd had enough pretense over the past couple of weeks to last a lifetime.

"I'm listening," he said. "And before you ask, this is my niece. It's perfectly okay to talk in front of her. We work together. It's a package."

He glanced across at Billie, and she was almost grinning. Almost.

The man called Thorpe nodded. "All right. The reason for my call, Mr. Stein, is that I understand you've been involved in a case recently . . ."

Jack leaned forward. "Whether I have or haven't, I'm not sure what that's got to do with you, Mr. Thorpe."

Thorpe cleared his throat, looking slightly uncomfortable. "Um, yes. Well, let's just say I believe you've been working on something that's of some importance to us."

This was suddenly getting interesting.

"And who might 'us' be?"

"I represent a large corporation. It doesn't matter which corporation at this time, Mr. Stein. Suffice it to say, we have interests in something you may have acquired recently."

"Okay, go on . . ."

"We would be very eager to have that item in our possession."

Jack laughed. "Don't tell me. Wait. It's a metal tablet about sooooo big." He spread his hands in illustration. "Is that right?"

"Ahh," said Thorpe. "I see you know what I'm talking about. Good. I have indeed called the right man, then. We would like to make sure the item was returned to us."

Jack stood. Interesting that he'd used the term "returned." "I'm sure you would. Exactly how interested are you, Mr. Thorpe?"

Thorpe didn't even blink. "I'm sure we could come to some arrangement."

"Well, how about this?" said Jack. "How about you convince me that the item belongs to you in the first place. How about that?"

Thorpe stared out from the wall. He took a couple of seconds to answer. "I can assure you that we have a legitimate claim. All that really needs to be established is how much it will take for you to release it to us."

Jack turned away from the wall, took a couple of paces and then turned back. "Okay, I've got another question for you then." He drew the moment out. Thorpe was watching attentively. "Does the name Van der Stegen mean anything to you? Or maybe Warburg?"

Thorpe paled visibly, then regained his composure. Jack wondered how that whole Outreach Industries power play had ended up. Whether Warburg was still around. Probably. Probably very little had changed in the big corporate. Van der Stegen and Warburg were still probably playing their little games together, juggling for position even now.

"I think that's immaterial," said Thorpe. "All you need to know is that we have a legitimate interest in the object and we're prepared to pay for its return."

Jack nodded slowly. "So tell me how you knew to contact me."

"We have our resources, Mr. Stein."

"Yeah, I'm sure you do. Well, I'm afraid I've got some disappointing news for you, Mr. Thorpe. News that I'm sure you'll enjoy passing on to your bosses. I don't actually have the object in question anymore."

Thorpe's eyes narrowed. "What do you mean?"

"Right about now, I think it's probably very safe

where it is and it's not going to be going anywhere in a hurry. I would say it's probably quite comfortable sitting in some evidence room at the Yorkstone police building. If your bosses would like to negotiate with them, then tell them to feel free. I don't think they actually own the Yorkstone police. And that's about all the help I can give you. Now, you can go away and leave us alone. Oh, and give them my regards, will you?"

Jack didn't give Thorpe a chance to say another word. He ended the call and turned to look slowly at Billie. She was watching him with an expression he could almost think was respect.

Slowly, he walked over and stood in front of her. "At least that's going to frustrate Outreach. Even if they try and get the artifact back from the police, it's not going to be much use to them, and who knows how long it's going to last anyway." He shrugged. "But even if it does hold together for a while longer, it's not going to be any good to them."

She nodded. "You meant to do that all along, didn't you?" she said.

Jack nodded, watching her expression.

"You could have told me what you were planning," she said. There was clearly something warring within her. "It's not fair that you couldn't trust me enough to tell me."

"No, Billie, listen. It wasn't like that. I wasn't really sure myself till right at the end. You, of course, helped me get there. I wouldn't have managed it without you. But I needed everything to be right. It wasn't that I couldn't trust you; I couldn't trust myself. And with that Galvin woman involved . . ."

"I knew it!" she said.

He shook off the implicit accusation.

"Okay, look. The final thing I want to do is this . . . I

want to put together all the dream notes I've made, all of the research stuff, everything into one package. I've made a start on it, but there's still some work to do."

"Uh-huh," she said. "What for?"

He crouched down in front of her. "Well . . . I don't know if it'll be any use, but just in case it is, I want to send the whole lot, one big package, to Dr. Hervé Antille at the University of Balance City. What do you say?"

She stared at him for a moment, then smiled. She leaned forward and threw her arms around his neck. "That's great, Jack," she said. "That's really great. Thank you."

She withdrew her arms and sat back again, still smiling, but looking slightly awkward. She bit her lip. "Can we do it now?" she said a moment later.

"Sure," he said, and stood, this time returning her smile with a little more ease. "As soon as I have the rest of the notes together."

Things were going to work out just fine. He didn't need any strange sensation working in the back of his brain telling him it was the case. He could just feel it.

Roc Science Fiction & Fantasy
COMING IN OCTOBER 2004

KINGDOM OF THE GRAIL by Judith Tarr
0-451-46004-9

Roland is a knight who has sworn to free the great
wizard Merlin, who is imprisoned in an enchanted
forest. But to save Merlin, Roland must first confront
a powerful, ancient enemy.

DOG WARRIOR by Wen Spencer
0-451-45990-3

On the run from a fanatical cult, Ukiah Oregon is
surprised to discover Atticus Steele, a brother he
didn't know he had. And he's even more surprised
to learn that Atticus is involved with trafficking an
alien drug that could get them both killed.

MECHWARRIOR: DARK AGE
HUNTERS OF THE DEEP
by Randall N. Bills
0-451-46005-7

The Clan Sea Fix is about to be torn asunder.
ovKhan Sha Clarke wants to rule his own faction
of warriors and take his share of wealth, glory, and
power. But ovKhan Petr Klasa knows about Sha's
rebellion and will stop him at any cost.